An Irish Summer

Also by Alexandra Paige

Weekends with You

An Irish Summer

A NOVEL

ALEXANDRA PAIGE

AVON

An Imprint of HarperCollinsPublishers

AN IRISH SUMMER. Copyright © 2025 by Alexandra Paige. All rights reserved. Printed in the United States of America. No part of this book may be used or reproduced in any manner whatsoever without written permission except in the case of brief quotations embodied in critical articles and reviews. For information, address HarperCollins Publishers, 195 Broadway, New York, NY 10007.

HarperCollins books may be purchased for educational, business, or sales promotional use. For information, please email the Special Markets Department at SPsales@harpercollins.com.

Avon, Avon & logo, and Avon Books & logo are registered trademarks of HarperCollins Publishers in the United States of America and other countries.

FIRST EDITION

Interior text design by Diahann Sturge-Campbell

Shamrock and plane illustrations © Indiloo; Graficriver/Stock.Adobe.com

Library of Congress Cataloging-in-Publication Data has been applied for.

ISBN 978-0-06-331656-0

25 26 27 28 29 LBC 5 4 3 2 1

To the Emerald Isle, to letting go, and to finding love in unexpected places

Chapter 1

Today was going to be a good day.

The weather was unseasonably warm for early May, I had just enough oat milk left in the fridge to make a latte, and my favorite jeans were clean and folded on the top of the pile. And when I got downstairs to work, the lobby of the bed-and-breakfast was quiet enough that I could spend some time organizing the vendors we had on file and preparing the invoices for the banquet we were hosting next week.

Any day that I had extra time to spend on events was a good day. Especially when that day started with a cloudless, sunny sky and the perfect coffee. I was on cloud nine.

Which is exactly where life wants you to be before it swoops in and pulls the rug out from under you.

"Chels, do you have a second?" Helen, the owner, materialized in the lobby with a wrinkle between her eyebrows.

"I, uh, yeah, of course," I said, getting to my feet. "Is everything okay?" I closed out of the tab I was working on and came out from behind the desk, following her into her office. The last time I followed Helen into this office was when I applied for this job six years ago. In the time since, we'd conducted all our business at the reception desk, in the small dining room, or in front of the bay window in the lounge.

She motioned for me to sit as Jack, her husband, entered the room and closed the door behind him.

"What's going on?" I asked, frantically looking between them and hoping someone was going to speak before I started to assume the worst.

"We're closing O'Shea's . . . in a month," Helen said. It was the last thing I heard before my blood was thundering so loud in my ears I missed everything else. The room started to spin, and I felt for a second like I might pass out. It was only when Jack reached out and touched my shoulder that I came back into my body and tuned back in. "The choice is yours, Chelsea," Helen said as she slid a brochure across the table, the words *The Wanderer* printed in emerald green across the top, stopping just short of my folded hands. I grabbed it by the corner if only to stop myself from picking my cuticles, but I had no intention of opening it.

"I don't understand," I said. "You're just . . . closing O'Shea's? Can you even do that?" I supposed I knew they could, but I was reeling. I'd need to hear the spiel a few times before any of it could register. I'd been working and living at this bed-and-breakfast since I graduated from college, and I hadn't even considered the possibility that it might not be an option someday. And that day was apparently a month from now.

Jack rubbed the back of his neck, searching for something to say, then reached for Helen's hand. "It's a lot, we know," he said eventually, "but we're getting old, and we can't run the inn forever, so when the opportunity to sell came around, well, it was the right choice, I'm afraid." He exhaled all at once, and I wished I could do the same.

"You didn't want to just, I don't know, hire someone new to run it?' *Like me*, I refrained from adding aloud. "Or sell it to someone who planned to keep it as an inn?"

"Unfortunately, what's best is full closure," Helen said, though it sounded like she'd practiced that line before this conversation. Which I supposed was possible. Given how long we'd known one another, it was likely the O'Sheas could have predicted exactly how this was going to go. If only I could have been so lucky.

"And you're selling the whole building?" I clarified, knowing it was true but hoping it wasn't. "My apartment included?"

Helen and Jack exchanged a glance as if wordlessly trying to determine which of them had to drop the hammer. In the end, Helen lost. "Yes," she said, not quite meeting my eyes. "Your apartment included." After a beat, she spoke again. "But you don't have to be out for another month, so you have some time."

Time to do what, exactly, I wasn't sure. I didn't need time. I needed a job. And a place to live. And a month was hardly time at all.

"You've been the best employee we've ever had," Helen said, as if that might somehow soften the blow. "You're hardworking, dedicated, creative. You've made some real improvements around here over the years. And that's why we wanted to offer you the opportunity to relocate to the hostel." She gestured to the brochure with a manicured finger, and I released it from my hand like it was suddenly on fire. "My sister said they have an opening for some seasonal work so we thought you might like to go for the summer."

"To Ireland," I said. Even as the words came out of my mouth, I knew it wasn't a real possibility. The only real possibility was finding another job in Boston and doing it fast.

"To Ireland," she confirmed, her smile teetering between sympathetic and overly enthusiastic. For whose sake, I wasn't entirely sure.

"Thank you," I said, "but I'm sure I can find something else in the city. I wouldn't want to trouble your sister, and I don't know if moving to Ireland is for me."

"You don't have to make any decisions now," Jack said, clocking my attitude and looking to his wife for support. "Just know the offer is on the table. And there's more to Ireland than rocks and bagpipes, you know. It's a beautiful country, and the Wanderer is a lovely property. Plenty of amenities, great managerial opportunities to get involved in and boost your résumé, lots of networking connections with professionals all over the world."

I tried and failed to swallow the lump in my throat. Tears collected in the corners of my eyes, threatening to escape if I thought for another second about all I was losing.

Working at O'Shea's was mostly all I'd known. And Boston was definitely all I'd known. How naive was I to think I didn't need a backup plan? A feeling dangerously close to betrayal swam in the silence between us, making it hard to look Jack or Helen in the eye.

"Thank you," I said eventually, afraid I would regret saying anything else.

"We're so sorry, Chels," Helen said. "We hope you understand." I wanted to tell them it wasn't an issue of understanding, that I understood perfectly well and I was just being selfish, but it was better not to say everything I was thinking. Instead I nodded, slipped the brochure into my tote, and headed for the door.

"Promise us you'll think about Ireland," Jack said before I made it out of the office. "I think it would really suit you."

I tried to force a smile, but it probably looked more like a grimace. Boston suited me. Knowing where I was and what I was doing suited me. Having a plan to pitch Jack and Helen for more responsibility and a raise this year so I could save for a down payment on a condo where I would live until I was married and bought a house in the suburbs suited me. Eventually moving into a more partner-oriented role at O'Shea's in the next ten years suited me. Working at a hostel in a foreign country surrounded by strangers with no real plan for the future definitely did not suit me.

Once I was out of the inn and onto the pavement, I followed my feet on autopilot to my favorite coffee shop down the block. It was where I often did my best thinking, so I could only hope it was also where I would do my best job hunting. I might not have been totally sure about where to begin, but I *was* totally sure about *when* to begin. If I was going to stop my life from crumbling entirely to ruins, I needed to get my résumé out there before I hit rock bottom.

Armed with a hazelnut latte and a window seat, I opened my laptop and stared listlessly at the home screen. Even before I'd gotten the job at O'Shea's, I hadn't done the traditional kind of job hunt. I'd been in this very coffee shop the week of my college graduation when I spotted the Help Wanted flyer tacked to the community bulletin board, and I was in the B and B's lobby with the flyer in my hand before my coffee was ready. Helen, Jack, and I had an instant connection, and I was hired within the week, living in the apartment on the third floor within the month. Easy as one, two, three.

I wondered if I'd ever get so lucky again. Or if my current circumstance was karma for how easy it had been in the first place.

Before I could get my pity party off the ground, I opened every job searching website I could think of and vowed to have a few viable options saved before I finished my latte. I typed in phrases like "hospitality + general manager" and "event planner" and even "concierge," hoping to increase my chances of finding something. I scrolled through pages and pages of jobs with entry-level salaries, overnight hours, unrealistic qualifications, and intentionally vague descriptions. I also scrolled through pages of jobs in dangerous parts of the city, jobs too far outside the city, and jobs posted years ago that might never have even been in the city in the first place.

And by the time my latte was little more than an empty glass in a puddle of condensation, I hadn't saved a single posting.

This was going to be harder than I thought.

I closed my laptop, promising myself I'd try again first thing tomorrow with a clearer head. Maybe I just couldn't weed out good jobs because I was still reeling from the news. Still clouded with the heartbreak of losing the job I loved, and still trying to accept that I had to move on, even if I didn't know what I was moving on to.

What I did know, however, was that no matter what that next step was, it definitely wasn't going to be Ireland.

WHEN I LEFT THE COFFEE SHOP, it didn't feel right to go back to my apartment just yet, especially since it wasn't going to be my apartment for much longer, so I followed the invisible thread to my parents' house. No matter how old I got, or how insane they sometimes made me, there was no denying the sense of comfort in my childhood home. And the more time the news had to settle in, the more I needed that comfort.

It was a fifteen-minute walk, which meant I only had to hold myself together for that much longer. Only had to put one foot in front of the other, slow and steady. I knew how to do slow and steady. Hell, until an hour ago I'd been building my entire future on slow and steady.

The sun was setting as I climbed the stairs to the front door, casting the brick house in an orange glow. My parents' cars were both in the driveway, so I skipped fumbling in my bag for the keys and knocked on the door instead.

"Chelsea, girl," my dad said, swinging the door open and studying me on the steps. "Did we have plans tonight?" He ushered me inside, taking my bag from my shoulder and hanging it on the hook in the foyer. "Wendy, did you know Chels was coming over tonight?" he called to my mother up the stairs before I could answer his question.

"No, we didn't, sorry. I just got some news, so I figured I'd come by," I said, shedding my denim jacket and hooking it over my bag. "I hope that's okay. You didn't have plans tonight or anything, did you?"

"Who, us?" My mother joined the conversation as she wound down the steps, kissing me on the cheek when she reached the foyer. "Plans? Don't be silly. What news? Are you okay?" She held my face in her hands. The speed with which she could become gravely concerned came with the territory of being a Jewish mother, and I should have expected this as soon as I opened my mouth.

"Yes, I'm fine, everything's fine," I lied, if only to settle her nerves for a minute.

By the time we settled around the kitchen table with glasses of wine, I had hardly braced myself to repeat the conversation I'd just had with Jack and Helen.

After a deep breath, I dove in. My voice wavered somewhere

around the part about having to find a new job, and the tears were flowing freely by the time I got to the part about having to move out of my apartment.

"Oh, baby," my mother said once I finished, reaching for my hand. "We're so sorry." I tried to wave her off, pretending it would be fine, but we both knew I didn't believe that.

"You know, Chels," my dad said, "finding a new job in hospitality isn't your only option for the future."

I knew exactly where he was going with this. "Dad, please—" I started.

"I'm just saying, you know you could always join us at the office." He nodded toward my mom, who clucked her tongue back in his direction.

"For the millionth time, I'm not a podiatrist," I said, hating how much I sounded like a whiny teenager.

"And for the millionth time," my mother said, "we aren't looking for a podiatrist. But our receptionist is going on maternity leave in a few months, so you could always fill in while she's away. And the benefits are fantastic, Chelsea. Really, the health insurance is the best you're going to get out here at your age."

"Oh, wow," I said. "Great health insurance. A job as a receptionist at my parents' office. Just what every woman is looking for in her late twenties."

"These things are a privilege, honey," my mother said, leaning closer to me. "Health insurance. A family. Job opportunities. I know you're upset, but that isn't an excuse to be ungrateful."

Even though I was an adult, my mom didn't let up. She was never a woman to let anything slide, especially disrespect, and I knew I was out of line.

"You're right," I said, turning the stem of the glass in my fingers.

"I know."

"And thank you." She nodded but said nothing. "I'm just not sure that's what I want for my future."

"Why not?" my dad asked. "You were a receptionist at O'Shea's, weren't you? I thought you liked that kind of stuff."

"Hospitality and podiatry aren't exactly the same," I said. "And I wasn't just a receptionist, you know. I was planning events, organizing functions, that sort of thing. It's going to be hard work to find something similar, but that's still the plan." Anxiety crept into my voice when I thought back to my failed search not even an hour ago. "And then there's the issue of where I'm supposed to live." I raked a hand through my hair, letting a few curls obscure my face when they fell back down. "I could only afford the apartment above the inn because Jack and Helen cut me a deal. I could never find another place that cheap, and even if one did exist, I couldn't find it in a month."

"Not with that attitude."

"Dad, I'm serious."

"So am I," he said. "It's a self-fulfilling prophecy, Chels. If you decide nothing is going to work, then nothing is going to work. You might as well give up now." My mom swatted him in the chest, and he only shrugged, a gentle smile forming at his own joke.

"I know the receptionist position at the office doesn't have the best salary, but you could always live here," my mom said, gesturing upstairs in the direction of my old bedroom as if this was obvious. "At least until you could save a little cash. This is your home, remember?"

The thought alone of moving back home and working as a receptionist for my parents was suffocating. And the more we talked about it, the more I felt the walls closing in.

And the more appealing Ireland was actually starting to sound.

"Thanks," I said, searching for a way to say *absolutely not* without offending her. I came up empty, so for the second time today I said nothing else.

"Think of it as a stepping stone," she said. "I mean, you want to settle in a suburb of Boston eventually, don't you? Have a steady job, live in a nice house, be near your friends and family?"

"I mean, yeah, but—"

"But what? This is how you're going to get there, honey. Sometimes we have to make sacrifices." She took a big swig of her wine, keeping her eyes locked on mine.

She was right, to some extent. That was what I wanted, wasn't it? What I planned for? The steady job and the nice house in the Boston suburbs? That's what they had, and what everyone else in my life seemed to have, and what I definitely wanted to have. And at the end of the day, there was happiness in security, wasn't there? Wasn't happiness a roof over your head, food on the table, book club, local farmers' markets, the things that shaped my childhood?

"Besides"—my dad shrugged—"what else are you going to do?"

The question crowded the air between us. There was no way I was really considering this, was there?

"I could, uh, I could move to Ireland," I said before I could think better of it, my forced laugh echoing around the kitchen. My mother's gasp was quick to follow.

"You could *what*?"

"That was Jack and Helen's solution." I tried to play it off like I thought it was ridiculous, but once the words were out there, I no longer had such a clear picture of where I stood. I mean, I *knew* it was ridiculous, but so was struggling through the summer here and ending up in my parents' office, wasn't it? "Helen's sister runs a hostel in Galway," I continued, "and she offered me a job for the summer if I wanted to get away while I sorted things out."

"Well, that sounds like one hell of an opportunity, doesn't it?" My dad's smile was growing by the minute, his eyes darting back and forth between my mom and me. "What? You two don't think so?"

"Alan, be realistic."

"What's unrealistic about that? Sounds like a job, housing, an adventure. Chelsea girl, why didn't you mention this sooner?"

"I don't know. Because it's kind of crazy," I said. "I have no business in Ireland."

"And what business do you have in Boston now?"

"Alan," my mother scolded. "She has plenty of business in Boston. Like coming to work at the office when Megan leaves."

"No, he's right," I said, surprising myself. "Without the job and my apartment, I have nothing in the city, do I?"

"Oh, I didn't realize we were chopped liver. Would you look at that, honey? We mean nothing to our own daughter," my mom said, bringing a hand to her chest.

"Ah, yes," I said. "The Jewish guilt card. Nice play." She winked, as if the compliment wasn't sarcastic. "But still," I backtracked. "I'm not sure there's anything for me in Ireland, either."

"That's a bold claim for someone who's never been to Ireland," my dad said, eyeing me from his spot across the table. "What makes you so sure it isn't for you?"

"It isn't the city," I said, gesturing vaguely around me like it was obvious. "I'm not a country girl, you know that. I'm sure all the space and the quiet is nice for some people, but not for me." Too much quiet made my head spin.

"Galway isn't the middle of nowhere," my dad said, suppressing a chuckle. "It's a city too, you know. Maybe not this big, but one worth experiencing I would think. Don't you think so, Wen?"

"Sounds like a big risk," my mom said. "We have no idea what the hostel is like, or the people, or the room you'll be staying in. And this doesn't really contribute to your future, does it? It just delays the inevitable?"

"If she has nothing lined up anyway, would it kill her to take a few months to figure out said future?"

"She's right here, you know," I said, gesturing to myself, frustrated they were talking around me like I was a child. At least my dad had a little faith in, well, whatever decision I was about to make.

"Is that even something you might like?" my mother asked. "I know you like hospitality, honey, but would you really like working in a hostel? It's a far cry from O'Shea's. And don't you think you'd be homesick? You have such a nice life here, and I just—"

"You don't think I could do it."

"What?" She set her wineglass on the table. "Chels, that's not what I'm saying; I'm . . . it's just that—"

"It's just that you don't think I could move to a foreign country for the summer. You don't think I have it in me."

I didn't even want to move to a foreign country for the summer, did I? I thought it sounded like a terrible idea from the minute it left Helen's lips. But that was before I realized my back was against the wall.

"I just don't think you'd be happy doing it, that's all," she conceded. "And I want you to be happy, honey."

I swallowed the groan that threatened to escape my throat.

"Have you talked to Ada about it yet?" my dad asked, saving me from the direction this conversation was headed.

Ada had been my best friend since we met at the local summer camp when we were kids. The only real time we spent apart was four years of undergrad, but when we returned to the city after graduation, it was like we had never been apart at all.

"Not yet," I said. I'd been too stunned to call her this afternoon, and I wasn't looking forward to rehashing the news again. But I had a feeling I knew exactly what she was going to say. She was one of those people who trusted her intuition and her intuition often favored the bold.

"Might not be a bad idea to give her a call," he suggested, sipping his wine with raised eyebrows. "Get another perspective." He nodded toward the door, giving me an excuse to get out of this kitchen and clear my head. Coming here wasn't exactly a mistake, but it wasn't quite the comfort I'd hoped it would be. If anything, I was leaving more confused.

Chapter 2

"Go to Ireland, Chels," Ada said down the line as if it was the most obvious decision in the world. I was lying on my couch, which wouldn't be my couch for much longer, counting the ceiling tiles while I waited for her to continue. "I mean, it's kind of a no-brainer, isn't it?" She sounded out of breath, and I wondered if she was on a run.

"Are you working out?"

"Ew, no. I'm walking up that big hill to the Whole Foods," she said. "Stop deflecting. You called for advice, and I'm giving it to you. Take the Ireland gig."

"Should I be concerned by how eager you are to get rid of me?" I knew I was still stalling, but I was afraid of what might happen if I stopped.

"Very funny," she said, and I could hear her eye roll over the phone. "Honestly, Chels, the fact that you asked my opinion at all, when you definitely knew what I was going to say, tells me you already know you want to go." I made a sound that was somewhere between a laugh and a scoff. "Seriously. What's stopping you?"

"I don't know, maybe that I don't know anything about the

country? Or maybe that my entire life is here, in Boston, where I want it to be?"

"Okay, first of all, there's Google," she said, and I laughed, despite myself. "And this gig isn't forever. You'll be able to be back to your Boston life in no time. Which, might I remind you, at this moment doesn't consist of an apartment or a job, so."

"Any more salt you'd like to rub in the wound?"

"I'm just saying. You have to rebuild some of your life here anyway. So might as well do it from over there."

"How am I supposed to rebuild my life *here* from three thousand miles away?"

"Did you call me for advice, or did you call me to complain? This hill is hard enough without having to argue with you, so I'm happy to hang up if you don't want to talk about this."

"You're right, you're right, I'm sorry," I said, a little embarrassed by my tone. "I called for advice."

"Good," she said, and I was relieved when I heard the smile return to her voice. "Then my advice is this: take the gig. We have technology now, you know. You can look online for a job and an apartment here while you're over there, so that excuse doesn't exactly hold up. It's not every day you have the opportunity to move to Ireland."

"And the opportunity to move to Ireland is something I should want?" I asked. Ada scoffed so loud I had to pull the phone away from my ear. "Oh, don't scoff like you've been there and you know all about it," I said, calling her bluff before she even had a chance to speak. "You're a city girl just as much as I am."

"Okay, so maybe I haven't been there, but it seems beautiful, doesn't it? The grass always looks so green."

"That's because all the photos you've seen are probably on Instagram," I said, and we both laughed. "Besides, what am I supposed to do with green grass?"

"Some time outside wouldn't kill you, you know."

We both knew I wasn't exactly the tree-hugging type, but she was probably right. Any time I'd spent outside in the past few years was just a side effect of living in a walkable city, despite the abundance of parks in the area. I wouldn't admit it to her, but fresh air might do me some good.

"And isn't Galway a city?" she added when I didn't say anything. "Not like Boston, maybe, but it isn't like you're going to be in the middle of nowhere."

All I did was groan in response. I supposed she had a point there too.

"I guess it would be an easy way to avoid a gap in my résumé," I ventured.

"That's the spirit! What else?"

If you gave Ada an inch, she would take a mile. And frustrated as I was, I couldn't deny her energy was working.

"Uh," I fumbled, "it would also diversify my experience and make me seem more flexible?"

"Attagirl!"

I leaned into the building momentum. "And it's definitely a *plan*, even if it isn't my long-term plan. It's a job and housing. That's what I need right now, so I can't exactly complain. And I'll probably learn some transferable skills that will make me more marketable to a wider variety of jobs, which will benefit my career in the long run."

"Maybe a little too practical for my taste, but yes!" She chuckled, and I was surprised to find I did too. Ada was a romantic, the spontaneous, freewheeling kind, but she'd never been anything but supportive of my goals, career and otherwise. She may not have been a planner herself, but she recognized how important it was to me. "I know it isn't ideal, Chels," she said, softening her voice a little. "I know how much you love a plan, and I know you hoped to be promoted at O'Shea's. But I don't think moving to Ireland is the worst option. Maybe not your first choice, but I really think this'll be good for you. And somewhere deep down, I think you do too."

This was the problem with having the same best friend your entire life. She always knew exactly what I needed to hear, but I couldn't hide anything from her. She knew what I was thinking even before I did, and unlike me in this moment, she was brave enough to say it out loud.

"Thank you," I said, trying to unravel the knot of emotion constricting my throat. "You're right."

"Always am. So, it's settled, then?" she asked, returning to her usual tone. "Because I just walked into Whole Foods and need to focus. I don't want to hear Ben complain again about how bad I am at grocery shopping."

Was it settled? Could it really have been that easy?

"Chels?" she prompted when I didn't respond right away.

"It's, uh, yeah," I said, but my voice was breathy and a little manic. "I guess it is? And Ben's right. You are terrible at grocery shopping."

"Only someone as type A as you two would think grocery shopping was something you could be bad at. But I'll attribute your temporary insanity to the aftermath of having just made a huge decision. Anyway, call me later so we can discuss what you're packing!" Before I could even respond, she hung up.

And that was that.

I fished the brochure from my tote, squinting at it in the

semidarkness of my apartment. Only the string lights around the window were on, accompanied by a few candles on the coffee table, but it was enough.

The glossy photo on the cover depicted a smiling group of backpack-clad travelers in the entryway of the hostel, arms slung around one another like old friends. I flipped it open, catching key phrases in the same bold green font from the cover: *seasonal work, make lifelong friends, explore all Ireland has to offer.*

I rubbed my eyes with the heels of my hands, trying to stop the room from spinning. I wasn't really going to do this, was I? Even as I asked the question, I knew the answer. I needed a plan, and here it was. Temporary, maybe, but as the benefits began to outweigh the drawbacks, the decision was clear as day.

I was moving to Ireland.

Chapter 3

I'm so glad you decided to do this," Helen said, standing beside me in the empty space that used to be my apartment. "I think you're going to love the Wanderer. It's even more charming than it is here," she whispered. "Not that I'd ever admit that to Lori."

"It'll definitely be an adventure," I said, because that was what people said about leaving the city for the country, wasn't it?

"It's going to be great. I spoke to my sister this morning, and they're thrilled. The current receptionist is leaving tomorrow, so Lori will be able to turn the room over in the next few days and have it ready for you when you arrive at the end of the week. It might not be your own apartment, but it's really cozy."

The end of the week. The end of this era, and the start of the next. I was moving in slow motion while everyone was bustling to get ready around me. Helen's sister, Lori, was scrambling to turn over one of the staff rooms above the hostel; Ada had forced me to go shopping nearly every day this week; my parents were hustling to help me get the entire contents of my apartment into storage. Yet it felt impossible to believe I was actually leaving.

"And I really get to live there without paying rent?" I asked again, still in disbelief.

"The seasonal workers all do," Helen said. "That's why the pay is so low. You're mostly compensated for the accommodation. And the property has a gym, laundry on-site, a few common areas for socializing and recreation, a bar, and a small restaurant space, so it's really quite a nice arrangement."

That was more than I could have said for O'Shea's, I supposed. Not only would I be saving on rent, but I'd be saving on extortionate gym fees, and I'd have more than one room to hang out in if I needed a change of scenery. It wasn't all bad.

But still, it wasn't this. My now former apartment was so empty even the sound of our breathing echoed off the bare walls. Gone were the antique lamps I used in place of the overhead light, the stacks of books I had wedged in every available corner, the colorful collection of candlesticks that cluttered the coffee table. A faint urge to cry pricked the back of my eyes, but a deep breath and a shake of my head was enough to suppress the tears.

"Thanks, Helen," I said, fearing I'd hardly said it enough since she announced the opportunity.

"Ah, don't mention it," she said, waving me off. "Just a little summer work, that's all."

"Not just for the job. For everything. The years at O'Shea's, this apartment, for looking out for me even after you fired me," I joked, trying to cover the wobble in my voice with a laugh. "I don't think I ever thanked you properly."

"Go over there and make me proud," she said. "That's how you can thank me. Do good work for Lori, and don't make me regret recommending you." We laughed quietly, not quite looking at each other. "And go easy on yourself, will you, Chelsea? I know this might not be ideal but try to get something out of it. You might surprise yourself."

"Yeah," I said, thinking she was wrong but hoping she was right.

After another silent moment looking at the empty apartment, Helen closed the door: an action as literal as it was metaphorical. In just a few short days another door would be opened, and I would be on the other side.

THE REST OF THE WEEK passed in a blur of buying rain gear, combing the travel section of the drugstore, and shoving the last of my things into suitcases. I spent more time than I cared to admit weighing and taking things out and weighing again. The packing was nearly as stressful as the move itself.

"I would be excited if I were you," Ada said on my last night home, the two of us sharing a bottle of wine on my parents' couch. "Who doesn't love a good adventure?"

"Me," I said, pouring a sizable swig into my mouth. "Adventures stress me out. Maybe you should go instead."

"Don't threaten me with a good time. Let's think of at least one thing you can be excited about. Besides the boring job stuff. Come on," she said, putting her glass on the table and turning to face me.

"This feels like a therapy exercise," I said. "Do we have to?"

"Don't make me make it five."

"Fine," I said, crossing my legs under me and turning to face her. "One thing . . ." I narrowed my eyes, and she gave me a smug nod in return.

"I, uh, I don't have to pay for breakfast anymore?" I tried. "Or rent?"

"Okay," Ada said, trying to maintain her enthusiasm. "That's . . .

something! Are there any other perks besides free breakfast and no rent?"

I thought for a minute, trying to think of something real. If Ada was patient enough to tolerate my bullshit, the least I could do was take her exercise seriously. It was for my own good, after all.

"I guess I'll probably learn a lot," I said eventually, slowly, like I was testing the idea. "I haven't really traveled on my own, and I've obviously never worked in a hostel, so I'll probably learn at least something about myself and my career while I'm there."

"Yes!" Ada said, beaming. Her smile alone made me glad I played along. "Look at you. Already embracing your new-life life."

I laughed, returning to my wine. "I've hardly done anything yet," I said.

"Everyone has to start somewhere."

Normally someone as chronically optimistic as Ada would get under my skin, but she had been such a fixture of my up-bringing that I had long since gotten used to it. Maybe in this case I could even learn a thing or two.

We spent the rest of the night with low-budget Netflix rom-coms, a second bottle of wine, and nonsense chatter to avoid talking about how much we would miss each other. It was only a few months, but it was the longest Ada and I would be apart since college, which felt significant.

"All right, this is it then, isn't it?" she asked as we made our way to the foyer, prolonging our goodbye.

"Don't make it sound so final." I forced a laugh, and she smiled in return. "I'm coming back, you know."

"You say that now," she said, "but what if you fall in love with Ireland and never want to come home? Or worse, what if you fall in love with a person and never want to come home?"

"Relax," I said, rolling my eyes. "I can assure you; I will do neither." I may have been open to finding love in Boston, but I had no interest in finding love in Ireland. What sense did it make to fall for someone in a place I only planned to spend the summer?

"If you say so," she said, opening her arms to me. I stepped into the space, and we hugged for a long time, pulling away only to laugh at our own drama. "And you're sure you've packed everything you need? Toothbrush? Outlet converters?"

"Yes, Mom," I said. "Triple-checked. Which you know because you were there."

"You know, I've heard the Irish are sarcastic people. You'll fit in just fine," she said, and I rolled my eyes. "Good luck, Chels. Text me as soon as you can once you're there, okay? I want to know you made it safe. And I want to hear about how terrible the communal bathroom is."

"Not helping," I said, shoving her toward the door. "But you know I will." We hugged once more, said goodbyes and I-love-yous, and blew a hundred kisses to each other as she made her way to her car. I watched her taillights disappear down the street, missing her already. How was I going to survive in a new environment without my best friend? Or any friends, for that matter? I shook the thought from my head, knowing full well if I didn't, it would keep me up all night.

I was naive, really, to think I'd sleep at all. Night came and went, and I did little more than toss and turn and stare listlessly at the ceiling.

AND THE FOLLOWING DAY passed in much the same way. It was nearly impossible to focus on anything with a midnight flight looming in the distance, so I moved through last-minute logistics like a zombie until it was time to leave for the airport.

"Chelsea girl, time to go," my dad called from the foyer, and I heard the jingle of his keys.

My luggage thudded on every step from my room to the foyer like a countdown, ushering me toward the door. It felt eerily similar to the morning I first left for college, except UMass was ninety-four miles from home, and Galway was nearly three thousand.

"Ready?" my dad asked at the bottom of the stairs, taking my suitcase from my hand and replacing it with a tumbler of green tea.

"And if I wasn't?" I said, my voice quiet.

He kissed me on the temple. "I know you are," he said. "And I'll remind you any time you forget." I exhaled slowly, leaning into the brief moment of relief. "You can be excited and scared at the same time, you know," he added, hardly above a whisper.

I didn't have to tell him he was right.

"All right, then, you two should be off," my mother said, coming out from the kitchen and bringing us both back into reality. "Don't want you to miss your flight." We all knew I had more than enough time, nearly four hours, in fact, but I was equally eager to get the last goodbyes out of the way.

My dad was driving me to the airport, so he loaded the car while my mom and I went through the same routine Ada and I did last night. Hugs, kisses, good-lucks, rogue tears, poorly timed jokes, and constant reminders to call as soon as I landed.

"And remember, honey," she said as I walked down the front steps to the car. "You can always come home. There will always be space for you in the house and in the office."

I knew she was trying to be comforting, but her words had

the opposite effect. All they did was remind me what I needed to do to get my life back on track.

"Thanks," I said, sliding into the passenger seat of the car. "I'll call you when I land." She blew a kiss from the steps, my dad put the car in reverse, and we were off.

Logan Airport wasn't particularly crowded, so I got through security with plenty of time for an overpriced cocktail before I had to be at the gate. Fortunately, my dad always slipped me some cash when he dropped me at the airport, so the cost of the cocktail stung a little less.

I'd only been on a few long-haul flights in my twenty-eight years of life, and none of them were without a return ticket a few days later, so a massive Aperol spritz was in order.

A few sips of my drink steadied my nerves, and I exhaled for the first time all day. This was happening. I'd be boarding the plane before I knew it, leaving my life in Boston behind. I said a silent prayer that I'd sleep through most of the flight, hoping I could arrive in Galway without having had a six-hour panic attack on the way there.

Thanks to the spritz my eyes were heavy by the time the wheels were up, and my journey was officially underway.

Chapter 4

The pilot had given us a weather update as soon as we were on the tarmac at Shannon Airport, an hour from Galway, but the "gentle mist" she described was more of a cold, spitting rain that clung to my hair and my face and my clothes as I waited for a taxi. A few buses had already come and gone, with their drivers announcing the number of stops they were making on the way to Galway.

"Are you sure, there, lass? Save you a couple euros, it will," one of the drivers had said through the door at me, grimacing at the taxi stand.

"Thank you, but that's okay," I'd said, trying to sound confident in my decision to get a cab, when really I should have said *I have no idea how to get to where I'm supposed to be living for the next two months and I've never been to Ireland before and I have no real idea what I'm doing at all.*

"Suit yourself." He'd shrugged, closing his doors and rejoining the flow of traffic. When a cab finally arrived and we'd discussed the astronomical fare to get me to the hostel, I made a mental note to learn the bus system after all.

As we drove away from the airport and onto the highway, reality settled into my bones alongside the cold rain that seeped through my clothes. I felt how I imagined Dorothy must have felt when she woke up in Oz. Only instead of a rainbow, I was greeted by slate-gray skies and overlapping shades of soft greens for miles and miles. I leaned my head against the window, letting the glass quell my anxiety and cool the burning in my cheeks.

After miles and miles of the very nothingness I was so afraid of, seemingly out of nowhere, the countryside became a small village, and I felt the pressure of my impending arrival. The village seemed mostly residential, save for its own small high street. I clocked a few shops wedged between pubs and markets and parks, though the rest of the village seemed to be small cottage-esque homes with gardens triple their size. Its colors were wind-worn and faded, but it seemed impossibly determined to remain cheerful in the face of the temperamental Irish weather. For a fleeting moment, I envied that resolution.

Toward the end of the high street, the taxi slowed to a stop outside what revealed itself to be the Wanderer. The facade was unassuming, wedged between what I assumed to be the hostel's bar and a small grocery store, and if it wasn't for the colorful bunting draped over the awning, I might have missed it altogether. After paying the painfully high fare and thanking the driver, I hauled my suitcase from the trunk and turned to face what would be my home for the summer.

"You must be Chelsea." An older woman, undoubtedly Lori, came bustling out of the front door with her hand outstretched. She sounded so much like Helen I felt my heart squeeze in my chest.

"Yes, hi," I said, trying to sound cheerful despite the exhaustion from the flight. "You must be Lori."

"What gave it away, my good looks? Or did Helen leave that

part out?" Lori pretended to push a lock of hair over her shoulder despite her pixie cut, and a quiet laugh slipped from my lips. If it wasn't for their matching caramel eyes and their identical voices, I never would have believed they were sisters. Where Helen was reserved and put-together, Lori seemed to be the creative hippie type.

"Let's get you inside," Lori said before I responded, draping an arm around my shoulders and leading me through the doors.

The lobby of the Wanderer looked exactly like the brochure, only the colors were somehow brighter and gaudier in real life. A neon sign reading *fáilte*, a word I quickly learned to mean "welcome," blinked erratically behind the reception desk, casting the left side of the lobby in an artificial glow. The right side seemed to serve as one of a few common areas, boasting a pool table, a few vending machines, and a handful of mismatched beanbag chairs.

"Like what you see?" Lori asked, watching me look around. I hope my face didn't give anything away. I wasn't sure *like* was the right word so much as *processing*. Truthfully, it reminded me a little of my undergraduate dorm, only somehow more run-down. The carpets were shredding at the edges, the wood paneling was chipping off the walls, and there were a few bugs in the light fixtures.

"Yeah," I said, hoping I sounded convincing. "Looking forward to seeing the rest of the place." That part wasn't a lie, at least. I was dying to see my room, mostly because if I didn't lie down in the next ten minutes I was liable to fall asleep standing up.

"Let's get to it, then," she said. "The grand tour awaits." She motioned out of the room, bangles clanking loudly up her arm as she did so, and I obeyed.

"So, the rooms you're seeing now are the guest rooms. We have four-person to twelve-person dorms, all mixed gender, and a small handful of private rooms. There are communal bathrooms on each end of the hallway, and all guests and staff have access to this laundry room." She swung a door open and I peered in at the stacks of old washers and dryers, trying not to wince as their cacophonous thumping flooded the hallway. It was a far cry from the in-unit arrangement I had in Boston, which I tried not to think about.

"And just down here we have the gym," Lori said as we rounded another corner. A few foggy glass windows framed the "gym," which was hardly more than a few old treadmills and a sparse stack of free weights. I never thought I'd miss paying nearly two hundred bucks a month for an unnecessarily bougie Pilates studio, but I never thought I'd be living in a hostel in Galway, either, so there was a first for everything.

For a second, I wondered if Jack and Helen had actually ever been here.

"And over here," Lori said, pulling me back into the present, "we have another common area, this one with table tennis, a projector, and loads of board games." She talked as we walked, swinging open doors and greeting staff and guests along the way. I kept my gaze ahead of me, offering only shy smiles when someone forced eye contact, too overwhelmed by the space itself to register new faces. "The common areas are a great way to meet people, so I'm sure you'll be spending a lot of time in them. Best to jump in right away!"

I offered a wordless nod, trying, and failing, to appear grateful. I hadn't even put down my luggage and was already expected to socialize? Play board games? I was more of a one-martini-at-happy-hour-with-Ada-then-home-by-eight kind of girl. I was still processing the state of the communal laundry room, so I had a feeling it would be a while before I jumped in on the group game night.

"And up here," she said as we climbed a narrow set of crooked stairs, "are the staff rooms. Yours is room two, right here on the left." She opened the door with a brass key, and I stood motionless in the doorway.

Helen had told me the room was cozy, but I hadn't realized "cozy" was code for "minuscule." The single bed shoved into the corner of the room reminded me of the one I slept on during my week sleepaway camp, nothing more than a wooden frame and a paper-thin mattress. The only other furniture was a small desk beneath a window and a wooden wardrobe to match the bed frame. I fumbled along the wall for a light switch, only to learn all I had was a floor lamp with a pull string.

"This is . . ." I started. "Thanks, Lori." I was too tired to say anything else. And the tone in her voice on the tour was too proud for me to ever let it slip that her sister had massively oversold the property, even if it was the truth. All I wanted to do was flop face down on the bed and close my eyes, hoping that when I opened them, I would be back in Boston. On my fourteen-inch mattress with my ambient fairy lights.

"I hope it suits you," she said, raising her eyebrows in my direction. Had I given something away? Could she tell I was deeply out of my element and, quite frankly, terrified?

"It's great," I said, reminding myself not to complain about free rent to the woman putting a roof over my head. I could do that with Ada later.

"If you need anything, just— Oh, Collin! Come in here for a minute, would you?" She called to someone in the hall. I fought to suppress a groan. The last thing I needed was to be introduced to anyone right now. I was disheveled, certain the bags under my eyes made me look like I'd been in a boxing match, and I wasn't exactly in the friendliest mood.

"No need to trouble anyone," I started, desperate to be left alone, "I wouldn't want to—"

"Chelsea, this is Collin." She held her hands up like she was on a game show, framing Collin like the grand prize. And for the second time since I walked into this room, I was paralyzed.

Collin wasn't much taller than me, which meant his eyes were that much closer to mine. They were such a clear green they looked like marbles, and I had to swallow twice so my mouth didn't dry out completely. His sandy hair matched the faint freckles that dotted his cheeks, becoming scarce as they crept to the angles of his jaw, which made sense to me. I too would be wary of approaching something so sharp.

"Aye, pleasure to meet ya, Chelsea." He extended a calloused hand, and I tried not to notice how it felt in mine. I was busy contemplating how I felt about the sound of my name in the Irish accent, and I didn't have the brain capacity at the moment to do both.

"Collin is kind of our jack-of-all-trades," Lori explained. "He's mostly the hostel tour guide, you know, taking visitors around the country, but he also does a bit of bartending and sometimes some farm work off the property." Collin's wide smile at her description was lopsided, but his teeth were surprisingly straight.

"She oversells me," he said, nudging Lori. "I'm mostly a pain in her arse." She laughed, perhaps a bit too loud, wiping nonexistent sweat from her brow.

"Ah, and he's humble," I joked, though I wasn't sure why.

"She's clever, this one, is she?" he said to Lori, still looking at me.

"She is," I answered, running a hand through my hair before planting both hands on my hips. I was too tired for however it was he was looking at me, and it was dangerously close to seeping into my tone.

"Really, Chelsea, if you want to see more of the country, he's your guy," Lori said. More of the country? I hadn't even seen anything beyond the route from the airport to the hostel, and my eyes were closed for half of it. And I didn't need a guy, tour guide or not, so she could squash both of those ideas, really.

"Duly noted," I said, trying to be polite. "I think I'll just focus on seeing the hostel, for now. You know, settling in and all."

"Right," Lori said, a blush creeping onto her cheeks. "I suppose you want to unpack and lie down for a bit. If you're feeling up to it later, please join us for a drink at the bar next door. If Collin's on tonight, he'll pull you a mean pint of the black stuff."

"I'm always on," he said, and I had a feeling he wasn't talking about the bar.

"I would imagine anyone with that job would have to be. It takes a lot to pull a lever and fill a glass with Guinness, doesn't it?" Why couldn't I stop myself? They were just on their way out . . . why couldn't I have let them go?

Collin's loud, low guffaw eclipsed Lori's, bouncing off the walls of my tiny room. "Don't let any of the locals hear ya saying that," he said. "They'll boot you right on out of here."

At this point, that might not have been the worst thing.

"This one here might give you a run for your money, Collin," Lori said, pointing at me with her thumb, still chuckling softly.

"Only one way to find out," he said. I chastised myself for noticing the way his tongue rested against the back of his teeth when he smiled, then looked beyond them both into the hallway, hoping they would go back to leaving. "Right, then," he said, taking the hint. "We'll be off. See you at the pub, then, Chelsea."

"Don't count on it," I said, smiling softly so he knew I wasn't trying to be rude. And because something about him made *not* smiling a challenge.

He slapped a hand against his chest, and I tried not to study the length of his fingers. "She's going to break my heart already too, isn't she?" he said to Lori without breaking eye contact with me.

"You seem to have that covered all on your own," Lori said. "Now let the woman unpack. We'll all catch up later."

I hoped by *later*, Lori really meant *tomorrow* or *next week*. The only thing I planned to do later was take a long, hot shower, unpack, and get under the covers with a book as soon as the sun set.

IF I THOUGHT the communal laundry room was bad, nothing could have prepared me for the communal bathroom. Sure, I shared a bathroom in my undergrad, for a year or two when I was hardly twenty years old. As an adult woman, it was more daunting than I could have imagined.

The bathroom on my end of the hallway was shared by rooms one through six, though I had yet to meet any of the occupants. There were three of everything: stalls, urinals, sinks, showers.

Thinking the shower would be "hot," however, proved to be even more of a pipe dream. Lukewarm water trickled from a removable showerhead, which I had to hold directly against my head for the water to penetrate my waves. I hoped someone else in this block of rooms had red hair, otherwise, I would be the obvious culprit for constantly clogging the shower drain.

I managed to make it out of the bathroom unnoticed, but on the short walk back to my room, I was intercepted by a woman around my age, with cropped curly hair the color of dark chocolate and a flawless olive complexion. She looked like a painting.

"You must be Chelsea," she said, echoing Lori's words from my arrival. "I'm Florence."

"Word travels fast around here, doesn't it?" I said.

"The hostel is like a small town within a small town. I mean, technically Galway is a city, but it doesn't feel like that at all. Everyone knows everything pretty much as soon as it happens, especially at the Wanderer," she said. "Oh god, sorry. That was intense for your first day." She must have clocked my facial expression. We both giggled, and I was relieved to meet someone capable of recognizing that fear.

"It's all been intense for a first day, to be honest," I said, trying to keep my voice light. "I take it you're not seasonal, then?"

"I used to be," she said. "But that was years ago. I planned to go home to Italy after my first winter, but never got around to booking the flight."

"Wow," I said, unable to hide my surprise. She just walked away from her life?

"I know, I know, not for everyone. A testament to the Wanderer, though, you know?"

If she was trying to sell me on this place, I wasn't buying it. Between the cold shower, the closet-size bedroom, and the way everyone apparently knew everyone else's business, it was more of a testament to Florence than anything else.

"I guess so," I said, turning in the direction of my room, signaling an end to the conversation. I had the opposite effect.

"Are you heading to the bar tonight? I have to work, but it's usually pretty popular on Saturdays, so it would be a great way to meet everyone else."

"Ah, I don't know about that," I said. I gestured to my appearance for effect, hoping she'd take notice of my sweats and realize I was in no shape to be at a bar. Or still having a conversation in the hallway, for that matter.

"Are you sure? Collin's bartending tonight, I think, and he—"

"Pulls a mean pint of the black stuff?" I repeated Lori's words from before, trying not to laugh at how ridiculous they felt in my mouth.

"You sound like an Irishwoman already," Florence said. "I take it you've met Collin, then?"

"I have," I said, trying to ignore the blush creeping up my neck.

"He's something, that one," Florence said, seemingly more to herself than to me. I hummed in agreement. "Well, if you change your mind, you know where to go."

"Thanks," I said, eager to get back into my room. "Nice to meet you, Florence."

"Call me Flo. Everyone else does." Her smile was warm, and I returned it to the best of my ability. She disappeared down the hall as I closed my door, and I relished the solitude. Finally. I put my shower caddy away, then sat down with my phone for my obligatory updates. First my parents, then Ada.

I gave my parents the abridged, parent-friendly version: everyone is nice; my room is fine; I'm settling in; yes, I've eaten; getting started tomorrow; yes, I'm five hours ahead here, so yes, it's 9:00; yes, I'm going to sleep soon because yes, I am exhausted, will call you again when I can, love you, bye.

As soon as Ada picked up the phone, however, I dove right in.

"Slow down," she chided me after a few minutes of my rambling.

"Seriously, Ada, what the hell have I done?"

"You've moved to Ireland, like you planned, and now you adjust. Which is to be expected when you move to a new country," she said like she was talking to a kindergartner.

"Adjusting would have been easier if any of this actually matched my expectations," I argued.

"You barely had any expectations," she replied with a laugh.

"This isn't funny, Ada," I said.

"I know. I'm sorry. I shouldn't have laughed. But I do think you need to take a deep breath."

"I'm trying, but it's so claustrophobic here. Have I mentioned how small it is? I can reach my wardrobe from my bed, and you know how short my arms are. I have no idea how anyone lives like this. Or why Helen chose to leave this out. Do you think she did it on purpose?"

"I see you haven't gotten any less dramatic since you left," she said.

"Was I supposed to change my personality when I got here?"

"No, Chels." She sighed. "But it might not kill you to lighten up. You want to survive there, don't you?"

"Do I?" At this point, it felt like it might be more trouble than it was worth. Would it really have been so hard to sort myself out in Boston?

"Are you kidding me?" she said. "What's the alternative, huh? You come home, move back into your childhood bedroom, and answer phones from foot patients for the rest of your twenties?" She had me there. "You aren't seriously thinking of bailing, are you?"

"No," I groaned. "You're right. I'll stay at least until I work something out in Boston. Which I'm getting started on first thing tomorrow, by the way."

"Knock yourself out," she said. "As long as you aren't spending it feeling sorry for yourself, I don't care what you do with your free time. Though I do think you should spend some of it with, what's his name, Charlie?"

"Collin," I said, then immediately regretted telling her about him in the first place. "But it doesn't matter what his name is because we are never going to need it."

"Famous last words," she said, and I could hear her smile down the line.

"Goodbye, Ada."

"Fine, fine. Call me later this week once you get a few shifts out of the way. And try to smile once or twice, if only so you don't forget how."

"Aye, aye, Captain."

"Smart-ass."

"Love you," I said.

"Love you, back. Talk soon."

By the time we hung up it was dark outside, the rain was coming down in sheets, and going to the bar was even less of an option than it was when I'd gotten out of the shower. Everyone else seemed to think being waited on by Collin would ease the nerves that came with my arrival, but I knew it would do exactly the opposite. I slipped under the covers, pulled them over my head, and set an alarm for first thing in the morning. I needed every second of sleep to prepare for whatever my first day of work had in store.

Chapter 5

"Chelsea, this is Lars. He'll be training you this week." Lori gestured to the man standing next to her, who stood well over six feet tall and bore a striking resemblance to a Ken doll. "He's the recreational director now, but he spent some time as a receptionist in the past, so he knows the ropes. You're in good hands."

I smiled, fighting a yawn, and shook his hand. Between the jet lag, the plastic mattress, the roaring wind, and the creaking from every corner of the hostel at all hours of the night, sleep didn't come as easily as I'd hoped.

"It's a pleasure," Lars said in a Dutch accent, nearly crushing my hand as we shook. "Ready to get started?"

"Ready as I'll ever be," I joked.

"That's the spirit." His voice was louder than anyone's should ever be at this hour, and it became instantly clear why he'd been promoted to recreational director. This kind of enthusiasm would have wasted away behind a reception desk.

For me, the morning passed in a blur. It wasn't a ton of information, and it wasn't entirely different from working at O'Shea's, but the combination of the lack of sleep and the foreign environment made it difficult to process. For Lars, however, the morning passed in streams of light and color. How could anyone be so excited about organizing spreadsheets and answering landlines?

"You're a fast learner, there," he said as he supervised me making a booking over the phone.

"I have a lot of experience," I said. "I used to work in a bed-and-breakfast back home in Boston, doing reception and some event planning on the side and whatever else."

"That explains a lot," he said. "Most of our seasonal staff are untrained, so this process usually requires a lot more work on my end. But you're making my job nice and easy this morning." His smile was blinding.

"Well, I aim to please," I said.

"How'd you end up here, anyway? What happened to the bed-and-breakfast?" If everyone was this nosy, I understood how word traveled so quickly.

"It closed," I said, willing to share only the facts. "The owners, Lori's sister and brother-in-law, sold so they could retire."

"Ah, I see," he said. "And you didn't want to stay in Boston?" Was this interrogation part of the training?

"I-I, uh . . ." I stuttered. "I'm just taking a break, that's all. Returning as soon as the summer is over." *Or as soon as I line up a job and an apartment*, I refrained from adding aloud.

"Pity," he said, busying himself by shuffling a stack of papers on the desk. "I have a feeling you'll be good here."

The compliment was surprising and it warmed me for a second. Someone thought I would be good here. Then I felt the instant pressure of having to live up to anyone's expectations, so I pushed the thought from my mind and refocused on the training.

"Thank you," I said, trying to remain neutral.

"Did Lori mention some of the other stuff you'd be doing besides running the desk?" he asked, and I felt my eyes widen.

"Other stuff?"

"Nothing crazy, don't worry. We all just pick up odd jobs here and there. Whatever we need to do to keep the hostel running. Sometimes it's housekeeping, helping Flo in the kitchen, picking up a bartending shift, whatever it is. It's a real community feel around here."

The thought of having to change strangers' sheets repulsed me, but a group of people supporting one another at work sounded . . . nice. We hadn't had a ton of staff at O'Shea's, and even so, we hadn't interacted much. Everyone kept to their own jobs, but here, I sensed I was going to have to get used to the opposite.

"And you mentioned event planning back home, yeah?" Lars clarified.

I rubbed the back of my neck, suddenly weirdly insecure even though I was the one who volunteered that information. "Yeah, but I know that's your thing here, so I'm not trying to step on anyone's toes. Just here to answer phones." I hoped my smile hid how awkward I felt.

"I'm mostly in charge of the athletic stuff," he said. "Kayaking, hiking, cycling, yoga, that sort of thing. So we could use someone around here to organize some other events, now that I think about it. Maybe you could help out that way instead of changing sheets. If you're keen, of course."

Was I keen? I hadn't realized it might have been a possibility, but it would look good on my résumé. And a good résumé would help me get out of here. And anything was better than changing sheets.

"That sounds great," I said, trying to return his friendly

smile. "Thanks." He nodded in response, wordlessly resuming our tour.

LARS AND I SPENT the rest of the day reviewing some of those odd jobs, changing over guest rooms, visiting Flo as she prepared for the dinner service, going over the weekly schedule of outdoor activities and tours, and meeting some of the other staff.

"Is every day this busy?" I asked Lars as we closed out our last booking of the day.

"Sometimes busier," he replied. "People always seem to think working at the hostel is going to be easy, but it's hard work. It pays off in a big way, though, since we get to meet all kinds of interesting people and show them such a beautiful place. Helping people make lasting memories is quite the reward for the workload."

Busier? If that was the case, when was I supposed to look for jobs? Apartments? How would I set up my life back in Boston for my return? I forced the panic from my chest, reminding myself I still had nights and off-days. I could find the time, right?

"At least we don't have to work around the clock," I said, trying to gauge how much free time I would actually have. "Those days off are probably superrelaxing."

"If you use them to relax," he said, leaning back in the desk chair and spinning it around. "But if I'm honest, most of us play as hard as we work. We use the free time to explore Ireland, or go down the pub for a few too many pints, or to travel wherever else we can find cheap flights. There's never a dull moment. Which leads me to our last stop of today's training," he said, getting up from his chair and gesturing out the door.

How could we possibly have more to do? I was exhausted, and I'd desperately hoped closing down the phones was the last item on our agenda. "To the bar," he said. Of course. I should have known.

His broad smile told me there was no way I was getting out of this. He was in charge of my training, after all, and I prided myself on my work ethic. If that was the last stop for today, so be it. A drink might actually feel good.

AN OVERHEAD BELL ANNOUNCED our arrival as we walked through the door, but no one turned to look. Groups of people, travelers and locals alike, I assumed, crowded around tables, barrels, and barstools, talking over one another and swigging heavily from pint glasses. It was more crowded than I anticipated, and I followed Lars closely as we weaved around the throngs to the bar.

We slid onto two stools near the wall, which was covered in notes, Polaroids, and ticket stubs from years and years of passing travelers. I studied them, imagining the lives of these people. Had they all come to Galway just for fun? Had any of them been forced from their job and their apartment and backed into a corner? Or was I the only one pathetic enough to flee the country to avoid having to move back in with her parents? And if they did come to Galway for fun, what exactly did they find?

If I was honest, I hadn't done as much traveling as I felt I should have by my age. Every time I considered planning a trip, something came up at work, or it was too expensive, or Ada was too busy to take time off and I didn't have the courage or the desire to travel alone. So I probably had a lot to learn about what travelers found *anywhere*, not just Galway.

"And what'll it be for you, then?" A deep voice broke my reverie, redirecting my attention to the bar.

Collin was drying a pint glass, looking at me with expectant eyes. His short-sleeve shirt revealed a collection of small tattoos scattered over his forearms, which flexed as he dried the glass. I fought against the hypnotic effect of his spinning the rag around and around, trying to answer his question.

I scanned the taps before remembering there was only one option. "Well," I said, pretending to look for another bartender, "I was hoping for a Guinness, but I'm not sure there's someone around here who can pull a good one. Lars, any suggestions?"

"Lars, do not answer that," he said, and Lars raised his hands in surrender, signaling he wouldn't say a word. Collin turned to me, releasing the glass and leaning on the bar. "And what is it you know about pulling a good Guinness, hmm?"

"I know it can't be that hard." I shrugged my shoulders. "Pull the lever, fill the glass, what more is there?"

"Already slagging me off, are ya?" He flashed a wicked grin and I stalled, searching for a response.

"Already what?"

His grin turned to a laugh and it made me want to crawl under the bar. "Slagging me off," he said again. "Like teasing, getting under my skin, you know." I felt flustered thinking about teasing or getting under his skin.

"Right," I said, feeling the banter slip from my fingers.

"You've a lot to learn," he said, but not unkindly. "Starting with this."

I watched him sling a glass under the tap, tilting it just so, pulling the pint with expert hands. When the glass was nearly full, he stopped the tap and let the beer settle before continuing. I watched the color turn from chocolate to ink, silently embarrassed that I didn't know this really was an art. By the time he was finished, a perfect Guinness sat in front of me. Black as night, label on the pint glass turned outward, an inch of milky foam resting on top.

He slid it toward me, resting his elbows on the bar and his chin on the heels of his hands. On both wrists he wore thin, fraying leather string bracelets and, for a second, I wondered where they came from. "Go on," he said, glancing from my eyes to the glass and back again. "Give it a go."

"I know what a Guinness tastes like," I said, not fully ready to admit I was out of my depth here.

"You've had one in Ireland, then?" he said.

"Well, no, but—"

"Then you've no idea what a Guinness tastes like."

I narrowed my eyes, and he did the same. It was a standoff, and I was fighting uphill. I tried not to notice his gaze travel to my lips as I sipped the beer, but the way his eyes lingered made it impossible to ignore. Ada would have loved this.

"It's fine," I said, trying to keep my voice steady.

"Of all the things I thought you'd be," he said, running his tongue over his teeth, "I didn't have you pegged for a liar."

I hated the way my stomach buzzed at the thought of him having thoughts about me. And he was right. I was a liar.

"Do you always go around making these accusations about your coworkers?"

"Well, it's not every day they come into my bar and lie to my face, now, is it, Lars?" Collin looked to Lars for support, who repeated his earlier hand gesture.

"Leave me out of this one, mate," Lars said. "I've been here long enough to know not to mess with anyone disparaging the black stuff."

"Clever bloke," Collin said, nodding in his direction. "You might learn a thing from him too while you're at it."

"More than I'll learn from you, I suppose," I said.

"You're stalling."

"I am not."

"You are," Lars said, going back on his word.

"Fine," I said, reaching the end of my rope. "It was surprising." Collin crossed his arms over his chest, raising his brows in a way that urged me to continue. "It was lighter than I thought it would be. And less bitter." That was all I would give him. I would never tell him I actually liked it.

"I think a lot of things are going to surprise you about Ireland, Chelsea," he said, going back to cleaning glasses, apparently satisfied with the ending of our Guinness debacle.

"Don't you have other customers to bother?" I asked, sharply. I'd heard that line enough from everyone in Boston, so I definitely didn't need to hear it from him. We both looked over his shoulder to see a small group forming at the other end of the bar, undoubtedly waiting for his attention.

"I got 'em," Lars said, sliding off his stool and heading behind the bar. He really wasn't kidding when he said they picked up each other's slack. How did he still have the energy for work?

"We're done here, anyway," I said.

"We . . ." Collin started, replacing Lars on the stool beside me, "are just getting started."

My breath caught in my throat. Had Lars and I been sitting this close? Collin was thin and angular, but his presence so close to me was overbearing. I risked spinning my stool to face him, not quite sure what I was getting myself into but unwilling to back down.

"You like telling people what to do, huh?" I asked, sizing him up. He wore a plain white T-shirt with surprisingly few wrinkles and a pair of tan jeans, cuffed at the ankles. When he rested one of those ankles across his knee I caught a glimpse of more faded black ink, and for a torturous second I allowed myself to imagine the rest of his tattoos. The rest of his body. What it might look like under all the earth tones.

What was I doing? I came here for a job and a place to live, not to flirt with some arrogant tour-guide-bartender-farmer-handyman who seemed determined to make decisions for me.

"Only with their best interest in mind," he said, answering the question I'd forgotten I'd asked. "Part of the territory as the resident tour guide. Though usually when I give advice, people accept it. Especially out-of-towners. You might look Irish with that red hair of yours, but that Boston accent isn't fooling anybody." He smiled at my surprise, leaning back on the stool, and sipping a beer of his own.

"How'd you recognize the accent?"

"Been around it quite a bit. I spent a summer there myself, years ago. Lori's sister, Helen, has a bed-and-breakfast with her husband. Did some seasonal work for them in 2017, the first summer they opened."

Guinness nearly shot from my nose.

"That's where I used to work!" I said, clearing my throat before my enthusiasm got the better of me. "I started there that fall. I can't believe you know Helen and Jack."

"I can't believe we missed each other," he said, eyes glinting. "To think we could have met years ago."

"Ah, yes. My summer after college was really missing a nosy tour guide intent on disrupting strangers trying to have a peaceful drink after a long day."

"Ouch," he said, bringing a hand to his chest for effect. With his fingers splayed wide, his hands looked twice the size they did when he was pulling the pints. "Besides, we're hardly strangers."

"We don't know anything about each other."

"So, tell me something about yourself." He smiled, and I knew I walked right into that.

"Hmm." I pretended to think. "Oh, I have something good," I said. "A fun fact: I'm exhausted. And I would very much like to pay for this pint, go back to the hostel, take a long shower, and go directly to sleep."

Collin laughed, bringing his glass to his lips and taking a slow sip, wholly undeterred by my attitude. "Tell me something real and I won't even charge ya for the pint."

"Fine," I conceded, figuring it might get me out of there quicker than arguing. "What is it you so desperately need to know?" Apparently, the single pint was getting to my head.

"Why don't you like it here?" he asked, any trace of jest gone from his tone.

"What?" I asked, though I heard him loud and clear. "I do like it here. What makes you think I don't? I mean, it's new to me, obviously, but I don't dislike it." My rambling betrayed me. I didn't want to offend anyone, but I was a terrible liar.

"Aye, Chelsea, I've seen you around today. You've been looking ready to leg it since you got out of bed."

I didn't need a translation here. He sounded surprisingly hurt by this, as if my not liking Ireland was a personal attack.

"It's only been one day," I said by way of excuses. "And it was long and I'm jet-lagged and trying to catch up, that's all."

"It's just usually most people show up in Galway for the summer bright-eyed and ready to jump right into the craic, you know? See what Ireland has to offer. And you seem intent on avoiding the craic at all costs, if I'm honest."

"Have you yet to figure out I'm not most people?"

"Oh, lass. That much I've known since you walked in the door."

A flush spread over my chest, and I hoped he didn't notice. "Really?" I raised an eyebrow, secretly nervous about where he might be going but trying not to show it.

"Course," he said, taking a long swig. "You've got an edge to ya. And that's not to say I don't like it." Another sip. "And don't even get me started on how you look." He dragged his eyes over the length of my body, making no attempt to hide the desire behind his gaze.

On cue, Lars wandered over and refilled both pints. My mouth was a desert, and I was desperate for a little liquid courage. The one was no longer going to cut it, and I needed something to do with my mouth that wasn't opening and closing it while searching for something to say.

"Make a deal with me," he said suddenly when I failed to respond, no longer concerned about his initial question.

"And why would I do that?"

"Because you aren't totally thick, and you might want to actually enjoy yourself this summer."

I took another swig, staring him down. "Tell me what it is before I agree."

"Let me show you the country," he said. "Properly. I know you don't seem to think Ireland is much of anything. But, if you're willing to see it, I mean really see it, it'll continue to surprise you. In all the best ways. Hell, it still surprises me, and I've lived on the west coast my entire life." His voice changed when he talked about the country and I couldn't pinpoint exactly why, but it made me nostalgic.

"So, what?" I asked. "Like a day trip, see the sights, hit all the highlights, come back here?"

His laugh was low, and it rumbled through me like distant thunder. "One day is hardly going to cut it, and the highlights aren't what you think they are. We'll take our time. See it little by little. We have the whole summer, after all. And by the end, I guarantee you won't want to leave."

The daunting length of the season stretched out before me. Whereas I'd previously been hoping it would pass in the blink of an eye, I was beginning to realize it would do the opposite. That's how time seemed to work here.

"I'm not so sure about that last part," I said, confident in at least that much. There was no chance I didn't go right back to Boston as soon as I had the opportunity.

"I'm just asking you to trust me," he said. "That's all. And to give Ireland a chance. I promise, she'll be good to you."

I was stuck here anyway, until I could find a way to get myself out. Trying to enjoy it might not be the worst thing. It didn't mean I'd stop actively trying to leave, but it might lower my cortisol levels a little, which definitely wouldn't hurt. Besides, even I wasn't stubborn enough to deny a proposal like that, from a man who looked like this.

"And you're sure this isn't just a chance to get more business as a tour guide? Boost your reviews, make a few tips? Surely, there's something in it for you." I couldn't resist one last opportunity to rib him and I was missing the levity that had disappeared from this conversation.

"It's on the house." He smiled. "Staff get to use all the amenities the Wanderer has to offer, for free. The only thing in it for me is the joy of sharing my love for this country. And the fact that I'll get to prove you wrong, of course."

"We'll see about that." By this point in the conversation, we were wearing matching smirks, and I hoped Lars wasn't listening.

"Whatever you're worried about, Chelsea, let it go. I've got you." To him, it may have been a throwaway comment, but to me, it was a rock at the base of my throat. A warm current just under my skin. Three words so unexpectedly intimate all I could do was nod.

"So, do we have ourselves a deal?" He extended his hand, and I narrowed my eyes before I shook it. "Say yes, Chelsea," he said, dropping his volume so only I could hear. The depth of his voice vibrated in the space between us, and even if I hadn't planned on agreeing before, those words might have been able to change my mind.

"We do."

He beamed, and it was almost impossible not to do the same. Whatever it was about him that got under my skin the way it did should have been a warning sign. A waving red flag, a blaring alarm, something that sent me running in the opposite direction. Instead, it was pulling me in headfirst.

Our handshake lingered just long enough for the heat of his hand to make its way through my body, and I hadn't the slightest clue what I'd just gotten myself into.

Chapter 6

A pounding headache woke me just before the sun and I scrambled in my nightstand drawer for ibuprofen. I tried to give it time to kick in, tossing, turning, and hoping to fall asleep again, but it became hopeless as the sun crept higher into the sky.

Before I got out of bed, I let my eyes roam around the room. My denim jacket already hung over the back of the desk chair, my journal and an expensive candle were arranged in the windowsill, and a pair of New Balance sneakers sat near the door. Everything else had already found a home, despite the size of the room: toiletries arranged carefully in a caddy, clothes folded and hung neatly in the wardrobe, essential oils and lip masks and melatonin tucked into the drawer in the nightstand.

When I managed to pull myself out of bed, I changed into leggings and a windbreaker, plaited my hair into two French braids, and slipped out of my room undetected. The fresh air of a morning walk would surely help the hangover, and I had time to kill before I had to be at the reception desk.

Outside the hostel, Galway was silent, save for the gentle sounds of nature before humans were awake to muffle them. A grassy field stretched behind the Wanderer and curled around a pond I hadn't noticed until now, and I felt it pulling me into its orbit. I followed my feet as they dragged through the damp grass, carrying me down a makeshift trail. Careful not to walk too far, I noted landmarks as I went. A small shed, a lopsided bench, the remnants of a vegetable garden.

"I didn't expect to see you out here so early." A rumbling voice cut through the silence. I whipped around, both relieved and startled to see the voice belonged to Collin.

"And I didn't expect anyone to give me a heart attack so early, so I guess we're both surprised," I said. He chuckled, and it echoed over the water.

"What brings you out at this hour?" he asked, turning his wrist over to look at his watch.

"A woman can't just get up early and go for a walk?"

"Didn't quite have you pegged as a morning person, that's all."

"And what did you have me pegged as, hmm?" I crossed my arms, knowing I was taking the bait.

"Oh, you know. Just away with the fairies is all."

I most certainly did not know. His accent was challenging enough on its own, made only more difficult by the slew of idioms I didn't understand.

"Away with the fairies?" I asked.

"Just out of touch a bit. Distracted. Like your body is here, but your mind is someplace else." That was putting it lightly.

"Does being away with the fairies mean I get to miss the early morning ridicule?" I asked, raising my eyebrows at him. "Do I get to do whatever the fairies are doing instead?"

"Aye, you want to know about the fairies?" He ignored my jab, and I watched his eyes light up at my question.

"You may have piqued my interest," I confessed.

"I don't know if you're ready yet," he mused, eyebrows lowered as he pretended to study me. "Fairy stories can't be wasted on skeptics." The longer we stared at each other, the more I realized he was serious.

"So you're a storyteller too, huh?" I asked. "That's your, what, eighth job here? Ninth?" I pretended to count on my fingers, though I really couldn't keep track.

"Storytelling is not a job," he said, still serious. "It's an art. Especially in Ireland."

Duly noted. My cheeks reddened at yet another thing I felt I should have known before I arrived. Or maybe at the way he sounded when he was talking about art.

I checked my watch, secretly hoping it was time to return to the Wanderer and get to work. There was a certain intimacy creeping into the early morning that I wasn't prepared for, and I needed to get myself in check before he could see the effect he had on me.

"Always eager to get to the next thing, are ya?" he asked, nodding toward my wrist. For a man with a million jobs, he seemed to have plenty of time for observation.

"Just want to make sure I'm not late," I replied, forcing his question to stay on the surface. If I let it in any deeper, I might have to consider it.

"Ah, you've got plenty of time for that still. Mornings are slow in Galway."

"So I'm learning." We fell into step beside each other, tracing the path back toward the hostel.

"I'm thinking we start your formal education this weekend. Neither of us has to work on Friday, so we can jump right in."

"How do you know I don't have to work on Friday?"

"Schedule's posted in the staff room," he said, smiling in a way that made me want to roll my eyes out of my head and into the pond.

"Sounds like you have it all figured out, then," I said. "Do you even need me?"

"Deal's a deal," he said. "We shook on it, remember? You wanted nothing to do with Ireland, I charmed you into agreeing to let me show you the country, now you're bound to fall in love with it before the summer's over . . . ringing any bells?"

I wish I didn't remember, I wanted to say. *I wish I hadn't been thinking about the feeling of my hand in yours since you let it go.*

"Friday it is," I said eventually, taking a deep breath.

"Right then," he said. "You can exhale, you know. I'll go easy on ya at the beginning. We can start slow. Work our way up to the big stuff."

"Do I even want to ask what the big stuff is?"

"All in good time," he said. I hummed, and we walked in silence the rest of the way. For a supposed storyteller, he was painfully cryptic. I had a feeling the week was going to crawl to Friday, which meant I was going to have to find a way to pass the time that didn't involve trying to uncover Collin Finegan's secrets.

We reached the hostel just as the night staff was turning over, and Flo was already laying out a small breakfast buffet. As soon as the bell chimed above the door, she snapped her head in our direction.

"Good morning, you two," she said, crossing her arms and leaning back against the buffet table. "I take it drinks went well last night?"

"No," I said, perhaps a bit too quickly, nervous she had the wrong idea. "I mean yes, drinks were fine, but we were just—"

"Found this one on a walk at sunrise," Collin said, gesturing to me with his thumb and grabbing an apple off the table. Flo swatted his hand as he disrupted her display, and he took a large bite an inch from her face. The juice from the apple clung to his lips, and I hated myself for noticing.

"Ah, enjoying Galway, are we?" she asked me.

"Just trying to get a little fresh air before work, that's all," I said. Why was everyone so concerned with whether I liked Galway?

"She's going to be enjoying it soon enough," Collin said with his mouth full. "Taking her out on Friday."

"Not *out* out, like on a date or anything," I corrected, though Flo hadn't said a word. "Just a tour."

"She wishes it was a date," Collin said, tossing the core of the apple into the trash like a basketball.

"Like hell I do," I said.

"Oh, Chelsea." He laughed a smug-ass laugh, shaking his head just slightly enough to notice. Whether he was unfazed or faking it was impossible to tell, which only flustered me even more.

"Have a nice day at work, ladies," he said without giving me enough time to think of a witty response, then disappeared down the hallway.

"Is he like this with everyone?" I ventured once he was out of earshot.

"For the most part," she said, and while I wasn't sure what kind of response I was looking for, there was no denying the inexplicable pang of what might have been disappointment. "Some more than others. You'll get used to it." We shook our heads and settled into our work. Flo continued arranging fresh fruit and stirring bowls of porridge. I made myself comfortable behind the desk and tried to force myself not to care that Collin treated everyone the same.

Once the phone started ringing, it hardly stopped. Who knew this tiny hostel in the west of Ireland would get so much activity? I'd soon taken a handful of bookings for the next few weeks, answered some questions about our "amenities," and fumbled around with a map while trying to give directions to a lost German couple.

AFTER THE PHONE LINES SETTLED in the late afternoon and the bookings were up-to-date in the computer, I ventured into my own journey of trying to sort my life back home. I had just opened Google and searched "hospitality jobs Boston" when Lars appeared over my shoulder, slapping his big hand on the desk beside me.

"Leaving us already, are you? I thought we had until the end of the summer, at least."

I forced a laugh despite my frustration that he was snooping and also interrupting. "We do," I said, trying not to think about that length of time, "but I still need to have something lined up for when I leave."

"And how's the search going?"

"This is as far as I've gotten."

"And as far as you're going to get, I'm afraid," he said. "We have a hen do coming in this weekend, and they're looking for something special."

"What does that mean for me?" I asked, fearful of his answer. "And what on earth is a hen do?"

"It's like, uh . . ." He snapped his fingers looking for a phrase I might know. "Bachelor party? But with ladies."

"Ah, a bachelorette," I said.

"Right," he confirmed. "Didn't you used to do stuff like this back in Boston? Parties and whatever?"

"I did, but only after I'd been working at the bed-and-breakfast for years. Not on my first day," I said.

"I tried to warn you." Lars grinned. "As soon as you sign a contract here, you're as much a part of this as anyone else, which means you aren't exempt from picking up the odd jobs. And in this case, we think you're the right person."

Intimidated as I might have been by the task on my first day, I couldn't deny I was flattered. And throwing myself into planning an event would be the perfect distraction.

"Thanks, Lars. I'd be happy to," I said before I lost my resolve. It was just a hen do at a hostel. How hard could it be?

"You're a star," he said, punching me lightly in the shoulder. "Knew we could count on you."

I was formatting the itinerary before he even left the room.

An hour of googling later and I was armed with a list of Galway's greatest pubs, all of which seemed to have live music, along with a single winery that offered a tasting, two spas located in hotels, a boat cruise, the website of a local photographer, a coupon for a group booking at a hair salon, and the contact information for a party bus company. Maybe I wasn't as rusty as I thought.

I had the rest of the week to make some calls and solidify the schedule, so I made a to-do list to keep myself organized. If I was going to do this, I was going to do it right.

Besides, something had to pass the time between now and Friday.

Chapter 7

By Thursday, I had a detailed itinerary for the bachelorette party printed on lilac paper and gift bags stuffed with things I pulled together from what I could find in the storage closet. Lori was so excited I had organized their weekend that she gave me the green light to use whatever I could find, so I collected soaps that had been donated by a local shop but never used, white cotton slippers, stacks of coupons for local eateries, and plastic sunglasses. It wasn't perfect, but it was the best I could do on short notice.

The women were set to check in tomorrow night, but I was assured I didn't have to be around to meet them since it was my day off. The itinerary had all the details, and Lars was working so he could give any additional recommendations.

Once the arrangements were made and everything had been settled, I had nothing else to do but wait for tomorrow to come. And not for the hen do.

I had spent most nights this week tossing and turning alongside the creaking floorboards and groaning pipes, trying not to listen for sounds down the hall. Especially from room five, which I saw Collin duck into the other night for the first time.

"I can't believe you're going on a date already," Ada had said on the phone one night when I told her about my impending plans. "You haven't been on a date since what's-his-face. That tech start-up guy? The one who only talked about himself and his mom?"

"It's not a date," I had told her for what had to have been the hundredth time, ignoring the reminder of my last one. "He's just, I don't know, showing me around Ireland or whatever."

"Chels, seriously, how can anyone be pissed about that? You have a personal tour guide. A really hot one. What's the problem?"

"You haven't even seen him," I'd reminded her. "You don't know if he's hot."

"Chelsea Gold," she'd said. "He's Irish. And he has tattoos. And green eyes and messy hair and he's a bartender. I don't have to see him to know he's hot."

I'd regretted everything I'd told her about Collin, but somehow I couldn't have stopped myself.

"It doesn't matter either way," I'd said. "The problem is that he *is* hot, and I'm just out here while I sort my life out. My focus for this summer is solely filling a gap in my résumé and finding a job and an apartment back home. Which means no men for me this summer. And no men ever who don't fit into the married-by-thirty-five-home-in-the-Boston-suburbs plan for the future."

"Keep telling yourself that."

As much as I loved Ada, sometimes she made me want to smack my head into the wall.

It also made me miss her. And the rest of my life at home. The only full-time positions in Boston I'd seen posted all week were a breakfast attendant at a hotel near the airport and a server at a local banquet hall.

I WOKE UP on Friday before my alarm and spent the extra time standing in front of my open wardrobe, staring mindlessly at my clothes. Collin and I had agreed to meet in the lobby at nine with no other instructions, so I hadn't the slightest clue how to dress.

After checking the weather app a dozen times despite the fact Ireland often saw four seasons in a day (which I now knew was no longer just an idiom), I settled on a white cotton T-shirt, straight-leg jeans with rips in the knees, and a pair of sneakers. A classic.

I put my hair in a ponytail, then took it down, then put it back up. I was being ridiculous. We were probably just going to be hiking around or looking at the ruins of some castle. I had no one to impress, so it didn't matter at all what I looked like.

I took my hair back down from the ponytail and headed to the lobby with five minutes to spare. Collin was already down there, sitting with his feet on the coffee table and dragging a toothpick back and forth between his teeth.

"You look like a farmer," I said.

"I look like you," he said, looking up and down at both of our outfits. He too was in jeans and a white T-shirt, only he had an army-green flannel layered on top and a battered pair of boots on his feet.

"One of us has to change," I said.

"Well, I look too good to change, so it can't be me," he said. "And you also look too good to change, so it looks like we're stuck like this. Are ya ready?"

The compliment sounded so natural coming out of his mouth I almost missed it. I clenched the inside of my lip between my teeth to avoid grinning and nodded toward the door.

"Lead the way."

"My specialty." He smiled, staring at me for an extra second before leaning down to grab a wicker basket I hadn't noticed before.

"What's in the basket?" I asked, following him toward the door.

"The usual," he said. "Bleach, knives, zip ties—"

"Very funny," I interrupted. "You'd make a terrible serial killer."

"What makes you so sure?"

"A serial killer would never own a picnic basket."

"So you do know what's in here after all."

I rolled my eyes, and my stomach rolled over with them

"This isn't, like, a date or anything, right?" I said.

"It isn't a date, Chelsea," he said. "You'd know if it was a date."

I exhaled, though I didn't like whatever feeling was mingling with relief. We crossed the street to a gravel parking lot, and I followed Collin's path to a small truck that looked better suited for a farm than the road.

"This is your car?" I asked, trying to keep my tone neutral. "Where are we going?"

"You ask too many questions," he said, opening the door for me then circling to the driver's side. "Your first lesson about Ireland is trust."

He turned the key in the ignition and after a few seconds of protest, the truck sputtered to life. "I've already learned trust," I said. "I'm out here letting you show me your beloved country, aren't I?"

"It's not about trusting me," he said. "It's about trusting her." He nodded out the window to what I assumed was Ireland in general, then threw the truck into gear and pulled into the street.

I tried to relax in the seat, maybe even look out the window while we drove, but it was nearly impossible when I had no idea where we were headed. And when I could see the ripples in his jaw as he clenched it around the toothpick.

"It's a bit of a road trip," he said as we reached the highway. "Nothing crazy. A few hours both ways. But figured I'd warn ya."

"You figured you'd warn me after we got in the truck?" Collin rubbed the back of his neck with his hand, and for a second I thought he might be embarrassed. "It's fine," I continued. "I don't mind being in the truck." He dropped his hand back to the wheel, both of us settling in for the ride.

"We're going straight across the country," he said. "Right down to the east coast there."

"I thought we were starting small."

"A picnic is small," he said, knowing that wasn't what I meant. "Besides, it's only a matter of time before we're cliff jumping, so enjoy this while it lasts."

"Cliff jumping?" I turned to face him so fast I gave myself whiplash. He snorted, looking in my direction just long enough for me to catch the way his teeth lined up right over each other in two perfect rows. "You can't be serious."

"A little adventure never hurt anyone," he said.

"That is absolutely not true."

He shrugged, his smile lingering on his lips. "Let's not get ahead of ourselves," he said. "Focus. Look out the window. Try to enjoy this."

I sighed, turning my gaze to the open window. Since we were on the highway, there was little more to look at than a smattering of trees or an open grassy field.

"It looks like Massachusetts," I said after a minute. He made a noise low in his throat I knew was frustration, but it raised the hairs on my arms. I dug my nails into the palms of my hands, trying to stop my train of thought before it got any further away from me.

"You are proper difficult, you know that?" he said, shaking

his head. "Look closer. And maybe for more than a minute this time."

I didn't know what I was supposed to be looking for, but I looked anyway. Something acoustic played from the old radio, tinny and far away.

AND EVENTUALLY, IT stopped looking like Massachusetts. The fields turned to rolling hills, which stretched for miles in all directions. Cattle and sheep dotted the endless green, and ruins of castles stood frozen in time. It wasn't hard to lose track of how long we'd been in the truck, and I'd almost forgotten Collin was there at all until his voice interrupted my aimless gazing.

"That used to be a cathedral," he said, watching me study a crumbling stone structure on the side of the road. "It was set on fire sometime in the thirteenth century, but the ruins have remained untouched since."

"How do you know that?" I asked. There were structures like this all over the place, and I had no idea how he could possibly tell one from the other.

"I'm more than just a pretty face, you know."

"No one said you had a pretty face."

He gasped in mock offense, slapping his hand to his chest. "You humble me, Chelsea."

"Someone has to."

He rolled his eyes, then settled back into drumming his fingers on the steering wheel and cutting tight corners of country roads.

"What about this one?" I asked, gesturing out the window to a dilapidated stone wall shaped like a square.

"Oh, that one used to be used for human sacrifice."

I whipped my head in his direction just in time to catch a smile at the corners of his mouth.

"Now you're just making shit up," I said. "And you're a terrible liar, you know."

"I'll have to work on that," he said. "Not that you could teach me anything."

"What's that supposed to mean?"

"You've one of those faces," he said. "The kind that tells everyone everything you're feeling, even if you don't want to."

"You've known me for a week," I said, trying not to sound defensive. "You couldn't possibly make that observation."

"You'd be surprised how observant you become when your jobs consist almost solely of people-pleasing."

I thought about him tending bar and shuttling tourists around the country and doing odd jobs on the farm and telling stories to those who have apparently earned them. He had a point.

"Does sharing these observations usually please people?" I asked.

"People who are willing to be pleased," he said. I bit my tongue so I wouldn't smile, especially when I could see how bad he wanted me to.

We rumbled past a sign welcoming us to County Wicklow, followed by a few directing us to a place called Glendalough. I refrained from asking questions because I knew answers were coming, but it was becoming increasingly difficult as I felt we were getting closer to our destination.

After what felt like an eternity, we pulled into a parking lot at the base of a hill, and Collin turned off the truck. "Ready?" he asked.

"As I'll ever be," I said. "Can I ask now what this place is?"

"I'll explain on the walk." He grabbed the basket from the back, and I forced myself to look away from the way his long fingers flexed around the handles. From our position at the base of the hill, I couldn't see much more than more hills and more ruins in the distance. But I followed, anxiously awaiting the grand reveal and silently worrying there might not be one.

I was trying to focus on steadying my breathing so as not to seem so out of shape when we reached the top of the hill and came face-to-face with a cemetery bathed in golden sunshine. Rows upon rows of mossy headstones leaned into one another, reaching out from overgrown grass and long-abandoned dirt paths. A few larger structures missing walls and ceilings, and another in a cylindrical shape, occupied the space between the tombstones, all of which sat just slightly off-kilter.

"You brought me to a cemetery?" I asked.

"A sixth-century monastic settlement," he corrected. "And some of the most beautiful lakes you'll ever see, but we aren't there quite yet."

I hummed, running my fingers over a tombstone and trying to read the name beneath the moss. I usually found cemeteries depressing, but this was undeniably beautiful. Each headstone rested at a different angle, moved by hundreds of years of shifting earth.

"It used to be a city," Collin said as we wove our way around the ruins. "A proper one, with farming and religion and that. Real peaceful for the monks."

"What happened?" I asked, turning my gaze to the round tower jutting into the sky.

"Vikings," he said. I waited for him to continue, but he stopped talking in favor of looking at me looking at the pillar. "Grand, isn't it?"

"What happened to the monks?" I spun in a slow circle, studying the rows of graves surrounding the skeleton of what had once been a cathedral. Collin chuckled softly at what I imagined were my endless questions, and I turned to face him for his response.

"Some died," he said, "and others fled to new settlements. But it was par for the course, really. A lot of Irish history at that time was dying and fleeing, I'm afraid."

"How do you know so much about history?"

"Storytelling," he said, as if that one word said it all. "Ready to see the lakes?"

"If the picnic is happening at the lakes, then absolutely," I said. "I'm starving."

"Might it kill you to focus?" he asked.

"It will, actually," I said. "Thanks for asking." He nudged me with his shoulder and my skin tingled at the contact.

We walked along a path under a canopy of trees, in and out of the sunlight. Collin swung the picnic basket in the space between us, and I was thankful for the distance. He'd taken his flannel off when the sun came out, leaving his forearms out in the open, and I noticed the tattooed cherries on the inside of his elbow. And the umbrella on the bone of his wrist. The scattered collection of art that might tell me everything about him if I only asked.

Before I even had a chance to contemplate whether I'd ever do such a thing, the trees cleared. The gravel path turned to dirt and the water stretched in front of us, and my breath caught in my lungs. Sunshine sparkled on the blue-green water, and mountains dipped low in the center of the lake in a perfect V. Wispy clouds followed the path carved by the mountains, reflected in perfect streaks of white between the deep greens of the trees.

"Deadly, isn't it?" Collin said from behind me, his voice quieter in my ear than it had been in the cemetery. I giggled at the slang, grateful for the opportunity to cover my surprise at how close we were standing.

"That's one way to describe it."

"The Irish call it the 'valley of two lakes,'" he said. "That's the translation of Glendalough."

"It's a pretty word," I said, eyes trained on the valley and ears trained on Collin's voice.

"Say it."

"What?"

"Try it out," he said. "Irish words feel good on the tongue."

"It wouldn't sound as good in my accent," I said, conscious of the fact neither of us needed to know how anything felt on the other's tongue.

"Aye, don't be embarrassed," he said. "Yer accent isn't so bad. And besides, the Irish language is dying, so we need as many people to use it as possible. Even if it's just a word."

"Do you speak it?"

"You're stalling again."

"Glendalough," I said, tasting the language in my mouth. It didn't sound right, and I could feel heat creeping onto my cheeks in the silence that followed.

"Fair play," he said with an approving nod, which made me feel sillier. He didn't have to be looking at me like I just announced he won the lottery. It was just a word. "And I do speak the language a bit," he said. "My grandparents tried to teach us when we were kids, and of course we learned it in school, but I don't use it a lot, so it's gone to shite."

"Maybe you should use it more," I said. "I heard it's dying."

His smile stretched to his ears, and I snagged the picnic

basket from his hands to give myself something to do other than stare at his face. "Picnic time?" I asked, holding it up, and he laughed.

"Picnic time."

We found a grassy spot by the water and spread a blanket on the ground, ignoring that it was damp and uneven. Collin unpacked the basket, laying sandwiches and fruit and two cans of beer between us.

"I can't take credit for anything," he said before I could react. "This is Flo's doing." I wasn't huge on the idea of our coworkers knowing what we were up to, especially Flo and her wiggling eyebrows, but I was too thankful for the food in that moment to care.

I picked up a sandwich, studying it through the plastic wrap. "Is this—"

"A Tayto sandwich." Collin laughed. "An Irish delicacy."

"But it's just—"

"Crisps on a sandwich?" He chuckled again, taking it from my hands and unwrapping it. "Take a bite."

"You're bossy."

"Part of the job," he said, holding the sandwich out to me. "Give it a try."

I took a bite under the scrutiny of his gaze, trying to keep crumbs from dusting my lap.

"Bang on, right?" he asked almost immediately. If my mouth wasn't stuck together by the dryness of the white bread and the chips, I might have returned his smile. Instead, I had to focus every muscle in my jaw on just chewing and swallowing.

Before I could open my mouth to speak, he cracked the tab on a beer and handed it to me. "You'll need this," he said. I took a grateful swig, washing down the bite.

"It's dry," I said.

"But it's delicious," he said.

"But it's delicious," I repeated, finally able to laugh. I handed it to him and he took a bite twice the size of mine, and I watched the corners of his jaw as he chewed.

"A delicacy, huh?" I asked.

"A proper one, at that. Used to eat these as kids when it was too hot to cook in the summertime," he said. "So you're getting more Irish by the minute, you know."

"I thought the goal was to make me like Ireland," I said, "not to make me Irish."

"All in good time," he said, taking another bite. "Is it working yet?"

I considered his question. It was a nice afternoon, sure. The scenery was beautiful. But it wasn't home. Not by a long shot.

"I do like it more than I did last weekend," I conceded. "Well, this part, anyway. The history is interesting, and this is an incredible place. And it's definitely much nicer when the sun is out. But there still isn't a chance I'm staying," I added, perhaps too quickly. I tried to laugh in case it sounded harsh.

"Aye, what's so important back in Boston, then?"

"Other than my entire life?"

He shook his head, brushing his hands off on his knees and leaning back on his elbows. "Your view of life is so rigid," he said. "It can look like more than one thing, you know."

"Not for me," I said.

"It does right now. I mean, look at ya. Halfway across the world working for a hostel. I bet that wasn't in your plan."

I laughed, though it wasn't funny. "No," I said. "It wasn't. But I'm going to get the plan back on track. Go home, get another job, find another apartment, live happily ever after."

He didn't respond, but instead folded his hands behind his head and lay back on the blanket, turning his face to the clouds. "Lie down," he said eventually.

"Will you ever stop telling me what to do?"

"Maybe you'll have to stick around long enough to find out," he said. "But definitely not anytime soon." He shielded his eyes with his hand, and the sliver of sun that got through turned them nearly translucent. "I'm serious. Lie down."

I took another swig then joined him, flat on my back, facing the sky.

"Why are we doing this?"

"Bloody hell, Chelsea," he said, raking his fingers through his hair. "Because the sun is out. Because sometimes it feels good not to be thinking or planning or working or any of that. And because we both need a minute of peace and quiet, don't ya think?"

It was hard not to envy how easy it seemed for him to turn his brain off, to do nothing other than lie in the sun. Growing up in Boston hadn't exactly prepared me for that. But at the end of the day, city life soothed me in a way nature didn't. Most of the time, I felt more at peace on a subway surrounded by people or in a coffee shop than I did on an aimless walk, and I didn't see that changing anytime soon.

"What are you thinking about?" I asked after a few minutes, unable to tolerate the silence.

"I'm not," he said. "You should try it sometime."

"I don't believe you."

"You don't have to."

Collin's eyes were still closed, and it was infuriating how a person could be so cavalier. The lines on his face were smooth, and a tattoo on his bicep of what looked like a snare drum peeked out of his shirtsleeve. I had to close my own eyes to stop them from lingering over the rest of his body.

THE REST OF THE AFTERNOON passed as slowly as the clouds, and I fought to stay focused. To pay attention to how the gravel felt under my feet or how the sun felt on my back instead of how the stress felt in my chest that I wasn't yet any closer to getting my life back on track. I was surprised to find myself trying to focus on Ireland to distract myself from my life at home. And I was even more surprised it was working.

I watched the sun set as we drove back west, trying to match my breath to the rhythm of the road. It was the only way I could avoid thinking about my conversation with Collin on the picnic blanket. *Life can look like more than one thing, you know.* His accent got stuck in my head like a song from the radio, and I was determined to do everything I could to get it out.

I turned up the dial, letting the actual song on the radio permeate the sound of the wind. It was an Irish tune, which shouldn't have been surprising, with fiddles and bagpipes and other indistinguishable sounds. I focused on trying to under-stand what they were singing about, turning the volume louder as the song reached the chorus.

"Aye, Chelsea," Collin said, leaning his head back against the seat. "You are going to be just fine."

I wasn't sure exactly what made him say that, but I hoped he was right. Even if I'd never admit it.

Chapter 8

*W*ednesdays, I was beginning to learn from other staff members, and my own brief time manning the reception desk, were the quietest. It seemed the people who called in advance had already booked their weekend trips, and the people who didn't weren't yet close enough to the weekend to panic. The phones rang off and on, most of our guests were out and about, and I had a second or two to myself to do what I came here to do.

I'd been combing every job site searching for something in event planning or general management for days, but was coming up empty.

Had I known Helen and Jack were going to sell O'Shea's when they retired, I would have been more diligent about networking, or joining LinkedIn, or whatever else my corporate friends were doing. I would have made connections or leveraged my inner circle or contacted alumni or whatever else they tell you to do before you graduate and move into the job market. I wouldn't have been so complacent.

This Wednesday morning, however, I scrolled long enough to find a posting for a senior events coordinator at a boutique hotel called Hotel Blue just outside Boston.

It is near the water, and the website features a series of links that look like neon signs, only much classier than the ones in the Wanderer. From the photos, it appears the lobby is cluttered with monstera plants and velour furniture, and there is a bar armed with colored glassware and a bartender with a mustache just beyond the reception desk.

Senior Events Coordinator sounded far more legitimate than any side work I'd done in event planning before, and I wondered if I was even qualified for a job like this. If I had the experience necessary to be a "senior" or a "coordinator" of anything.

But there was a reason I opened the link in the first place, and a reason my heart was hammering in my chest, so I owed it to myself to at least apply.

Just as I was conjuring every corporate buzzword imaginable to write a cover letter that made me sound qualified, Flo stuck her head into the lobby.

"*Ciao, tesoro,*" she said.

"*Ciao*, Flo."

"Do you have a minute? My sous chef cut his hand, and I really need to get this buffet out."

I looked from my computer screen to her pleading eyes, knowing well enough the answer around here was always yes. I closed the document but bookmarked the job posting, promising myself I'd return to it later.

"Happy to help," I said as she thanked me profusely in Italian and dragged me to the kitchen.

It wasn't long before we were in a rhythm, scooping ground beef into heated buffet trays, chopping tomatoes, shredding lettuce, and preparing other various fixings for a taco night.

"This is such a huge help," Flo said later in the day as we laid out the buffet just in time for some stragglers to wander in for dinner. "I hope I didn't pull you away from anything too important this morning."

"To tell you the truth, I was job hunting," I whispered, though no one in charge was around to hear me.

"Ooh," she mused. "Any luck?"

"I found something just outside Boston," I said, "but I'm not exactly qualified."

"That's not even a thing anymore," she said, waving her hand like she was swatting a bug. "What's the job?"

"It's a boutique hotel looking for a senior events coordinator," I said. "But I've only ever done event planning on the side, and even that has been on a small scale, so I'm not sure I could do it full-time."

"Where's your confidence, huh? You're an American woman with no confidence?"

"Is that a stereotype?" I laughed. "If so, I don't think I got the memo."

"Either way," she said, ignoring my question, "if you can't even convince me you're qualified, how are you supposed to convince them?"

She had a point. All I could do was groan in response and make a mental note to stop thinking of excuses not to apply. I *did* have event planning experience, and didn't everyone start small? The posting didn't say they were looking for someone with extensive experience. It only said they were looking for someone creative, dedicated, passionate. Someone with exceptional interpersonal skills and a sharp eye for trends. Someone detail-oriented and ambitious. Eager.

And those were boxes I *could* check. Hell, I was in Ireland planning bachelorette parties in a city I barely knew. That had to count for something.

"Did you always know you wanted to be a chef?" I asked. I'd been curious about Flo's story since I met her in the hallway, and now seemed as good a time as any to ask.

"Of course not," she said. "I had no idea what I wanted to do. We just cooked all the time at home in Italy, and then when I got here and they needed a cook I was decent at it, and I've been doing it ever since."

"Wasn't that scary?" I asked. "Just deciding to stay? Changing your life like that?"

"Not as scary as it would have been going home," she said. "My head would have exploded if I stayed in my family's house. Too many opinions."

"Is the Wanderer any different?" I asked. She hooted the kind of laugh that startled everyone in earshot, and I couldn't help but join her.

"You're catching on quick," she said. "At least there's freedom at the Wanderer. No bossy dads or judgmental aunts to be found."

"Only needy guests and nosy coworkers," I said.

"Speaking of," she said, and I knew exactly where she was going, "how was your day out in the country with Collin?"

I tried to keep my expression neutral and described our platonic, not romantic, day of hiking and picnicking. I left out any mention of flirty glances or touching knees and kept it to seeing the lakes and driving down the freeway and learning a bit of Irish history.

Flo hummed, tapping her fingers against her full lips, squinting her eyes. "Sounds like a date to me," she said eventually, to which I rolled my eyes.

"We're just friends."

"Yeah, yeah. When's the next one?" she asked.

"Tomorrow, I'm guessing. According to the schedule posted in the staff room, that's the next time we both have a day off."

"Look at you, checking the schedule," she said, raising her eyebrows.

"Just trying to plan ahead," I said. "I need to know when I can dedicate time to applying for jobs since I keep getting pulled to do other things every time I try." I nudged her so she would know I was joking, mostly.

"Well, you can confirm with him tonight," she said.

"What's tonight?" My only plans for tonight were to revisit the posting and be asleep before ten o'clock.

"Staff bonding," she said. "Don't tell me you forgot."

I had absolutely forgotten.

Lars mentioned something the other day about the staff getting together tonight for drinks and bar games, but I was so invested in responding to an email from Ada about an apartment I couldn't afford that I hadn't really heard a word he said.

"Right, bonding," I said, hardly able to hide that this was mostly new information to me.

"You totally forgot."

"Shut up."

"I can handle it from here," she said, nodding toward the door. "Your shift is just about over and Wednesdays are quiet, so you have some time to get ready."

"This is something I need to get ready for?"

"You know what I mean." She practically shooed me out of the room, and I raised my hands in surrender. I needed to wash my hair anyway, and I was dying to get out of the work polo.

The staff wing was quiet, so I undressed in my room and wrapped myself in a towel to head into the bathroom instead of going in my clothes.

I should have known the silence was too good to be true.

As soon as I turned away from my closed door, I bumped smack into Collin. Also in a towel.

"Oh my god," I said, wishing my hands weren't holding up my towel so I could cover my face in embarrassment. His laugh came from somewhere low in his throat, and I knew my blush had turned to blotches across my chest, which was exposed. "I'm so sorry," I said.

"Happens all the time," he said, shrugging. I envied his nonchalance. "Side effect of communal toilets."

"I can wait," I said. "You go first."

"They're communal, Chelsea," he said. "We can both go."

The longer we stood in the hallway, the harder it got to continue making eye contact. Especially when his shirtless body revealed a new smattering of tattoos, including a eucalyptus branch just below his collarbone and what looked like an antique mirror on the front of his ribs. I blinked a few times before I could catch the rest, determined not to make this interaction any weirder.

"You're right," I said, despite how badly I wanted to disappear back into my room and wait until he was done. "That is what communal means." *Duh.*

"After you." He held out his hand, and I followed the gesture on shaky legs. I'd been in the shower before at the same time as other staff members, including Collin for all I knew, but it was much easier when I didn't have to see them in towels beforehand.

I walked directly from the doorway into a stall, exhaling only once I was inside.

"I'm going to put music on," Collin said loud enough for me to hear over the running water. "Hope that's okay with you."

"And if it isn't?"

"I'm going to put music on," he said again, and I could hear the smile in his voice.

Before I could say another word, Ed Sheeran's "Galway Girl" blasted from Collin's phone speakers and filled the bathroom.

"You've got to be kidding," I shouted from my stall, trying to hide my laughter. How could a man be so hot and so corny at the same time?

"What?" he said. "A bloke can't enjoy a little Ed Sheeran in the shower?"

"Guilty pleasure?"

"No one should ever feel guilty about pleasure," he said.

I was glad he couldn't see me, not only because I was naked, but because I was sure I was blushing like a teenager. I'd thought our conversation had been light, but the deeper tone in his voice took us to a place I had no intention of going.

"Isn't this song a little on the nose?" I said eventually, trying to get back on solid ground.

"It's a classic," he said. "You don't have to read so much into everything, you know."

"I don't."

"You do."

Did I?

"I'm not arguing with you from the shower," I said. "Showering is supposed to be relaxing."

"It would be if you didn't insist on arguing with me," he said, effectively shutting me up. I had a whole night of him ahead of me and if I was going to survive, I needed to pace myself.

He shut off the water first, so I stalled long enough to hear him leave the bathroom before getting out myself. I looked in the hallway to make sure the coast was clear, then shuffled into my room.

I spent more time trying to forget what Collin looked like half naked than I did getting ready, and frankly, I failed at both. I forgot to put product in my hair, so my curls were unruly, and the image of Collin seemed to be burned on the back of my eyelids. Eventually I threw on a pair of loose ripped jeans and a battered crew neck sweatshirt from college and headed down the hall to collect Flo.

"You're lucky you're hot," she said as soon as she opened the door.

"Excuse me?"

"That's how you can get away with wearing house clothes outside the house," she said.

"Some of us don't have a choice," I said, looking down at my old sweatshirt and hoping its vibe was more curated vintage than just old. "We don't all have your style." She twirled in her doorway, flaunting a pair of cotton overalls and a patterned headscarf. I snapped my fingers in applause, and she looped her arm through mine to lead us downstairs.

MOST OF THE STAFF were already gathered in the bar, pulling their own pints and distributing pool cues. I was beginning to recognize everyone, and people stopped looking at me like I was a stranger.

I followed Flo to the bar, watching gratefully as she mixed us two gin and tonics. Helen had said there would be discounted drinks when she pitched this job, but I hadn't seen anyone on staff pay for one since I'd been here, so I was beginning to gather "discounted" really meant "free." She should have led with that.

"It's nice to see you with clothes on," Collin said from over my shoulder, just loud enough for Flo to hear. She swallowed a mouthful of gin down the wrong pipe, and her coughing fit broke the tension.

I shot him a glare, but he didn't seem to care at all. "We ran into each other on the way to the shower earlier," I said to Flo as soon as she calmed down. "Traumatizing for all parties, really."

"I'll let you two work on healing, then," she said, slipping out from behind the bar. I wanted to grab her arm and beg her to stay, but I knew she wouldn't even if I asked.

I turned to face Collin at the exact moment he leaned over me for something behind the bar, bringing us nose to nose. He smelled like shampoo and fire, and it reminded me of a candle my dad used to burn around the holidays.

I was standing as still as possible, trying to appear composed, when he produced a pint glass filled with darts from behind my back.

"Fancy a game?" he asked, still only inches from my face.

"Depends," I said. "Do you fancy losing?"

"Aye," he said. "Think you're jammy, do ya?"

"You think I need luck to beat you?" I asked, thankful I overheard that bit of slang from a guest last week.

"There's only one way to find out," he said, handing me half the darts. I hadn't played much since college, but I used to be a decent shot. If only I could steady my nerves.

I stepped up to the line, squinting one eye and aiming for the board.

"I took off tomorrow," Collin said just before I released the dart. I dropped my arm to my side and turned to face him. "I know you're off tomorrow, and it's almost been a week since

Glendalough already," he explained. "I think we're overdue for our next adventure." I wondered how he had time and energy to take me all over the country on his days off when that was quite literally exactly what he did on the days he was working, but I didn't ask. If this was just an extension of his job, I didn't want to know.

I narrowed my eyes, but I couldn't suppress my smile enough to look intimidating "Are you trying to throw off my game?"

"Is it working?"

I squeezed the dart in my hand, wishing I could turn the point on him instead. "No," I said, turning and throwing the dart straight into the board. It landed less than a centimeter from where I was aiming, and I threw a glance over my shoulder before I scored it in chalk on the wall. I still had it.

He clucked his tongue, taking a slow sip of his beer and watching me as I returned to the line. "Looks like it might be myself who needs the luck, after all," he said.

"Don't say I didn't warn you."

"Let's put a wager on it, then, shall we?" He twirled the dart in his fingers like a drumstick, leaning against a high-top table. I'd only shot once but I was feeling confident, so I accepted.

"What's on tomorrow's agenda?" I asked, looking for inspiration for the bet.

"I," he said, taking another swig, "am taking you to a hurling match." I furrowed my eyebrows, wordlessly asking, *What the hell is a hurling match?* "It's a traditional Irish sport," he explained. "Kind of like lacrosse, maybe, if I tried to compare it to something you have in America. You'll like it."

"How can you be so sure?"

He threw the dart, which landed nearly right on top of mine. "Do you trust me?"

"For now," I said. He hadn't given me any reason not to, and I couldn't deny how good it felt to let someone else make all the plans for once.

"Good." He smiled. "Everyone likes hurling. Even a pox like yerself."

"I'm not a pox," I said, despite having no idea what it meant. Although from his tone, I could tell it wasn't good.

"Keep telling yourself that, darling."

"Let's go double or nothing, then," I said, my irritation sparking my competitive edge. "You have to win darts and pick the winner of the hurling match to win the bet."

"A proper competition," he said. "I like the way you think. What's the wager?"

"What comes after hurling?"

"You think I plan that far in advance?" He raised his eyebrows, and I did the same, calling his bluff. "We're driving the Wild Atlantic Way," he said, fighting a crooked smile.

"If I win, I get to drive," I said. I wasn't sure whether I wanted to learn to drive on the left side so much as I knew my suggestion would irk him, but I was glad I said it.

"Absolutely not," he said immediately. "Unless you can afford to buy me a new truck after you crash this one."

"What makes you so sure I'm gonna crash it?"

"You do a lot of driving on the left side of the road in Boston, do ya? Besides, I'd have to teach you to drive stick first, and it would be a whole thing."

"If you're scared you're going to lose, Collin, you could just say so," I said, taking my place back on the line. I watched over my shoulder as he dragged his fingers through his hair, looking toward the ceiling for some sort of reprieve.

"You're on, then," he said. "And if I win, you don't even think about getting behind the wheel for the rest of the time you're here."

"Which is only the rest of the summer," I reminded him.

"So you say." I rolled my eyes, which made him laugh.

"Do we have a deal?" he said, echoing his question from that first night in the bar.

"We do." I clinked my glass against his, and we both downed most of our drinks in a few gulps.

We went shot for shot for the rest of the game, alternating on the top of the leaderboard and talking just enough shit to still be able to back it up. By the time we got down to the bull's-eye shot, I was two points ahead.

"You put up a good fight, you know," I said, watching him step to the line for his last shot.

"Catch yourself on," he snapped. He squared his shoulders, and I watched the way they rose and fell as he took a deep breath. His shirt pulled gently between them, and the top of another tattoo peeked out above the collar, just at the base of his neck.

After another dramatic breath he threw the dart, and we both watched as it stuck in the board two inches to the left of the bull's-eye. He brought his knuckles to his teeth, letting out a groan that dissolved every ounce of concentration I had left.

I swept my hair from my shoulders, trying to look nonchalant but really needing to cool myself down. "I take it you aren't used to losing," I said, trading places.

"I haven't lost yet," he said. "If you shoot anywhere in the green, we're going into overtime."

"Won't be necessary," I said. I aimed the dart, painfully aware he was just inches from my back. The second before the dart left my fingers, he whispered so close to my ear I could feel his lips.

"Don't miss."

The dart went flying, and not in the direction of the bull's-eye. It landed on the border of the red and green, and we both gasped loud enough to draw the attention of the crowd.

"That's green!" Collin shouted, pointing at the board.

"If by green you mean red," I argued. We both approached to take a closer look, Collin just over my shoulder as we studied the dart. It would have only taken a second to make the call from this distance, but we stood there for what felt like an hour.

It was red.

I turned around to gloat and found myself pinned in the space between Collin and the board.

"Anything you'd like to say to me?" I asked, expecting him to confirm it was, in fact, in the red.

"There are a lot of things I'd like to say to you," he said, yanking the dart from the board. I swallowed hard, probably loud enough for him to hear, but said nothing. "Starting with the fact you're a bleedin' melter, Chelsea."

"I swear you make these words up," I said. "Should I be offended or flattered?"

"It means you drive me insane," he said. "So I guess the choice is yours."

"In that case, I'm going with flattered."

"Do you want another drink?" he asked, collecting my empty cup and heading toward the bar. "I don't know about you, but I need another one."

"Every good celebration requires a drink," I said, smiling in response to his gritted teeth.

"Don't get ahead of yourself there. We still have tomorrow. It's anyone's game."

"Spoken like a true loser."

"Do you want the drink or not?" he asked, holding two glasses behind the bar. I made a zipping motion across my lips, throwing away the imaginary key. "Attagirl," he said.

"What are you making?" I asked after a minute of watching him mix a cocktail.

"It's a surprise."

"Let me guess . . . you think I'll like it?"

"Clever girl." He smiled. Once the drink was poured, he stuck a straw into the glass, plugged one side, then dripped a few drops into his mouth. He let them settle on his tongue while I watched with bated breath.

"Well?" I asked.

"Too bitter," he said.

"I like bitter."

"Surprise, surprise."

"Let me taste it."

I assumed he would hand me the glass, but instead he collected another few drops inside the straw and stretched it out to me. He brought his other hand to my chin, tilting it up with the tips of his fingers. Before I could even clock what was happening, in a public bar, no less, I steadied his hand with my own, opened my mouth, and drank from the straw. His hand was warm beneath my chin and the drink was cool.

The intimacy of such a mundane moment illuminated the path we were heading down, and I feared I was already in too deep to turn around.

"Well?" he asked. His eyes sparkled even under the fluorescent lights of the bar, and I knew it wasn't the cocktail that had gone straight to my head.

"Too bitter," I said. Too bitter indeed.

Chapter 9

"And then what?" Ada asked over the phone as soon as I finished telling her about the bar. I was still a little drunk, but I could hardly get through my doorway before I called her.

"And then nothing," I said, hating the notes of frustration creeping into my voice. "He fixed the cocktail, I drank the new one, we mingled with the rest of the staff, then I came up here so I wouldn't be too hungover for tomorrow."

"But did you want something to happen?" she asked. "You sound like you wanted something to happen."

"Does it matter either way?" I said. Lying to Ada was as useless as lying to myself, so I didn't bother pretending I hadn't thought about it. "I'm leaving at the end of the summer, so I have no business getting involved with anything. Or anybody. Besides," I continued, "he's a bartender and a tour guide. He treats everyone like this. It's his job."

"Any other excuses?"

"His full-time job is working at a hostel," I said.

"What's wrong with that?"

"I mean, it's great that he's happy doing it, but it isn't a career, you know? Like how does he support himself?"

"Slow down," she said. "I thought we were just talking about kissing the guy in a bar. Now we're worrying how he's going to pay a mortgage? Afford childcare?"

"You know what I mean, Ada."

"You sound judgy."

"We're just different," I said, though it came out more of a sigh. "We don't make any sense, so I need to reel it in before it gets any worse."

"At least kiss him first," she said. "I'm dying to know what it's like."

"You come here and kiss him then."

"Please," she said. "You know if I wasn't dating Ben I'd have been there already."

Ada always said things like this, which I ignored. She and Ben were so in love it made me nauseous, and sometimes she tried to offset it by jumping on the ball-and-chain bandwagon. She was horribly unconvincing.

I groaned into the phone, flopping onto my bed. "I can't," I said eventually. "It would be stupid since it has an expiration date."

"You say that now."

"You sound like Collin."

"Maybe I will come kiss him after all."

"Ada!"

"You'd be jealous, wouldn't you?" I could hear her smile through the phone.

"No," I said, though we both knew I would be. "And I'm sure he's already kissing someone else if this is how he's treating everyone who comes through the Wanderer, so I need to put it out of my mind either way."

"Good luck," she snickered.

"I'm serious, Ada."

"So am I," she said. "The man fed you a drink through a straw tonight, Chels. He put his beautiful bartender hands on your face and you loved it. You're not putting him out of your mind."

"Well, I don't have a choice, so. Consider it done."

"Whatever you say."

"I'm hanging up now," I said.

"To get a good night's sleep for your date tomorrow?"

"Good night, Ada."

"Fine, fine, message received. Good night, Chels. Love you."

"Love you back." I dropped my phone on my chest and stared up at the ceiling, rubbing my eyes with the heels of my hands as if that would do anything to get Collin out of my brain.

Unsurprisingly, it was hopeless. There was nothing I could have done in that moment that would have stopped me from savoring the *what-ifs*. What if these weren't the circumstances, what if I didn't have to hold back, what if he kissed me. What if I had the chance to find out what his lips felt like against mine, what his tattoos looked like under his clothes, what his accent sounded like when he said words only I was meant to hear.

I WASN'T SURE when I fell asleep, but a knock on my door at the crack of dawn woke me before my alarm. I expected Flo to be locked out or maybe Lori to need emergency coverage at the desk, so I pulled a hoodie over my head, ran my hands through my hair, and opened my door without looking in the mirror.

When I swung the door open to see Collin standing on the other side, I immediately regretted not so much as glancing at my reflection.

"Morning," he said, bright-eyed and grinning like he'd been up for hours. Where did he get all this energy?

"Am I late?" I asked, fumbling for my watch on the nightstand.

"No, no," he said. "I'm early. Just thought you might like to blend in with the locals today, that's all." He handed me a shirt, and I unfolded it between us. It was a jersey for what I assumed to be the local hurling team. "I know you're desperately trying not to embrace Irish culture, but you'll stand out at a match in regular clothes. Which I think you'd hate more than you'd hate looking Irish, to be fair."

Once again, Collin proved to be more observant than I was willing to give him credit for.

"Thank you," I said. "That was thoughtful."

"Don't sound so surprised."

I looked at my feet on the floor, trying to avoid wondering how anyone could manage to be charming at this hour.

"Anyway," he said, louder than he needed to, "I'll see you in the lobby in an hour then, yeah?"

I nodded. "Anything else I need to know while I'm getting ready?" I asked before he turned to leave. "To blend in with the locals, I mean."

"Trainers," he said, kicking my bare foot with his. The contact of our skin was just enough to pull me fully from sleep and into the day. "And those plaits you do sometimes."

I smoothed my hand over my hair, wondering what else he's observed. "Surely all the locals aren't wearing braids, are they?"

"No." He smiled. "I just like it when you do."

With that, he drummed his hands on the doorframe a few times and disappeared down the hallway. I stood still for a few seconds with my hand still in my hair, staring into the empty corridor. If that was the energy he was bringing to the morning, what did that mean for the rest of the day?

I shook the thought from my brain and focused on getting

ready, reminding myself we were just two friends going to a hurling match.

My hopes were dashed as soon as I pulled the silky jersey over my head. How was anyone supposed to be platonic while wearing each other's clothes? The jersey was perfectly over-sized, and I stood in front of the mirror for a second too long, examining the way Collin's clothes looked on my body. Then I immediately distracted myself to avoid thinking about the way Collin's clothes look on Collin's body. And the way Collin's body would look without Collin's clothes.

With only ten minutes before I needed to be in the lobby, I did the exact thing I told myself I wasn't going to do: I braided my hair.

For the second time, Collin was already slumped in a lobby chair when I arrived.

"Lars," he called out of the room as soon as he saw me. "Come get a look at this."

"Oh, stop. Lars," I said down the hallway, "don't bother. There's nothing to see here." Lars showed up a second later, despite my protest.

"She's a proper Galway supporter now, isn't she?" Collin said, crossing his arms and smiling down at me like a proud parent.

"What have you done to her?" Lars laughed. "Chelsea," he said, "get out while you can. Before you know it, he'll have you working on the farm and playing the fiddle."

"Oh, feck off, mate," Collin said. "You got to admit she fits right in, doesn't she?"

"Don't say yes," I said, pointing my finger at Lars.

"Maybe it's just the jersey," Lars said. "And the red hair, of course."

"Don't you have work to be doing?" I asked, shooing him out

of the lobby. We could hear him chuckling to himself as he made his way back down the hall.

"Told ya the red hair made you look like one of us," Collin said, flicking one of my braids off my shoulder. I went to swat his hand away but he grabbed my wrist before I could. "And you did the plaits," he said.

"Only because it keeps my hair under control in this weather," I said, nodding out the window at the darkening sky and fighting a smile.

"So you say." He let my wrist slip through his fingers without breaking eye contact.

"Are we sure it's not going to rain on us?" The more I looked out the window, the more menacing the clouds looked.

"It's Ireland, Chels," he said. "It's gonna bloody pour."

The sound of my name, or the first half of it, anyway, echoed in the empty lobby. Had it not been my name, it might have just been an indiscernible sound under the thick blanket of his accent. But it was my name, and it settled around us with the weight of the clouds.

"Are ya ready, then?" he asked, looking from my head to my toes and back again, probably because I was standing there like an idiot.

"Yeah, yeah. Let's do it."

THE STADIUM WAS already pretty rowdy when we arrived, given the match was between Galway and Dublin, and I had to shove my hands into my back pockets so I wouldn't reach for Collin's as we wove through the crowd. Though he didn't seem to get the hands-to-yourself memo, because he took every opportunity to rest his fingertips on my lower back while we wound our way to our seats.

"So," he said, nodding toward the field. "Double or nothing, huh?"

"As long as you're ready to hand those keys over," I said. "And I want Galway."

I wasn't sure whether the sound that came out of his mouth was more of a gasp or a laugh, but it was loud enough to make me jump either way.

"She wants Galway," he announced to no one in particular. "Proper culchie now, are ya?"

"Excuse me?" I said.

He laughed, clapping his hand on my shoulder. "Someone from outside of Dublin, that's all. Not a city lass."

"I am a city lass," I said. "Just not that city."

"And how's your city treating ya?" he asked. The question hung in the air just long enough to sting before it dissolved into the crowd.

"Fine, thanks. I applied for a great job last week, actually," I lied. "Event planning at a boutique hotel outside the city." I made a mental note to actually apply when I was done running around Galway, doing whatever it was we were doing.

"Aye," he said after a beat. The following silence was deafening, even in the roar of the stadium.

"So, do we have a deal?" I asked, trying to get back on track.

"It's hard to say no to you, you know. Even if it does mean betting against my own city."

"Game on, then."

His smile returned, hitched up more on the right than the left, and I tried to let the moment slip behind us. There was no reason for it to be tense when we talked about my life in Boston, so I wouldn't let it be. And I'd apply for the job when we got back to the Wanderer so I wasn't a total liar.

The match moved at lightning speed, and I had to strain to hear Collin over the noise of the fans. He explained the rules, but between his accent and the jargon I wasn't sure I caught a word. Not that it mattered. I knew how to read a scoreboard, more or less in this case, and I could see the numbers next to Galway were higher than the numbers next to Dublin. And I could see the wrinkles between Collin's eyes deepening as the match neared the end.

"Have you recovered from the first loss?" I asked. "In time for the second loss, I mean?"

"Let me ask you something, Chelsea," he said, leaning dangerously close to my ear. I put my hand around it as if to say *I'm listening.* "Do you ever stop talkin' shite?" he whispered.

"I thought I was supposed to be blending in with the locals." I laughed. "But if you can't handle a little friendly competition, you could have just said so."

"I just thought you'd leave me with at least a shred of dignity, that's all."

"Maybe you don't know me as well as you thought you did."

"Kind of hard when it feels like you're trying to keep it that way," he said.

Before I had a chance to respond, a big, fat raindrop landed directly between my eyes. I turned my face to the sky just in time to watch it open. The rain was loud on the metal bleachers, and I couldn't stop myself from putting my palms out like a child.

I turned to look at Collin, relieved to see the rain was enough of a distraction from our conversation. He pushed his hair from his eyes, then turned his palms up too.

"Told you it'd come bucketing down," he said.

"Not a hard prediction in this country, is it?"

"There she goes again," he said. "Taking every ounce of dignity I have left."

"Maybe you shouldn't be so willing to hand it over."

"Keep myself closed off like you, should I?" He was smiling, but his words burned in my chest all the same.

"I am not—"

The final whistle of the match triggered an eruption in the crowd, and I turned back to the field just in time to see the celebration on the Galway side.

"Fair play," Collin conceded, crossing his arms over his chest and looking up and down the length of my body. "You know how to pick 'em, don't ya?"

"Galway had to be good for something."

He rolled his eyes under lashes dark and slick with raindrops. Lashes I had no business staring at. "At least you're giving her a chance," he said. I resisted the urge to remind him he hadn't given me much of a choice.

By then the rain was coming down in sheets, and we were trapped in the slow-moving sea of other fans rushing to the car park. There was hardly an overhang, and I could feel the rain soaking into my skin under my clothes.

"Come on," Collin said, grabbing my wrist and pulling me from the crowd. "I know a shortcut." We stumbled backward against the current, bobbing and weaving until it spit us out into a dim corridor that appeared to be closed for repairs. "I think if we follow this around the back, we'll be near the truck by the time we're back out in the rain."

"Do you really think I'm closed off?" I asked before I could stop myself. The sound of the rain had been reduced to a steady hum in the distance, and the quiet in the corridor let his words seep in.

"What?" he asked, looking absentmindedly down the corridor for the right way to go.

"You said I'm trying to keep you from getting to know me," I said. "Did you mean that?"

He turned to face me, and I focused on counting the raindrops that dripped from his hair while I waited for a response. "Is that not the case, then?" he asked. "Tell me it's not true and I'll believe it."

"It's not you," I said.

"Let me guess, it's you? A classic."

"I meant that it's not you, specifically. It's just . . . the circumstances," I said, though even I knew it was lame. "Since I'm only here for the summer, there's no need for everyone to really get to know me, is there?"

"Is that what you always think? That the only people who should get to know you are the ones who are in it for the long haul?"

"We're different, Collin," I said, clapping my hands together. I wanted to blame my increasing frustration on my cold, wet clothes, but I knew that wasn't the case. "I've had the same best friend since I was a kid. She's been there for everything that's ever happened to me, so there's nothing to hide. But you're meeting new people every single day, people who come and go with the wind, which might be comfortable for you, but I'm not like that." I was winded by the time I finished talking.

"So you plan to just get through the summer without actually connecting with anyone?"

"It's not . . . I mean, when you say it like that, it sounds bad," I fumbled. "But I'm not good at meaningful connections in such a short amount of time."

"I don't think you're giving yourself enough credit," he said, taking a step closer. The space was already tight, so this put him only a breath away.

"It's only going to make it harder to leave," I said, barely audible over the rain.

"So now you're worried the leaving's gonna be hard?" The sheen on his lips made it impossible to look away from his growing smile, and it made me want to lie motionless in the car park in the rain for the rest of the afternoon.

"Aren't we supposed to be taking a shortcut?" I asked. "At this rate, everyone else has probably gone by now."

"And whose fault is that?" He laughed, and I was impossibly relieved at the sound.

I groaned at myself. "I just don't like when people have negative opinions of me, that's all."

Collin took only a step closer to me, but it felt like a leap in the narrow corridor. The wet jersey clung to him just tight enough that I could make out the lines of his body, which made me wonder what they would feel like under my fingers. The curves of his pecs, the hard plane of his stomach, the peaks and valleys of his collarbones.

"If you think I have a negative opinion of you, Chelsea, then you haven't been paying attention."

"Maybe I'm just thick," I said, mimicking his accent on the last word. If Ada had known I'd made a joke in a moment like this, she'd have killed me.

His laugh bounced around the tight walls, cutting through the sound of the rain. "You're something, all right." I answered with a cheesy smile, and he brought his fingertips to my chin, tilting my face toward his. "So is that smile," he said, far quieter than the laugh. I inhaled sharply but said nothing.

"Are ya ready, then?" he asked when I finally looked away

after a moment of excruciating, impossibly charged silence. "Once we get out of the stadium, we're going to have to make a run for it." Just like that, he was peering around the corner and we were back on track to the truck. And the lingering heat of his hand nearly set me on fire.

Making a run for it sounded grand.

BY THE TIME we got out of the rain we collapsed into the truck in a fit of laughter, soaking the seats and flicking water at each other. Any tension from the stadium washed away on the run, and it felt good to be back in friendly territory.

"Oh, watch your feet, there," Collin said, gesturing to where my sneakers were already soaking everything underneath them. I lifted them from a leatherbound journal I must have missed when I got into the truck before the game, but he snatched it up and tossed it into the back of the cab before I could inspect it any further.

"Secret diary?" I asked.

"Very funny."

"So, it is?"

"It's not a diary," he said. "It's just, it's a . . . a place where I write things."

"What kind of things?"

"Does it matter?"

"I thought we were getting to know each other," I said.

He sighed. "Just stories, that's all. It's nothing, like."

"What stories?"

"The fairy stories," he said, waving his hand like it didn't matter. "The Irish folklore. The yokes my family tells."

I was looking at him, but he was staring straight out at the road.

"Collin, that's—"

"It's just so no one forgets them," he said. "It's not a thing. And my family don't even think they should be written down in the first place, so it's not like I'm to do anything with them."

"You could let me read them," I said.

"They're much better out loud," he said.

"So tell me one."

He glanced in my direction and I offered a soft smile, hoping to encourage him without looking too eager.

"You can't be cynical about them, you know. There's no sense in telling a fairy story to someone who doesn't want to believe it." I nodded. I couldn't promise I would believe it, but I could promise I wanted to.

"Right, then," he said through a soft smile of his own. "Okay, Chelsea. Here's yer first fairy story."

I leaned my head against the back of the seat and kicked my shoes off, propping my feet up on the dashboard. And I listened.

The story rolled off Collin's tongue in a way that was comfortable without sounding rehearsed. Like he'd listened to it and repeated it a thousand times. Like he'd come from a long line of others who'd listened to it and repeated it a thousand times. His voice was just loud enough to be heard over the rain but with the softness you'd use to tell a story to a child. And as always, his accent was music.

In this story, a man passed a fairy hurling match on the way home from the pub one night. The fairies asked the man to be the referee, and since he feared what would happen to him if he declined their request, he obliged. They seemed happy enough that he was willing to referee, but as the game became more competitive, he began to worry what would happen if he declared a winner. Would he face consequences from the losing team? Is there a chance they could take him away?

He decided to take a risk, fudging the time and calling a draw with a minute left on the clock before anyone could score again. To his delight, the fairies were none the wiser. They thanked him profusely and invited him back, and while he agreed to return, he knew better than to follow through. If he was lucky enough to encounter the fairies and come out unscathed, there was hardly a chance he'd be so lucky a second time.

"Do you have a fairy story for every occasion?" I asked, silently wishing this story had been longer.

"Just about," he said. His smile was one of contentment, or maybe pride, even, and I had to force myself to look away.

"Why couldn't one of the fairies be the referee?"

"Aye, some say the fairies can't go about their business without someone from this side of the world."

"And what would have happened to him if he'd gone back?" I hadn't expected to become so invested, but couldn't help myself.

"Well," Collin said, "while it's possible he would have been so jammy a second time, it's more likely they would have done him some harm. Taken him in, made him ill, damaged his crops, like."

"Why?"

"Lots of theories about that one. The fairies just haven't always had an easy go of it, I suppose. They've a dark side. So it's good the lad kept a level head."

"Is that the lesson of this one?" I asked. "Keeping a level head? Good decision making and all that?"

"That much is up to you," he said, glancing over at me. "The fairy stories give you whatever you need at the time you hear them."

I hummed but said nothing by way of actual response. Would I ever stop being surprised by Collin?

"Thanks," I said after a while. "For telling me the story, I mean."

"Thanks for listening," he said. "And for at least having the decency to hide your cynicism." His wide grin made it seem like he was joking, but the undertones weren't lost on me. I could tell the fairy stories weren't always well-received and that a captive audience meant more than he was willing to let on. Lucky for us both, I could have listened to him tell stories all summer, whether or not I really believed them.

And whether or not I really believed them, I wondered what else they would give me.

Chapter 10

The dreaded task of updating my résumé only took about five minutes, seeing as the only change in my career since O'Shea's was the Wanderer.

I thought more about the fairy story in the days after the hurling match—about decision-making and levelheadedness—and I decided if the man was brave enough to referee the fairy hurling match, I could be brave enough to apply for a job.

"Lars," I called from the desk when the breakfast rush settled. "Can you come out here for a sec?" Thankfully, he appeared in under a minute, because if he had taken any longer the odds were high that I would have lost my resolve.

"What can I do for ya?" he asked, leaning his long arms on the edge of the counter.

"Does anyone ever use that projector?" I gestured to the device collecting dust in the corner of the lobby.

"To be honest with you," he said, leaning in, "I didn't even know we had a projector. What are you thinking?" He narrowed his eyes and tapped his fingers together like we were concocting some sort of evil plan.

"What about a weekly movie night?" I asked. The idea had only come to me about thirty seconds before I called Lars into the room, when I'd first spotted the projector, but now I was committed. We'd done "Scary Movie Mondays" in my dorm freshman year when we'd been trying to get to know one another and adjust to a new place, and I was beginning to think something like that wouldn't be a terrible idea here, either.

"Is this what I think it is?" he said. "You, Chelsea from Boston, are *volunteering* to get involved with the Wanderer community? Beyond the duties outlined in your contract?"

"Yeah, yeah," I said, waving him off. "I updated my résumé this morning, and since I'm including event planning here, I'd like it to be legitimate," I said.

"Ah, so you're still just trying to make it easier for yourself to leave? I'm onto you, Chelsea." I rolled my eyes, and he reached across the counter to nudge my shoulder. "Projector's all yours," he said. "Go wild."

"It's just a movie night." I laughed. "Do you think Lori will go for it?"

"Are you kidding?" he said. "There's virtually nothing Lori won't go for. And she'll be thrilled you're getting involved."

"It's just a movie night," I said again.

"Whatever you say."

I shot Lori an email for approval as soon as Lars left the lobby, trying to keep the ball rolling before I could change my mind. She answered almost immediately with nothing more than a string of emojis: thumbs-up, smiley face, movie reel, popping champagne bottle, red exclamation point. Then a follow-up: So glad you're getting into the spirit of The Wanderer!

I added it to the event calendar between Collin's tours and Lars's outdoor activities, settling on Thursday night as the recurring date. Beneath the event calendar on the bulletin board, I posted a suggestion sheet for guests to recommend movies. And to my surprise, there were a handful of entries on the sheet by the end of the week, one of which was circled and underlined by different colored pens.

MOVIE NIGHT WAS ON.

If only I could figure out how to work the projector.

No matter how many times I turned it on and off, unplugged it and plugged it back in, and pressed every glowing red button until it turned green, it wasn't showing a damn thing. Just as I was cursing the very idea of the movie night in the first place, I heard Collin's familiar low chuckle from the back of the lobby.

I turned around to see him leaning against the wall, arms and ankles crossed, watching me with a smirk.

"Can I help you?" I said, pushing my hair from my eyes.

"I think I should be the one asking that," he said. "I reckon I've watched you struggle long enough."

"Oh, how kind," I said. "I hope you enjoyed the show."

"Proper craic, if I'm honest."

"Are you going to help me now," I said, "or just stand there smiling like that?"

"Is the smile doing anything for you?"

"Not nearly as much as a working projector would be doing for me."

"In that case, time to see what I can do."

I stood with my fists on my hips while I watched him work, annoyed and thankful in equal measure.

"How do you know how to do everything?" I asked as he clicked the right buttons in the right order until the projector turned on, bathing the room in blue fluorescent light.

"You flatter me."

"Not on purpose."

"I didn't grow up with a lot of money," he said by way of explanation. "I've been doing odd jobs since I was a wain, and I've been at the Wanderer for more years than I'm willing to count, so the skills just kind of add up."

He didn't say any of this like it was a confession, but it still made me wonder what Collin's life was like outside the walls of the hostel. As the "face" of the Wanderer, it was easy to forget he had family outside of Galway who weren't twentysomething expats clad in embroidered polos.

"Well, I'm grateful for those skills," I said, watching as he adjusted the focus on the screen.

"You're cute when you're nice," he said, clapping his hands together once the screen was clear. "Ready for the movie night, are we?"

"We?" I responded. "Your work is done here. For which I am grateful, by the way. But you don't have to stick around. Hell, I don't even know if I'm going to stick around."

"Just gonna toss the film on and leg it, are ya? I like your style."

"It's not a style," I said. "They hardly need a babysitter. I'll come back down at the end to put the projector and the screen away, but I think that's where my job begins and ends."

"What are your plans for tonight then?" he asked.

"Applying for jobs," I said. And I meant it. I had found a few more openings over the course of the week in reputable hotels, and I intended on spending the duration of the movie at my laptop curating cover letters.

"On a Thursday night?" he said. "You should be on the gargle."

"I'm sorry," I said, "I should be what?"

"Out drinkin'." He grinned. "You gotta start learning some words around here, Chels."

"It's impossible to keep up." I played along, nudging him with my shoulder. "Besides, I can't understand your accent half the time anyway."

"Spend more time with me and you'll get used to it," he said. "Come down the pub tonight. Lars and I will teach you enough slang to keep you from sounding like an eejit."

"Lars isn't even Irish," I said.

"But he's been here long enough. Rubs off on ya."

"I have work to do."

"The work can wait," he said.

"If I never wanted to go back to Boston, maybe," I said. "But I do, so. Don't get any ideas."

"How could I possibly?" He looked amused, but I didn't get the sense he was really joking. "You remind us all the time."

"Which is why I need to get the work done tonight," I said. "If I can get a job, then you won't have to hear me talk about it anymore."

"Bittersweet," he said. "I quite like hearing you talk."

If he kept this up, I'd constantly be at a loss for things to say.

"Well," I tried, "maybe I'll be able to do it more if I can get this work done."

"Go on, then." Collin nodded in the direction of the staff wing. A few guests were beginning to settle in, and I looked around for others. "I'll press play once everyone is in here, don't worry."

"Thank you," I said.

"You can repay me by coming round the pub later."

"Don't push it."

"A bloke can dream."

"Good night, Collin," I said, channeling some semblance of resolve and turning to leave the lobby.

"See you at the pub," he called after me. I could hear his smile, and I kept my back to him so he couldn't see mine.

By the time I'd opened my laptop to a handful of job postings on open tabs, I was able to refocus. For the night, anyway. With an updated résumé that was slowly becoming less of a lie, I was trying to feel confident about my prospects.

I kept an eye on the clock so I'd be downstairs before the end of the movie and used the time to write and revise different versions of my cover letter: ones for event planning, ones for general managing, vague ones for front-of-house and other odd jobs.

Each somehow harder to write than the last.

Not only was it nearly impossible to effectively brag about myself without sounding somehow both arrogant and insecure, it was even more challenging to face my career goals, let alone express them in writing.

Why did I really want this job? Why did I want any of these jobs? *Did* I even want any of these jobs?

I dropped my head to my keyboard, wondering if the random collection of letters typed by my forehead could arrange themselves into some semblance of answers to my questions.

No. I knew myself. Of course I wanted these jobs. I'd always wanted these jobs.

Only I hadn't always wanted to be a full-time event planner, had I? I always wanted a job in hospitality in the city, sure, but on the managerial side. Had I even ever considered leaving all the administrative stuff behind for good? Could I even hack it? And was there even a real reason it had to be in Boston?

Those questions rolled around in the back of my head like marbles, and I snapped my head up from my keyboard and tried to get back to work before I was forced to play with them.

I started with Hotel Blue, then followed with a commercial chain near Faneuil Hall, and a new tourist center on the harbor. Just in case. Somehow it felt like the summer had only just begun and yet I was running out of time to be picky.

I picked up my phone before I could speculate on what might happen if I didn't find anything and shot Ada a text, as I'd promised to update her on the hunt.

> Three solid applications out tn. Keep your fingers and toes crossed. We need all the luck we can get.

She answered before I even put my phone back down.

> We don't need luck. You have talent. It's the employers who would be lucky to have you.

I read her text a few times, trying to believe it, before sending out two more applications for good measure, closing my laptop, and heading back downstairs. They were both straightforward managing positions, without much room for creativity, but the pay was decent and they were centrally located, so I definitely couldn't complain.

When I got back into the lobby, I was surprised to see at least fifteen people sprawled in the seating area. There were a few crushed beer cans between the beanbags, and the credits were just beginning to roll. And Collin was standing in the back, exactly where I'd left him.

"You stayed?" I whispered, joining him against the wall.

"Got absorbed in the film," he whispered back. "I'm a sucker for a young Meg Ryan. This had nothing to do with you."

"I never said it did."

"You didn't have to."

We eyed each other, only a few inches apart. I tore myself away to shut down the projector and thank everyone for coming, reminding them to leave reviews if they were happy with the service at the Wanderer.

"If I didn't know any better, I'd think you liked it here," Collin said as the last of the guests trickled out.

"Good thing you know better, then," I smiled.

"How'd the applications go?"

"Well, thanks for asking. Hoping to hear back soon." My voice faltered, and I couldn't stop it.

"You sound stressed about it."

"I am stressed about it."

"Let me take your mind off it," he said, grabbing me by the shoulders and ushering me toward the door. "The pints aren't going to drink themselves."

"Collin!" I protested.

"Your work is done, you've applied for boring jobs for your boring city life, now you can come out for the craic."

"My city life is not boring."

"Says you."

"It's sustainable," I said, too busy with the verbal argument to also push back against his hands.

"And this isn't?"

"Thank god we're heading to the pub," I said, laughing. "We're gonna need a drink if we're gonna have this conversation."

"Aye," he said. "Now you're getting the hang of it." I rolled my eyes and followed him into the pub, letting him order us two pints of whatever lager was on tap and silently promising myself I'd only stay for one.

"So you think this isn't sustainable, do ya?" He turned to me and took a long sip, watching me do the same.

"It's just, it's different from a salaried position," I said, trying to tread lightly. "And it's not exactly comfortable apartment living."

"So, it's just about a salary and flat for you, then? Having a nice doorman, giving half your paycheck to taxes?"

"It sounds worse when you put it that way," I said. "It's about security, I guess. Not having to worry about where I'm living or where the money is coming from. I know that sounds privileged, but it's the life I want for myself."

"White picket fence and a husband too, yeah? One of those finance blokes who wear a suit to the office every day?"

"I mean, it isn't the most important part of the equation, but if I happened to find a nice husband, I'd be happy with that. And I wouldn't care if he wore a suit to work."

"But would you care if he wore work boots? Worked for an hourly wage?"

"Where is all this coming from?" I asked. "Look, Collin, this life just isn't for *me*. I don't mean to be knocking it for anyone else."

"Just part of getting to know you," he said, taking a few large gulps as if to avoid having to say anything else right away. I followed suit, needing the buzz to gather myself. "This life isn't all that bad, you know. We quite like it here, to be fair."

"And had I grown up with this, I might like it too," I said. "But it's so foreign to me. Too foreign. I'm not like you or Flo or Lars or any of the seasonal staff who came and never left. I can't adapt like that. That's why I like to have a plan."

"What if a better plan comes along?" he asked. "Would you even know?"

"I don't think there is a better plan for me than the one I've had my whole life," I said. "That's really the only plan for me."

"Sure look, then."

Because Collin was usually so chatty, it was painfully clear when he decided he had nothing else to say. And if he liked Ireland and hostel life enough for the whole country, why did it matter if I liked it too?

We finished our drinks in silence just as Lars appeared between us, clapping us both on the shoulders with his large hands.

"Chelsea, glad you made it round."

"I was actually just leaving," I said.

"So soon?"

"I've already been here for one more beer than I told myself I'd have tonight, so I better get going before it snowballs."

"Chelsea," Collin said, getting to his feet at the same time I did. I meant to just hold up a hand signaling for him not to, but he was so close that my fingertips touched his chest in a way that surprised us both.

"Enjoy your night," I said.

"Fair play to you on film night, by the way," Lars said before I could leave. "Collin texted me saying it was a hit."

I looked at Collin, and we shared a small smile before I slipped out the door, just wide enough to take the edge off without dissolving the tension completely. I took a deep breath as soon as I left the pub, trying to ease the inexplicable ache in my chest. And as much as I hated to admit it, the Galway air worked its magic.

Chapter 11

I can't believe we haven't had more overlapping days off since you started here," Flo said, sipping a coffee across from me in a café in town. "We should have done this ages ago." She took another sip, then spoke again before I had a chance. "Though now that I think about it, I suppose you're always with Collin when you have days off."

"That's not true," I said. "I do other things with my days off."

"Like what? Applying for jobs and doing laundry and making obligatory phone calls home?" Flo laughed, and I couldn't help but join in despite myself. She was right. I hadn't done a ton with my time off other than keep things in order, and I'd been here too long for "adjusting" to still be an excuse. I'd adjusted just fine. So fine, in fact, that something deep inside me worried exploring the city would make me *too* well-adjusted. Comfortable, even. At home.

"Like getting coffee with you," I said trying to keep it light. "Duh."

"Cheers to that." She lifted her mug, and I clinked mine against hers. "Let's make a day of it," she said. "We're already in town, and the sun might actually come out. We could do anything."

"Within reason," I cautioned. Aside from the activities I had researched for the bachelorette party I still wasn't sold on the liveliness of the town.

"There's tons to do here," she countered. "We just have to get creative." I stared out the window, trying to get a glimpse of what we might get ourselves into. "Finish that coffee, *tesoro*. We're starting with shopping."

"Yes, ma'am," I said, swallowing the rest of my latte and following her lead. I knew Flo well enough by then to know I didn't have a choice otherwise.

The day was coming alive, and the buskers were already setting up shop in their respective positions, carefully dotted around the streets so you'd never be more than a few steps from live music, but nothing overlapped.

A gentle breeze ruffled the bunting strung between buildings overhead, and I felt like I was seeing Galway for the first time. The colors of the buildings and the flags were faded from the harsh Irish weather, giving the whole city a vintage feel.

"You're going to love this little market," Flo said, gesturing down a narrow side street.

I followed her around the corner, turning sharply into a flurry of market stalls. Vendors stretched the length of the street, selling wares from jewelry to candles to pottery to street food. It wasn't the biggest market I'd ever seen, but it might have been the liveliest. The music from the streets floated through the throngs of people, mingling with sounds of bargaining locals and sizzling fries and laughing children.

"Cute, isn't it?" Flo asked, waving to a vendor. "Every time I come down this way I end up spending money I don't have, but I can't help myself."

I ran my fingers along a canvas tote bag, tracing an Irish

phrase printed on the front. "I don't blame you," I said. "Everything is so . . ."

"Unique?" She finished for me. "That's the best part. Nothing else like it in the world."

Admittedly, I hadn't seen much of the world, but there was nothing like this in Boston. And if there was, the vendors would be aggressively pushing sales and children would be screaming and the music would be too loud.

We took our time combing over each stall, listening to the sellers marketing their products, touching crystals and hand-woven sweaters and wooden spoons.

"Claddagh rings," Flo said, watching me inspect a tray of glistening silver bands. "They're from right here in Galway, you know."

"What do they mean?" I asked. It was becoming clear that everything in Ireland was symbolic, so I figured this was no different.

"Loyalty, friendship, *amore*," she said, slipping one onto my finger. I studied the shape, the crown above the heart clasped between two hands. It was beautiful.

"We'll take this one," Flo said, already handing her card to the vendor.

"Oh, no," I started. "Flo, you don't—"

"It's bad luck to buy one for yourself," she explained, "so you have to accept the gift." She smiled, squeezing my hand and thanking the seller. She was impossible to argue with, and impossibly generous, so I kept my mouth shut.

"Now," she said. "Let me show you how to wear it." She explained that the different ways to wear it signified relationship status, eventually turning it on my right hand so the heart was facing away from me. "This means you're single," she said.

"And then when you and Collin eventually stop pretending you aren't into each other, you can turn it around to face you to show other people you're taken."

"Flo!"

"Don't act so surprised, Chelsea. We can all see you're inseparable."

"Then you all may as well be blind," I said.

"I don't know," she mused. "Lars said there was some tension in the pub the other night. No one has tension in the pub unless something is going on."

"It's Ireland. Everyone has tension in the pub," I said. "Besides, Lars is just trying to stir the pot. I can assure you, nothing's going on."

"Just don't forget to turn the ring around when you stop lying to yourself," she said. "Speaking of Lars, I think he has a group out in Salthill today. Should we pop over there? I could go for the sea in this weather."

Flo was smart to change the subject. I had no idea what Salthill was, but the day was getting hotter and my mind cloudier, so the sea sounded like a great idea.

"Let's do it," I said, desperate to get out from under her gaze. With Lars and the guests around there was sure to be less ribbing about Collin, which was appealing enough without the promise of the sea.

After a short text exchange, Flo confirmed they were indeed at Salthill, so we headed out of town and down to the seaside. We walked along the bay, turning our faces to the wind and letting the mist settle in our hair.

"This is the Promenade," Flo said as we walked down a flat stretch that bordered the water, lined with old fashioned streetlights and wooden benches. The gentle drop off was rocky before deep blue water stretched to the horizon, and I found it impossible to look away. "And those are the hills of the Burren." She nodded across the water at a landscape that looked photoshopped. Unusual rock formations carving paths through kelly-green hills, stretching lazily toward the sky.

"Is everyone around here a tour guide?"

"It just becomes a part of you," Flo said. "Whether you want it to or not."

I kept quiet, afraid to prompt more teasing about my unwillingness to embrace Ireland.

"And that's Blackrock," she said and pointed to what looked like a diving board standing at least twenty feet above the water. I snapped my head in her direction, and her smile confirmed my fear: that was exactly where we were headed.

"Tell me we aren't," I tried.

"Oh, but that would be a lie." Her smile doubled in size, and she grabbed my hand to keep me from running all the way back to the Wanderer. "Come on. It'll be fun. I think I see Lars up there now."

Sure enough, Lars was on top of the higher platform, gesturing wildly at what must have been his group from the hostel. We watched as he approached the end of the platform, looked back to confirm he had their attention, then jumped into the sea. I tried to count the seconds it took before he hit the water but closed my eyes after *one*.

"Flo, there is absolutely no way I'm going up there."

"It's a rite of passage," she said. "Everyone who comes to Galway in the summer jumps from Blackrock." She was still dragging me in the direction of the diving board, no matter how hard I tried to pull away.

"Everyone except me," I said.

"It's only, like, ten meters," she said as if ten meters was no bigger than ten inches.

"That's thirty feet, Florence."

"Afraid of heights or the sea?"

"Heights."

"Then you'll just have to jump quickly."

"I don't have a swimsuit," I said, searching for any viable excuse.

"Do you have a bra and underwear?" she asked. I rolled my eyes, knowing we both knew the answer was yes. "Then you have a swimsuit," she said. "Let's go."

As we approached the platform, I heard a mixture of accents, the familiar soundtrack at the Wanderer.

"You girls made it," Lars called to us as he clambered out of the sea, shaking water from his hair. Unsurprisingly, his body matched his Ken-doll face, and I wondered if that was part of how he convinced so many guests to jump from a thirty-foot-high diving platform into the sea.

"We did," Flo said, flinging her arms wide. "And this one's going to do the jump."

"I don't know which one she's talking about," I said, "because it definitely isn't me."

"Chelsea Gold, get your arse up here."

I recognized Collin's voice before I looked up at the platform, and I wasn't sure what was more unsettling: the fact that he was here, or the fact that he was talking about my *arse*.

"Of course you're here," I called.

"You say that like it's a bad thing," he yelled back.

"It is," I said. "Too much pressure."

"So give in."

His words were laced with undertones I was in no position

to decode. "Not a chance," I said, wondering if he could hear the wobble in my voice from all the way up there.

"She still hasn't learned she doesn't have a choice, has she?" he asked the other two.

"I tried to tell her it was a rite of passage." Flo shrugged. "But you know how she is about embracing Galway's customs."

"*She* is standing right here," I said.

"When really she should be taking her clothes off and getting up here," Collin said. As if I wasn't nervous enough, now I also had to think about the way it sounded when Collin Finegan told me to take my clothes off.

I looked from expectant face to expectant face, slowly coming to grips with the fact that there was no getting out of this. There were a few whoops and cheers from the guests as they plunged into the water, while the others watched our conversation and waited for me to make a move.

"Ah, lads, we shouldn't be surprised," Collin said eventually. "We all know Chelsea isn't a chancer. She isn't going to change her ways now."

I opened my mouth to protest, but he had backed me into a corner. If I said I was, in fact, a chancer, I'd have no excuse not to jump. And if I agreed with him, he would be right. I could barely make out his features from so far down below, but his expression was just cocky enough for me to know we were thinking the same thing.

"You're such a pain in the ass, you know that?"

"Heard it a few times." I could tell he was smiling. "Now, what's it gonna be, Chelsea? Are you going to be brave for once, or are you going to go for security, like you always do?"

"You have no idea what I always do."

"Is that your answer?"

"I'm going to kill you," I said.

"You'll have to come up here for that."

I wasn't sure if the burning in my chest was my nerves, my frustration with Collin, or my frustration with myself, but it was becoming less bearable the longer I stood down there looking up at him.

The breaking point came, however, when a beautiful, curvy woman in a tiny black bikini materialized beside Collin, announcing in a posh English accent that she would show us how it was done.

She trailed her fingertips along Collin's back as she passed him, stepping up to the edge of the platform and cracking her neck for effect.

"Watch and learn," she said to no one in particular, though her words spread icy fingers through my chest. She dove from the platform with more grace than I've probably ever done anything and landed in the water with hardly a splash.

Collin stuck his fingers in his mouth and whistled through his teeth as she surfaced, and the ice in my chest turned to flames. Who was this woman?

And why was she touching Collin like he was more than just her tour guide?

And why the hell did I feel like this about it?

She sauntered out of the water with her long hair clinging to her back, then took a bow when she got to the sand.

"Who is that?" I whispered to Flo.

"Rhiannon something, I think," she said. "Checked in a few days ago."

"Do they know each other?" I asked. I knew I shouldn't have said anything, but I couldn't resist.

"Who, Rhiannon and Collin? Not until she got here, I don't think. But she's been hanging around the bar a bit. Or that's what Lars said, anyway."

Why hadn't I noticed her before? And what was she doing hanging around the bar when she came all the way here for vacation?

"She's a little over the top, no?" I asked, once again unable to keep my mouth shut.

"If jealousy is your way of convincing me nothing is going on with Collin, you're doing a hell of a job," she said.

"I'm not jealous," I said, perhaps a bit too quickly. "I'm just not sure we needed a whole performance just now."

"I guess you'll just have to give a better one," Flo said, shrugging in a way that suggested I had no other choice.

And she was right.

With my eyes locked on Collin and my teeth clenched, I reached for the hem of my shirt. I hadn't lifted it more than an inch when my friends and the guests erupted in a chorus of cheers, which admittedly forced me to unclench my jaw to laugh a little. It was too late to change my mind, so it was time to fully commit.

I pulled my shirt over my head and dropped my shorts to the ground, too focused on the stress of the jump to care I was in my underwear in public. Most of the crowd on the platform seemed to be wearing the same, so that was at least one thing I could have checked off the panic list.

"So she decides to be brave after all," Collin called from the platform, clapping slowly as I climbed the stairs. "What changed your mind?"

"Couldn't let everyone else have all the fun," I said, hoping I sounded more casual than I felt.

"You're the jealous type, then?" He crossed his arms, sizing me up. "There's enough fun to go around, you know."

I ignored his comment, fearful that if I said anything at all I would have to address that we might not have been talking about the jump, and that was the last thing I needed on my mind. The cheers might have gotten louder as I approached the edge, but the increasing volume of my heartbeat in my ears made it impossible to tell for sure. It may have only been thirty feet, but it felt like thirty thousand.

"I'll go first," Collin said softly enough that I might have been the only one who heard him.

"Why, so you can show off and make me look like an idiot?" I tried to laugh, but it got caught behind the lump in my throat.

"No," he said, more of a whisper now. "So I can be there in the water when you land."

"Like I'm a little kid," I said. I was fighting embarrassment with everything I had. I wasn't sure if he was helping or making it worse.

"It's a high jump, Chels. Sometimes it feels better with someone waiting for you down below, that's all."

I risked a glance at his eyes, the same blue green as the sea, though arguably more dangerous. There was a kindness in them that wasn't there before, and if my legs weren't wobbly enough from the height of the platform, they were jelly after a few seconds of eye contact.

"Yeah, but you don't—"

"I've got you," he said, flashing a crooked smile in the split second before he leapt from the platform and splashed into the sea. I watched as his head bobbed above the water and he ruffled a hand through his hair, pushing it from his eyes and gazing up at me.

"It's now or never," he yelled up at me. "You've got this. And I've got you."

Hearing those words again, at that volume, gave me the last bit of courage I needed. He wasn't lying. He had me, and I had to trust him.

I took a deep breath and jumped, and for a second, I realized why everyone did this. For a second, I was flying.

Then I was crashing into the water, water was up my nose, it felt impossible to figure out which way was up, and it wasn't until my head broke the surface that I realized I was in Collin's arms, which was likely how I'd gotten to the surface in the first place.

"I did it!" I shouted entirely too loudly for how close I was to his face.

"Told you you could," he said, pushing a wet lock of hair out of my eyes. Outside of this moment, that gesture might have stolen the breath from my lungs, but in this case the breath was hardly there in the first place, so it was easy to cope.

"Only you would use my moment of glory to brag," I said.

"Old habits die hard," he said. "But you're right. This was all you. Fair play to ya there, Chelsea."

"Thank you," I said. "For your help too, I mean."

He flicked water into my face, and I was finally able to let out a laugh for real.

"We should probably—"

"Are you two done?" a voice called from the platform. "Or am I going to have to jump right onto your heads?"

"—get out of the way," Collin was laughing as he finished his thought. We called apologies to the man on the platform, and I wondered how long we'd been floating there and how many others noticed.

Just before the man plunged into the water, I felt Collin's hands circle my waist once more, pulling me toward him and out of the way. Even under the cool water they were warm, and since they were just out of view of everyone on the sand, the gesture felt more intimate than it should have.

But that didn't stop me from being disappointed when he let go.

And it didn't stop me from wondering if those same hands had been on Rhiannon, either.

We swam to the shore, side by side, breathing heavily as we shook water from our hair and rejoined our friends at the bottom of the platform.

"I'm going to give you one more chance," Flo whispered as Collin caught up with Lars.

"Save it," I said before she could finish. She tittered and tossed me my clothes, and together we watched the boys rejoin the rest of the guests at the top. Rhiannon included.

"Clock's ticking, *cara*," Flo said, following my gaze. "If you don't make a move, someone else might."

"Then it's a good thing I don't plan on making a move," I said.

"Whatever you have to tell yourself," she said. "Come on. Let's get back and into the showers before the boys can beat us to it."

I let her drag me by the arm back to the Promenade, forcing my eyes from where Collin stood with Rhiannon overlooking the sea.

If Flo was right, I worried I really didn't have much time left. And if everyone else who jumped was right, maybe there was something to be said for taking risks after all.

Chapter 12

Dear Ms. Gold,

We thank you for your application and your interest in the concierge position at Lakeland Inn. We regret to inform you, however—

Damn it. I didn't even need to read beyond the second line to know what the rest of the email said. Hell, I didn't even need to read beyond the first. *We've filled the role, a more qualified candidate, an internal transfer, please keep us in mind in the future,* etc. etc.

I leaned across the desk and scratched this job from my list of applications, resisting the urge to rip the entire thing to shreds. I tried to remind myself I still had plenty of time, but it didn't stop the heat from pricking the back of my eyes.

Since having graduated from college, I'd tried to do everything right. I'd gotten a good job, moved out of my parents' house, worked hard, and made my bosses proud. And where had it gotten me? Not a single mistake along the way, and for what? What was the point of working so hard, or planning my future, if it didn't even matter in the end?

"Are you Chelsea?"

I looked up from the reception desk at a smiling couple, the ageless kind that looked like they could be in their early twenties or their late forties depending on the lighting.

"I am," I said. "Is there something I can help you with?"

I waited while they exchanged small smiles, hoping they weren't going to ask for something that required more emotional stamina than I had this morning.

"You're the event planner here, right?" one of the men asked, clasping his hands together like he was praying I'd say yes.

"I mean, I'm not sure if I . . . maybe?" I laughed. "It isn't in my job title, but I have planned a few events since I've gotten here. Have you heard of our weekly movie night?" I hoped to persuade them with an event that already existed, rather than have them ask me to plan something entirely new.

"We do love a proper film night," the other man said, clearly enticed by the idea. "What d'you think, Grant? We could stay in, cozy up with a film and a few drinks?"

"We were hoping you could arrange a cooking class for us," Grant said to me, patting his partner's hand. "You see, Liam here is a terrible cook—"

"Terrible is a strong word."

"—and we're moving in together after we get back from this holiday, and I can't be the only one feeding this family."

"It's a family of two," Liam said. "It's not that hard."

"Which is why you'll learn to do it."

They nudged each other, giggling in a way that suggested they forgot I was sitting right there.

"Anyway," Grant continued, remembering my presence. "Is that something you might be able to do?"

Their smiles were so contagious it would have been impossible to say no.

"Of course," I said, turning to my computer and slipping into customer service mode. "Let me have a look."

"And between you and me," Grant said, leaning across the desk and dropping his voice to a whisper, "it doesn't have to be an Irish cooking class. I think Irish food is terrible, if I'm honest."

"And if I'm also honest," I said, matching his whisper, "I totally agree. Just don't let anyone around here hear you say that or they'll be shoving cabbage down our throats until you leave."

"Please," Grant said. "Don't even say the word. It's been a day in Ireland and I already never want to think about cabbage again."

"I quite like cabbage," Liam said, crossing his arms.

"You also like American football and the Queen, so I'm not sure your opinions can be trusted," Grant said with a laugh.

"Do you want to keep cooking yourself dinner or not?" Liam said, to which Grant raised his palms and turned back to me at my computer.

"Well, what is something you can agree on?" I asked. "Is there a specific cuisine you both like?"

"What about Italian?" Liam said. "That way maybe someday I can learn to make that pasta dish from Giacomo's that you like?"

"Now we're talking," Grant said, kissing Liam on the temple. "Though I can't imagine that'll be something easy to find in Galway, will it?"

"In fact," I said, bells and whistles and strobe lights flashing around in my brain, "I know just the chef."

I WASN'T SURE Flo would go for it, especially given how few days off we had. But I hoped that once she met Grant and Liam, she would like them enough to make it work.

"How do you feel about coming back here for a drink later?" I asked the couple. "Our chef gets off after dinner, and I'd love to introduce you and set something up. I should warn you, she didn't go to culinary school but she grew up in Italy in a house with all her relatives, so if you're looking for traditional Italian—"

"That's perfect," Grant said. "Even better that way."

"Agreed," Liam said.

Once they left I made my way to the kitchen, where Flo was preparing grab-and-go-style sandwiches for lunch even though the hostel was mostly empty during the day.

"Florence, darling," I said, approaching the bench with caution as she had a giant knife in her hand.

"Chelsea, if you've come to ask me to blow-dry your massive head of hair again, the answer is no. You know how to do it, and my hands are already sore from all the prep work today."

I laughed, remembering the day last week I'd been too lazy and asked her to help. She'd had a pixie cut for years, and the whole scene was apparently traumatizing.

"I've learned my lesson," I said. "Besides, this favor is a better one, anyway."

"I'm listening."

I gave her the pitch, leaving out the part that I secretly hoped she might agree to do it more regularly. I had no intention of doing any extra work today, but once the ball got rolling it was hard to stop myself.

She leaned her hip against the counter, narrowing her eyes and crossing her arms over her chest. "What's in it for me?"

I knew this was coming. "Uh," I said, "the sheer glory of helping a lovely couple have a long and happy life together in their new home?"

"And it's just this once?"

"Sure," I said, but it came out as more of a question.

"Chelsea!"

"Come on, Flo! Don't you think it would be cool to share your talents with our guests?"

"I do share my talents with our guests," she said, gesturing to the sandwiches.

"You know what I mean," I said. "It wouldn't be all the time. Maybe once or twice a month at most. I could even help you do some prep stuff so you had more time for the class. I'm sure Lori would let you do it on the nights you were already working if you had some extra hands in here."

Volunteering myself for more kitchen duties wasn't exactly part of the plan, but again, I wasn't always sure what came over me when I started planning events.

"You're lucky I like you," Flo said. "And this is the only class I'm doing outside of regularly scheduled working hours. I mean it, Chels. But if you can get Lori on board for the others and you help me out in here, then you have yourself a deal."

I threw my arms around her neck, pulling her into a tight hug. She uncrossed her arms to hug me back, and we laughed at ourselves.

"Thank you, Flo," I said.

"Yeah, yeah," she said, swatting my legs with a dish towel. "Now get out of here. I have work to do."

"*Si, signora.*"

I settled back into my place behind the desk and opened my email, firing yet another message to Lori about starting an event.

And, in true Lori fashion, she approved it almost instantly and with enthusiasm bordering on aggression. We didn't see much of her physically on the grounds at the Wanderer, but I had a sense she was never more than a minute from the action.

By THE TIME Grant and Liam returned for drinks, I had already slotted more than a handful of regular classes into the summer calendar and brainstormed a menu with Flo for their date night.

"How was your day out in the city?" I asked them as we pulled stools up to the bar. Fortunately, Collin wasn't working tonight, so I could focus on Grant and Liam.

"Brilliant," Grant said, smiling even wider than he'd been that morning. "Galway is really something. Which I'm sure you know, since you live here."

"You must love getting out and exploring the city," Liam said while Grant ordered the three of us gin and tonics.

"We're trying to get her out there," Flo said, kissing my cheek as she joined us. "It's like pulling teeth sometimes, but we're working on it. I'm Flo." She extended her hand, shaking with both Liam and Grant, respectively.

I had known I wasn't getting out into the city enough, but I figured Collin would just keep dragging me out until I'd seen the entire country if he had it his way. But now my body buzzed with a mix of guilt and apprehension, suddenly afraid of leaving Ireland with no real stories to tell. I sipped my drink in an attempt to calm down.

"We can't thank you enough for taking the time to teach us to cook," Grant said. "Especially your traditional recipes."

"It's my pleasure," Flo said.

"You say that now, but only because you haven't seen this one in the kitchen yet," Grant said through the corner of his mouth, jerking his thumb toward Liam.

"Keep talking like that and I'll change my mind about the whole thing," Liam said. "You included."

Grant pretended to zip his lips, and Liam swooped in for a quick kiss.

"So," Flo said. "Tell me your story. I like to get to know the people I'm sharing my family recipes with."

At once, Grant and Liam launched into their story, finishing each other's sentences and leaving no detail uncovered. They met in university, but they hadn't started dating until they reconnected at a wedding in Scotland years later. Since then they've seen more than fifty countries together, and they finally feel ready to share a home (which to them feels like the biggest adventure of all).

I had my suspicions that Flo was a hopeless romantic, try as she might to deny it, and the way she devoured their story only confirmed my belief. It really was beautiful, the way these two very different men found a common ground on the road and built a brilliant life together.

"Paul," Flo called to the bartender whom I'd never seen before. "A round of Limoncello for us, please." She turned her attention back to Grant and Liam. "To you two," she said, "and your story. And may this Limoncello be the beginning of a long and successful Italian culinary experience for you. Especially you, Liam," she said, winking in a way that was so charming even Liam couldn't pretend to be bothered by the teasing.

Paul slid a tray of cordials across the bar, and I had to admit I was shocked Limoncello was something we had stocked here.

"And to you," Grant said, "our culinary spirit guide. And dear Chelsea, for setting this up." We raised our glasses to one another, clinking before we drank.

I dropped into the background, listening as Flo chatted with her new friends. They discussed the recipes she planned to teach them, what her life was like in Italy, the amenities of Grant and Liam's new apartment building, where they planned to travel next. The conversation washed over me, and I grew content sitting quietly in its warm glow.

Until Collin walked in. With Rhiannon close behind.

They were joined by a handful of others I recognized from Blackrock, but they only seemed interested in each other.

Although I felt tempted to run, I was determined to be more discreet. There was no reason for either of them to get under my skin in the first place, so leaving the bar wouldn't have done any more good than staying put.

"Who is that?" Grant asked, following my not-so-subtle gaze.

"Who, him?" I said, gesturing toward Collin with my thumb like I had no idea why Grant would possibly be asking about him. "He's the tour guide, and sometimes the bartender, and whatever else."

"And does 'whatever else' happen to include being your lover?" Grant asked, looking right through me. "Because your gaze tells me it does, but that woman on his arm tells me the opposite."

"Please, Chelsea," Flo said. "Do tell us."

I shot her a look that had no effect. She kept smiling, and I kept trying not to scream. "Nope," I said to Grant. "Just a friend." Collin must have felt us all looking at him, because he turned on cue and whispered something to Rhiannon before heading in our direction.

"Oh, shit." Flo giggled under her breath. I did not join her.

"Hi," he said when he arrived, and I could tell Grant was already charmed by that damn sideways smile. They exchanged introductions, and I forced myself not to notice how much more Irish Collin's accent sounded in conversation with their English ones.

"You're the tour guide, are you?" Liam asked.

"I am," Collin said. "Interested in getting out to see more of the country while you're here?"

"That'd be brilliant," Grant said. "Would love to hear from a local."

"See?" Collin said, nudging my elbow with his. The unexpected contact gave me more of a buzz than the Limoncello ever could have. "Some people are actually interested in what the locals have to offer."

"They're misguided," I whispered loud enough for Grant and Liam to hear so they knew I was joking. "We try not to hold it against them. They're good people."

"She's right," Grant said, turning his attention to Collin. "We are misguided. We thought you fancied the woman you came in with, but now we see we're wrong." He beamed at Collin, who rested his bottom lip between his teeth while he looked for a response.

"Please forgive us," Liam said. "My partner sometimes has one drink and forgets how to behave." He said the last part with clenched teeth, but Grant only laughed.

"Sorry, love, but I have to call it as I see it, that's all."

"Have I mentioned how much I like these two?" Flo said, nodding toward Grant and Liam.

If I didn't want to run from the bar before, I did then. Well, part of me anyway. The other part was desperate to ask Grant what made him think Collin fancied me instead of Rhiannon.

"It was a pleasure to meet you both. I've got to get back, but I'm sure I'll see you around," Collin said eventually, but not unkindly, looking over his shoulder to the group he had brought in.

"Don't sound so excited," Flo said.

As we followed Collin's line of vision, we watched Rhiannon call him over with perfectly manicured fingers. There was an empty space next to her on a small couch, and I didn't want to imagine Collin filling it. I also didn't want to imagine their knees touching, them staying until closing time, finding their way out of here together.

But just because I didn't want to didn't mean I wasn't going to.

"I should probably head out," I said, getting up from the stool and finishing the last of the Limoncello.

"We just got here," Grant said. "Stay for at least another."

Collin had yet to walk away, and I could feel his gaze burning through the side of my face.

"This was just for you two to connect with Flo, anyway," I said to Grant. "I've done my job. And now I should keep doing my job if 'Cooking with Flo' is going to succeed more than just this once."

"Always working, this one," Flo said.

"Someone has to," I teased.

"Well, we're very lucky to have met you," Grant said. "Thank you for putting this together. The Wanderer is lucky to have you on the staff, you know. All of you."

"We keep telling her that," Collin said, "but she's a terrible listener."

"Didn't you say you had somewhere to be?" I said, sharper than I intended.

"Didn't you say the same?"

We stared at each other for a second too long, during which I was sure I heard Rhiannon call his name.

"Feels a bit mad they aren't going to the same place, doesn't it? I mean, they obviously should—"

"Grant," Liam said. Surely this wasn't the first time Liam had scolded Grant for something like this, because Grant immediately sank back onto his stool and raised the palms of his hands in surrender.

"Well, I guess I should, er . . ." Collin started.

"Yeah," I said. "Me too."

We clambered around each other to say good night to our friends, then headed off in opposite directions. Collin back to Rhiannon, and me up to my bed. Alone.

WHEN I COULDN'T FALL ASLEEP, I called Ada. I tried to detail the last few days, but it was hard to get through more than a sentence without an interruption.

"You jumped off a cliff?" she shouted. "You, Chelsea Gold, jumped off a cliff? Into the sea?"

"Is that really so surprising?" I asked, though we both knew the answer.

"I'm as proud as I am stunned, really," she said. "I mean, who even are you? First, you move to Ireland, then you jump off a cliff . . . what's next?"

"I didn't *move* to Ireland," I said. "I just relocated. Temporarily."

"And how's the job hunt going?"

"Bleak. Really bleak. But that's not why I called."

"Oh, babe, I know why you called," she said. "Same reason you've called the last, like, four times."

"That is not true."

"You're right," she said. "There hasn't been another woman the other times."

"Don't say it like that."

"Like what? That's the problem, right? The other woman?"

"If you say 'other' it makes it seem like I'm his usual woman."

"Well, you want to be, don't you?"

"No," I said, "*you* want me to be."

"I only ever want what's best for you."

"And without having ever even met him, you've decided a random hostel tour guide in Ireland is what's best for me?"

"It's the most you've ever talked to me about a guy in a long time, and he seems to make you happy, when he isn't making you insane, of course. But even when he is making you insane, when was the last time a man made you insane?"

She had a point. Men didn't make me insane. In fact, they did the opposite. They all but bored me to death, to be honest.

"What's insane is the idea of pursuing this at all," I said. "He's obviously just interested in whoever is the newest face to come through here, and at the end of the day he lives in Galway and I live in Boston, so what's the point?"

"Last I checked you also live in Galway."

"Temporarily," I reminded her. "Are you trying to get rid of me?"

"I wouldn't dream of it," she said. "In fact, I might just come live there with you."

"Which would be great, if I actually lived here. But it's just a visit. Which is why getting involved with Collin is stupid."

"A summer fling is never stupid. Men with lots of tattoos and messy hair who make good cocktails and take you on picnics to parks with lakes are not stupid."

"Men are always stupid," I said.

"Ireland has made you cynical."

"Boston made me cynical."

"All the more reason to give Ireland a chance, then," she said.

"And by Ireland you mean Collin," I said.

"Bingo."

"We don't even know if he's interested," I whispered, suddenly nervous he might have come back from the bar and could hear me from his room. Then I remembered he probably wouldn't be alone if that was the case, which made me want to crawl out of my own skin.

"Chelsea, please," Ada said. "He tells you fairy stories. What man tells romantic fairy stories to a woman he isn't interested in?"

"An Irishman," I said. "It's a thing here. But even so, maybe his interest in me isn't the issue. Maybe the issue is he's also interested in everyone else."

"Maybe he's trying to make you jealous."

This thought had floated into my mind for a fraction of a second at Blackrock, then again in the bar, but I had snuffed it out like a flame. It was wishful thinking at best and embarrassingly delusional at worst.

"I doubt it," I said. "He wouldn't go through the trouble."

"Have a little faith, Chels."

"Even if I did, now what am I supposed to do?"

"Make a move, duh."

"Easy for you to say," I said. "You aren't here. And you haven't seen the other woman."

"No, but I have seen you," she said. "And I know that the 'other woman' couldn't hold a candle, regardless of how she looks."

"What would I do without you?"

"Doesn't matter, because we're never going to have to find out," she said.

"Thanks, Ada."

"Don't thank me yet," she said. "I'm not going to let up until you get out there and do something bold, so."

"Can't I do, like, baby steps? Work my way up to bold?"

"You lost that privilege when you moved to Ireland and jumped off a cliff. Sorry, babe."

I moaned but said nothing. There was no arguing with Ada, and in a way, she was right. I'd been bold before. I could do it again, couldn't I?

But right now I was exhausted, so bold Chelsea would have to wait until tomorrow.

After ending my call with Ada, I grabbed my toiletries and headed to the bathroom, planning to get ready for bed and fall into a deep, dreamless sleep. I felt myself winding down, until I heard his voice while I was washing my face.

"Figured you'd be asleep by now."

I wiped the cleanser from my eyes, acutely aware that doing so probably made me look like a child who forgot her goggles at the swimming pool.

"And I figured you'd still be at the bar."

"Couple more drinks and this lot would have been making a proper holy show," he said, stretching his arms over his head just enough to expose a sliver of his stomach. "Couldn't be arsed to stay around for that tonight."

"A holy show?"

"A scene," he explained. "Though after your performance at Blackrock, I'd think you'd know a thing or two about a holy show."

"I did not make a scene," I said.

"Aye, I have to disagree with ya there, Chels. It was quite charming though, I have to say."

"Does charming have a different meaning here than it does at home?" I was hoping he would say yes and that an insult might stop the heat spreading across my chest, but I should have known better.

"Hardly," he said. He looked at his watch, which obscured a tattoo of what looked like a key that intrigued me every time I caught a glimpse. "What's keeping you up, then?"

"Just catching up with my best friend from home," I said, hoping he wouldn't probe.

"Did ya tell her how much you're loving Galway? How much the Wanderer has changed your life?"

"No," I said, "because I'm a terrible liar."

"Looks like I'm going to have to try harder," he said. "Might have to really start making my case."

"Seemed to be working for Rhiannon," I said. It took everything in me not to cover my mouth with my hand, willing the words back inside. He laughed, rubbing his hand over the back of his head.

"I'm sorry," I blurted. "That was . . . I don't know what that was."

"Lucky woman, you are," he said, joining me at the sink. "Even jealousy looks good on you." He turned the water on and started washing his face before I had a chance to respond, so I had to raise my voice over the faucet.

"I'm not jealous."

"I can't hear you," he said, face still in the sink. I crossed my arms and waited, only to be jarred by how good he looked when he was finished. The water turned his lashes dark and heavy, and the usually wild strands of hair in the front were slicked back from his face. He looked like he did after platform jumping, when he was inches from my face, wide-eyed, his hands on my hips under the water like a secret passing between us.

"You were saying?" he asked, leaning back on the counter.

"I'm not jealous," I repeated. "I was just making an observation."

"And that observation is that you think I'm trying to sell Rhiannon on Galway, is it?"

"It's that you're trying to sell her on *something*," I said. He laughed again, but I did not.

"You do know being a tour guide is my job, don't you? I'm contractually obligated to try to get people to like it here."

"Is that why you've been showing me around? Because you're contractually obligated?"

"Ah, come on. It's not like that with you, Chels."

"Then what is it like? If it isn't just part of your long list of jobs."

"If you have to ask, that means I'm not doing a good enough job of showing ya." He took a step closer, but we were interrupted by the sound of Lars's voice down the hall.

"I'm just going to have a quick shower first," he was saying to whomever he was with. "I'll be right back. Wait in my room for me, will you?"

A second later he swung open the bathroom door, seemingly surprised to see the two of us standing there, likely too close for coworkers who just happened to share a bathroom.

"Didn't expect to see you two in here," he said. "Am I interrupting something?"

"Are *we*?" Collin swooped in before I could die of embarrassment. "Seemed like you and whoever you were talking to in the corridor thought you were having a private moment."

"Last I checked you weren't the only one allowed to shag the guests," Lars said with a chuckle. I didn't laugh. Collin didn't either. Instead, we locked eyes, but his expression was unreadable, even in the bright light of the bathroom.

"Ah, so you are shagging the guests after all," I said, recrossing my arms and trying to look more smug than inexplicably crushed.

"It's not like—"

"I've said too much," Lars said, putting his fingers to his lips. "A few too many pints'll do that to me."

"You've said just enough. Enjoy your night," I said to Lars.

I was out the door before he could say anything else, and I felt Collin two steps behind me.

"Chelsea," he said.

I turned to him and raised my eyebrows to signal I was listening, though he only had about thirty seconds before I backed through my doorway and called it a night.

"He isn't talking about now," he said. "We've all done stuff like that since we've been working here. Especially when we've been here a while. It's just, I don't know. What happens in here sometimes."

"You don't have to explain anything to me," I said. "What you do in your free time is none of my business."

"I don't want you thinking I'm the bloke who shags all the guests."

"Does it matter what I think?"

"Do you really think it doesn't?"

We stared at each other, the only sounds the running water in the bathroom and our breathing.

"I don't know what to think," I said eventually. I was beginning to realize I might have overreacted about Rhiannon, maybe even misjudged what was really going on, and I probably owed him the benefit of the doubt. I'd have wanted it if the roles were reversed.

"Let me make it easier for you," he said. "Let's drive the Wild Atlantic Way this week. I'll tell you everything you want to know."

"What makes you so sure I want to know anything?"

"We wouldn't still be having this conversation if you didn't," he said. "Besides, I do believe you won a bet, and I am a man of my word, so it's only fair to follow through."

"Fine," I agreed. "But only because I want to drive."

"Whatever you have to tell yourself."

"Good night, Collin," I said, ducking into my room and closing my door.

"Sweet dreams," he called from the other side, so cheerful I almost had to laugh. Almost.

Chapter 13

ight, then," Collin said as we approached his truck. "We're really doing this?"

"I thought you were a man of your word."

We squinted at each other for a second against the bright morning sun before he wordlessly handed over his keys.

"Thanks a million," I said, smiling at his eye roll.

A few days of distance (and Rhiannon's departure) evaporated the tension from that night in the bathroom, so I decided to follow through with our plans to drive the Wild Atlantic Way.

Collin was right; there were things I wanted to know about him. About his history, about whether he treats every woman who passes through the Wanderer the same. About what the hell we were doing here.

"All right, so it's a manual transmission, yeah?" he said as I hopped into the driver's seat. "So to turn it on, step on the clutch and the brake, there." I did as I was told, fighting a smile. "Then you put it in gear, so push this up and to the left, then ease off the clutch and—"

Before he had a chance to finish speaking, I sped out of the parking spot.

"Christ, Chelsea," Collin said, grabbing the handle on the door. "What the hell are ya doing?"

"You didn't think you were teaching me to drive stick, did you?" I threw it into second gear, pulling up to the road. I may have been confident in driving the truck, but I definitely wasn't confident in doing it on the opposite side of the street.

"God," he shook his head as he laughed. "It's your goal to keep making me look like a fool, then, is it?"

"I mean, if the shoe fits . . ."

I could feel him staring at me, incredulous, but I didn't risk a glance across the truck. I had to stay focused.

"All right, then, if you're so confident, why don't ya get out on the road there?"

I looked back and forth at the passing traffic, trying to determine both when I had an opening and exactly which way to pull out. And if I wasn't nervous enough, I had the weight of Collin's gaze boring into the side of my head.

"Not so easy, is it?"

"It's your truck we're in," I reminded him. "So if I crash it because you'd rather make fun of me than be helpful, that's on you."

"That's dark, Chelsea."

"It's true."

"Right, then," he said, clapping his hands together and focusing on the road. "In the interest of not getting us killed, I think I'll help you out a bit."

"Chivalry isn't dead after all?"

"Stop faffin' about," he said. "Focus on the road."

"Yes, sir."

Once I had a window between cars, I pulled onto the left-hand side of the road, but not without an involuntary scream.

"You're fine," Collin encouraged. "Grand, even. I'll tell you what to do next."

I continued driving in silence, trying not to think about how nice it would be to always have someone telling you what to do next.

There wasn't much traffic, but that didn't stop me from thinking every car we passed was going to hit us head-on.

"You can breathe, Chelsea," Collin said after a while.

"I know that."

"Then why aren't you doing it?"

I shot him a look, which I regretted as soon as I saw the way his eyes caught the sun. Two sage-green planets, turned to glass by the brightness of the morning. He looked impossibly relaxed, slouched in the seat with his forearm out the window, so I figured maybe he was right. I could breathe.

"Lean into the curb on the left, stay wide on the right," he said as I turned onto another side street. "Lean left, wide right."

"Lean left, wide right," I repeated.

Fortunately, we were close to the highway, so it wasn't long before all I had to do was drive straight.

"Yer a fast learner," he said as I picked up speed to merge with the other cars.

"I have a decent teacher."

"Normally, I'd be offended by 'decent,'" he said. "But from you, I think it's quite the compliment."

"Whatever you have to tell yourself."

He clucked his tongue but said nothing else, and I resisted a smile at my little victory. It was time two played at that game.

"Where exactly are we headed?" I asked after another few minutes of silence. "Aren't those cliffs somewhere over here?"

"First of all, if another Irish person catches ya calling the very sacred Cliffs of Moher 'those cliffs' they'd kill ya, so watch yourself. And second of all, you aren't ready for the Cliffs. We're going in the other direction. Toward the castles."

"Why am I not ready for the Cliffs?"

"The Cliffs change people, Chels. Or they bring ya back to yourself. They can be quite a lot if you aren't in the right head-space."

I should have stopped being surprised when Collin talked like this. In a way that was serious. Contemplative. That made me feel like glass. Fragile and transparent.

But still, it caught me off guard, and I fumbled around for an answer.

"Are you saying I need to be changed?" I asked eventually, keeping my eyes on the road. "Or are you saying I need to come back to myself?"

"Aye, neither," he said. "Only the Cliffs can answer that." Before I could say anything else, he gestured out the window. "Right, so we're going to take this exit up here."

Still processing our conversation, I tried to refocus on the road. I downshifted to slow down, checked my mirrors, lost my bearings, and—

"Chelsea!" Collin shouted, reaching for the wheel and jerking us out of the way of an oncoming car and onto the shoulder of the exit ramp. I was sure the tire screeching was louder in my imagination, but that didn't stop it from feeling like we were in an action movie. A really bad action movie, where the main character had no idea how to drive and almost killed everyone else just trying to get off the highway.

Once our breathing slowed and our heart rates returned to somewhat normal, we dared to look at each other. I was as mortified as I was terrified, and I'm sure it was written all over my face. I expected to see the same look on Collin, but what I saw was his usual crooked smile. Only his lips were pressed together, seemingly trying to contain a laugh.

It wasn't long before it exploded out of him like fireworks. It took me a few seconds of processing before I could join in, then the two of us sat laughing like children on the side of the road, half in the way of traffic, not caring a bit.

"Holy shit," he said as he regained his composure. "I thought the goal was *not* to get us killed."

"I thought you were going to help me." I wiped tears from my eyes.

"I *was* helping you."

"You were distracting me."

"Not on purpose," he said, and I groaned. "Besides, you've been distracting me since the moment you got to the Wanderer, so it's only fair."

"Not on purpose," I said.

"Thank god," he said. "If you'd actually been putting effort in, I'd probably have lost my job by now."

"I'm not so sure," I said. "I'd say you manage distractions just fine."

"Oh, come on," he said, leaning his head against the seat, also seemingly resigning to our position on the side of the road. "I told ya, Chels, I was just doing my job."

"And right now?" I asked. "This is also just doing your job?"

"You think I'd be working on my day off, do ya?" I rolled my eyes, and he went on, "We both know this is far from just doing my job. I meant it when I said it the other night, you know. It's different with you."

I wanted to ask how, to urge him to say more, but my heart was still in my throat from a minute ago and I wasn't sure how much more I could handle. Instead, I shot him a soft smile before unbuckling my seat belt, preparing to switch places.

"Wait, wait, wait," he said. "You're still on."

"After that performance?" I looked at him in disbelief. "God, no. We're switching seats. You're driving."

"That wasn't the deal," he said. "You're grand. Keep going."

"You're not going to make fun of me?" I was so surprised I couldn't resist asking aloud.

"Don't get used to it," he teased. "It's only because I want to survive the rest of this trip. As soon as we're back at the Wanderer, all bets are off."

"Lucky me."

"If we make it back to the Wanderer, that is."

"I thought you were being nice."

"You're right," he said.

Once I successfully merged onto the exit, the drive became far more comfortable. I was getting the hang of driving on the left, and Collin and I slipped back into small talk about the scenery and the weather and the current batch of guests at the Wanderer. The clouds broke across the sky to reveal a deep summer blue.

"This," Collin said after a few more turns, "is Sky Road." The pride in his voice and the gentle smile I caught from the corner of my eye reminded me why he tours for a living.

There might have been a lot of things about Collin that were still a mystery to me, but if there was one thing of which I could be absolutely certain, it was that he lived and died by Ireland. And for a second, I wondered whether I felt even close to the same about Boston.

"You'll want to be careful here," he said as we climbed higher along the road. "It gets tight, and these inexperienced drivers are a real hazard."

I whipped my head in his direction only to be met with that cheeky lopsided smile.

"Rude," I said, refocusing on the road in case he was right.

"It's easy to wind you up," he said. "Sometimes it's hard to resist."

"Well, try," I said.

"Oh, I've been trying."

With a slow inhale, I continued working my way around the curves in the road. And just as I started to find my rhythm, the Atlantic revealed herself beyond the cliffside. The water was a deep navy, streaked with white caps of small waves crashing against the rocks.

"Oh my—"

"Told ya," he said. "Pull over up here. We can switch now."

"My driving's that bad?"

He laughed, but softer than I was expecting. "I want you to see the whole view," he said.

Once Collin was behind the wheel, he adjusted the driver's seat and pulled back onto the road. I knew I was supposed to be looking at the view, but it was difficult not to watch him drive. Not to watch him turn the wheel with the heel of his hand, not to watch his forearms flex as he changed gears, not to watch him watching me.

When I was finally able to focus, I let my eyes trail along the horizon and admire the sea blend into the sky. I rolled down the windows to smell the salty air, letting my hair tangle in the breeze, not caring at all about what it'd feel like to rake the knots out later.

Eventually I pulled my head inside the window and leaned it back against the seat, trying to savor the moment. I hadn't been doing enough of that since I'd gotten here. Or any of that, really. My main priority since I'd arrived in Ireland had been trying to leave Ireland, which meant I was mostly missing all of Ireland.

"All right?" Collin asked, studying my face in glances.

"Grand," I answered, which made him smile.

"Don't have anything like this in Boston, do ya?"

"We have plenty in Boston," I said, trying to think of a single thing that might stack up to this view. He waited, but I said nothing.

"Sure ya do," he said eventually, laughing under his breath.

"Where does this lead?" I asked, dragging my gaze along the shoreline, desperate to redirect our conversation.

"Still so eager to get to the next thing, are ya?" He shook his head, and I resisted the urge to melt into my seat. "Must there always be a destination, Chelsea?"

"Well, no, but—"

"But nothing," he said. "It's okay to not know where you're going."

"In the car, maybe," I argued. "But not in life."

"Who told you that?"

"No one had to tell me," I said, though an image of my mother flashed in my mind. "It's just the way things are."

Collin hummed, a low sound from deep in his chest, and it reverberated around the truck's cab and straight down my spine.

"What?" I asked.

"I didn't say anything."

"But you made a sound."

"I'm not allowed to make a sound?"

"Not without telling me what it was about," I said.

"How hard are you really trying?" he said. "To find a job,

I mean. To know where you're going again. Because you're putting in more work at the Wanderer, and I'm wondering when you have time for the job applications, and if you actually want to—"

"Of course I'm trying," I said defensively. "And of course I want to find a job and move home. Nothing's changed."

"Say it like you mean it and I might believe you."

"Where is this coming from?" I asked, rolling up the window and pushing my hair from my face.

"I just think you're happier here than you're willing to admit, that's all." He raised his palms suggesting he had nothing else to say, but that didn't work for me.

"And what makes you the authority on that?" I asked.

"I have eyes, Chelsea."

"What's that supposed to mean?"

"Stop asking questions you already know the answers to," he replied. "I can literally see you letting your guard down. You don't grit your teeth at the thought of exploring the country anymore. I'd say sometimes you're even excited about it. Unless that has nothing to do with Ireland, and everything to do with . . ."

The way he smiled told me he knew I knew exactly what he was going to say, and I was impossibly grateful he didn't finish speaking. Though in all honesty, it didn't make much of a difference. The energy in the truck was electric, and I studied the landscape beyond the window in a desperate attempt to distract myself.

I counted the cows that dotted the grass. The gulls that dipped over the sea. The breaths Collin took that sounded like he was about to say something but at the last minute changed his mind.

He was on his fourth when we rounded a curve and a castle came into view in the distance. It was a soft gray with turrets jutting into the sky beyond the deep green of the trees, nestled between a dense mountainside and a sparkling lake.

"Is that—"

"Our destination," he said. "Does it qualify for your list of acceptable places to be going? It's not anywhere on the corporate ladder or anything, but it's—"

"Beautiful," I said. For once, I had nothing else to say.

"Sometimes it's nice for things to just be beautiful, isn't it?" Collin asked, following the road along the direction of the water. "Not everything always has to be getting you to the next thing, or—"

"Collin," I said, "you're ruining it."

"Oh, I'm sorry," he said, "were you just embracing the moment for once?"

"I can do that, you know," I said.

"I'll believe it when I see it."

"I could do it better if you weren't riding me constantly."

"Oh, that's what I'm doing now, is it?" He raised his eyebrows, and I caught the innuendo a second too late.

"You're infuriating," I said.

"That's why you're here, then, is it? We've been running all around the country together because you can't stand me?"

It took everything in me not to slam my head against the window. I knew if I kept talking I'd be digging my grave deeper into the ground, but letting him win felt like a burial in its own right.

"Good point," I said. "Maybe this should be our last trip, then." His smile disappeared, and I had to bite the inside of my lip to keep a straight face.

"As you wish," he said. Goddamn it. "Though after you see the inside of the abbey, I think you might just change your mind."

"We'll see about that."

I could feel his smug grin without looking, and I forced myself to breathe deeply. Truthfully, I was excited to explore the castle, but I didn't want to give Collin the satisfaction of appearing too eager.

THE ONLY SOUNDS on the walk down the path to the abbey were the crunching of gravel underfoot and the idle chatter of other visitors. Collin and I walked close enough that our arms brushed every few steps, and the unexpected contact burned like embers.

As we got closer to the castle, though, even the electricity with Collin burned away. Kylemore Abbey was a marvel. Its dove-gray facade reflected in the lake below, blurring like a watercolor painting. The surrounding trees boasted shades of green I didn't even know existed, and the gardens sprawled in every direction. Every other castle I'd seen in Ireland so far had been in ruins, but this was remarkably preserved.

"Ready?" Collin asked as we approached the entrance.

"Aye, Collin. There you are?" The ticket attendant extended his hand, which Collin shook like they were old friends.

"Eamon, great to see ya," Collin said, patting his elbow. "Thanks for having us."

"Anything for you." Eamon gestured us through the door. "Say hi to yer father for me, will ya?"

"Anything for you," Collin echoed, saluting him as we made our way inside.

"Old friend?" I asked.

"Of the family."

"That was nice of him to let us in for free."

"No bother. Eamon's a good lad. Does a favor for us every now and again, and we do the same."

I nodded, trying also to listen to the other staff members as they prepared us for the self-guided tour.

"Don't bother," Collin said, tracking my gaze. "I'll tell you everything you need to know."

"How can I be sure?" I asked. "What if you decide to withhold critical pieces of Irish history?"

"Withholding isn't exactly my strong suit," he said, ushering me through a doorway with his hand on my lower back. The gesture tightened everything in me, and I missed the sensation before it was over.

Wandering through the castle felt like wandering through time—if you could overlook the velvet ropes and signage plastered on the walls. Each room was historically accurate, all gaudy curtains, gold-framed mirrors, and ornate upholstery.

We explored studies and drawing rooms and great halls; all the while Collin spun an elaborate history of the abbey. I listened as he told me of the early days, the Henry family, and the time they spent entertaining in their home.

"Must be nice," I mused. "No nine-to-five, no pressure, just rich people hobbies and the most gorgeous estate."

"You think that sounds nice, now?" Collin asked. "Not having a job and that?"

"If I was rich and this was my house, absolutely," I said.

"So, your work is about making a lot of money? Is that why you're so keen to find a job in Boston?"

"Everyone needs to work to make money. And with money comes stability."

"But at what cost?" he said. I kept my eyes locked on a marble bust to avoid looking at his. "Don't you think making less money and having more time for yourself might be worthwhile? More stability in the long run, no?"

"I have plenty of time for myself," I said, wondering if that was actually true.

"Enough that you're happy?"

This time I turned my gaze fully on him, but he remained staring at some artifact neither of us cared about.

"Why are you so concerned?" I whispered over a voice from a hidden loudspeaker chronicling the lives of Mitchell and Margaret Henry.

"Part of my job," he whispered back. "Gotta keep the guests happy."

"And you want to talk to me about working too much." I shook my head, and he fought a smile.

"Keeping people happy hardly feels like work," he said. "But I do make sure to give myself a break when I can. If I'm not taking care of myself, then I can't take good care of the guests."

"And right now is about taking care of the guests?" I teased. "I thought you weren't working today."

"I only said that to keep ya happy."

I smacked him in the arm, and he let go of the laugh he was holding. "And for what it's worth," I said, "it is about the work. I love helping people make the most of their vacations."

"I'm going to choose to believe you," he said, "but only because it's what Margaret Henry would do."

I scoffed, and neither of us said anything else.

We continued roaming the castle, dragging our feet on the glossy wood floors and resisting the urge to touch everything. Collin spoke only to tell me bits of history, and I didn't speak at all.

I listened to stories of ladies reading and sewing in the morning rooms, lavish dinner parties, the history of the Benedictine nuns.

"This," he said, opening his arms as we entered what was labeled "The Gallery Saloon," "is where the residents had happy hour."

A laugh slipped out of me into the silence, earning a glare from a security guard.

"I'm serious," Collin said. "They met here for before-dinner drinks. And probably again for after-dinner drinks. And mid-morning drinks, and all the other times they spent drinking without anything better to do."

"Sounds like the Wanderer."

"Now you're getting it," he said. "The Duke and Duchess of Manchester especially fancied this one."

"What's their story?"

"I'm glad you asked. The duke wasn't much of anything, but his wife, Helena, was a wealthy American. Her da practically funded their whole lives here."

"Nice gig for the duke, huh?"

"Except they changed nearly everything in the castle. They made tons of renovations, which the locals felt disrespected the legacy left by the Henrys, so the duke and duchess were mostly hated by the townspeople."

"Why did everyone care what they did with their house?" I asked.

"Haven't you noticed?" Collin said. "Everyone in Ireland cares deeply about everyone else's business."

"Oh, I've noticed," I said. "One of the many things I've learned from you since I've moved here."

He flashed a smile. "They also probably hated that she was American," he added after a moment.

"What's wrong with being American?" I asked.

"Depends who you ask. Some would say they're greedy, or ignorant, or self-loathing."

"And the Irish have it all figured out?"

"Look around, Chels," he said. "People are happy here. We know a thing or two about work-life balance. Doesn't hurt that there's a pub around every corner, but my statement stands."

I sighed, and his smile told me he knew he had me. People *were* happy here. And it wasn't just because of the pubs.

"I guess I can't argue with that," I said.

"Finally." He smiled.

"Thanks, Collin. For today, and the past couple weeks. I know I was difficult when I first got here, but I'm glad you forced me to get over myself."

"Someone had to do it."

"I'm trying to be nice!" I exclaimed, and he held his hands up in surrender.

"Don't mention it, Chels. It's been grand."

"Maybe your life is actually perfect."

He cleared his throat so suddenly I almost jumped, but he said nothing. Only offered an awkward half smile, motioning in the direction of the exit. His mood shifted so quickly I was certain it must have been because of something I said, but I couldn't figure out what it was. I was beginning to understand life here. That was what he wanted, wasn't it?

I walked wordlessly beside Collin to the truck, resisting the urge to say anything that would break the silence. Or make things worse. Instead, I followed his lead, settling in for the drive back to Galway with little more than the sound of the radio and the gears turning in my brain.

About halfway through the drive, he finally spoke. "My life isn't perfect, you know."

"What?"

"You said before that my life was perfect, but it's not."

I'd offended him with a compliment?

"I'm so sorry. I didn't mean anything by it," I said, turning to face him even though he was looking at the road. "Only that I really do think it's great."

He blew out a breath, and I waited. "I know, I know. That's what normal people usually mean when they say something like that. It's just, that's what my family always says, only they don't mean it the way you mean it. They say it like a dig at me. Like I left the family home to go live my perfect life, but they know it hasn't been perfect and isn't now, so they mean for it to sting. But you didn't." I kept waiting, in case he wanted to say anything else. I was beginning to realize while it was rare for Collin to be anything but positive, he had some skeletons just like the rest of us, and I wanted to give him space to air them out. "Sorry about that," he said after another minute.

"You have nothing to apologize for," I said. "I'm sorry about your family. That doesn't seem fair to you."

"Ah, family is never fair. Doesn't mean I don't love them." His voice softened. "They just get right under my skin sometimes."

I made a soft noise of understanding and he turned the radio back up, signaling the end of our conversation. The lines in his forehead disappeared, and I was grateful our silence this time was a contented one.

BY THE TIME we returned to the Wanderer the sun had long since set, and I was tired and hungry.

"Fancy a bite?" Collin asked, nodding toward the kitchen.

"Who's cooking?" I asked, narrowing my eyes. I definitely wasn't up for it, and I had no idea if any of his skills extended to the kitchen.

"Flo, earlier tonight," he said, and I was relieved. "Surely there's something left over."

"Lead the way."

We only turned one light on in the kitchen, leaving most of the room in the shadows. Collin found half a sheet cake in the fridge and pulled two forks from the silverware drawer. We leaned against the counter, slowly cutting pieces of the cake straight from the box.

"This was quite the day," he said after a while, licking buttercream from the back of his fork.

"It really was a roller coaster," I agreed, thinking our almost-crash on the way to the abbey felt like it was ages ago.

"Up, then down, then up, then down . . ." he said, dropping his fork on the counter and stepping in front of me, so close I could feel the warmth of his breath.

"We have to end on up, then, don't we?" I asked, dropping my fork beside his and meeting his gaze.

Our eyes locked over the cake. Our breath rose and fell in matching pace.

"I was hoping you'd say that," he whispered, slowly bringing his hands to my hips and pressing me against the counter. "Still willing to let me lead the way?"

Had I been one to speak my mind, I might have said *willing* felt more like *begging*.

It turned out a nod was all he needed, and within seconds, his lips were on mine and my head was spinning. I might have known a kiss was coming, but there was no way of knowing it would have felt like this. The floor disappeared from underneath me; the walls fell away; and I knew I would never have another first kiss as hot as this for as long as I lived.

When his teeth grazed my bottom lip, I let my hands slip under the hem of his shirt, relishing the feel of his body. I was sure he could feel my heart beating, but I was hopeless in slowing it down.

Collin pulled my hair and tilted my head back, deepening the kiss, clearly not willing to slow anything down. It took every ounce of self-control not to pull his shirt over his head and revisit the body I'd been trying and failing to forget since that day in the bathroom.

A low groan rumbled from his throat when I pressed my fingernails into his back. If I thought his accent would stick in my head forever, I had no idea what that groan would do to me.

Our breaths turned ragged as the kiss slowed, weeks of tension sparking erratically between us. The kiss was already seared into some deep, dark part of my memory, and I was replaying it before it was even over. The taste of buttercream would no longer remind me of birthdays, and I wasn't sure I'd be able to eat cake the same way again.

When we eventually separated, Collin pulled away just far enough to rest his forehead on mine.

Still a fraction of an inch from his face, terrifying thoughts started to creep in. How I no longer wanted to speed toward the end of the summer. How it was possible that one singular day altered everything I'd been telling myself since I'd gotten here. How it might have even altered everything I'd been telling myself long before that. How badly I wanted to do it again.

He laughed against my lips, as if responding to my racing thoughts. "Come on, Chels," he said, backing away and holding out his hand. "Let's get you out of here before you go down some rabbit hole you don't need to be in."

"I wasn't . . ."

"Catch yourself on." He smiled, smug as ever. Like his entire world hadn't been rattled by the last few minutes.

I took his hand and let him lead me upstairs to our hallway. My breath caught when he bypassed his door to walk me to mine. I was fumbling with my key, trying to figure out whether he expected to be invited in, when he spun me around and pressed me gently against the door.

"You're sending me right into the rabbit hole, you know," I whispered, trying to resist the urge to look over his shoulder and see if anyone could see us. His lips were so close to mine I could feel his breath, and the anticipation was setting my skin on fire.

"Then I should go before I make it any worse," he said, just as quiet, backing away at the exact moment I found myself leaning in, my eyes starting to close. I released the breath trapped in my chest, though it came out more like a huff. His laugh occupied the space between us, and I let my head drop back against my door.

"Be careful what you wish for." He smiled, walking toward his room.

"Only one of us is the wishing type," I said, "so I could say the same to you."

"I don't have to be careful," he said, unlocking his own door. "I know exactly what I want."

His door closed behind him before I could say another word, and I stood pressed against my own, trying to regulate my breathing. What the hell had I just gotten myself into?

Chapter 14

*L*ook at you!" Ada said as soon as she opened FaceTime. "You look great. Ready for the big interview?"

"I'm not so sure it's 'The Big Interview,'" I said. "It's just that tourist center by the water."

"Hate to break it to ya, babe, but at this point, any interview is a big interview."

"Ugh," I groaned. "Don't remind me. I miss you. And Boston. And iced coffee. All the drinks here are warm, even in the summer. I don't know how they live like this."

"Don't try to change the subject," she said. "And missing cold brew is a weak excuse to want to come home, just so you know. But you need to focus, here. This is important for you."

"Aye, aye, Captain," I said, saluting her. She rolled her eyes, and I knew she was right. Only it didn't feel as important as it did a few days ago when I originally scheduled the interview. Before the abbey. Before the kiss. Now, the interview didn't feel quite so big. Or so necessary.

"It would be okay if you changed your mind, you know," she said, reading the tone in my voice even from three thousand miles away.

"Why on earth would I ever change my mind?" I said, even though I was beginning to sense we both knew the answer to that.

"Oh, I don't know," she said. "Maybe you're into Ireland now. Maybe its kissing has charmed you into staying."

"I thought I was supposed to be focusing on my interview."

"You shouldn't have told me about the kiss, then," she said. And again, she was right. If you gave Ada an inch she took a mile. "You can be two things at once, Chels. You can be interested in this fling with Collin and trying to get your plans back on track at the same time."

"How does that make sense?"

"First of all, not everything has to make sense," she replied. "That's what makes life interesting. And the whole point of a fling is that it's short-lived, isn't it? Don't all summer flings burn hot and bright for a few months and then fizzle out come September?"

She had a point. Though now was not the time to define "flings," so I tried to let it roll off. Or at least roll elsewhere until I had the bandwidth.

"You're blowing my concentration," I said eventually, though we both knew that Ada wasn't the problem here. "I need to finish preparing and get this thing over with. I feel like an idiot in this shirt."

"You look like a goddess."

"Wish me luck."

"*Bonne chance*," she said, blowing me a kiss. "Call me later."

I agreed, ending the FaceTime and staring at myself in the reflection of my phone. It was the first time I'd really put myself together since I'd been living in Galway, and I hardly recognized myself. The freckles under my eyes were all but covered by a layer of foundation, and the unruly curls that had been framing my face all summer were slicked into a low bun.

While I waited for the hiring committee to join the video call, I looked over my notes one last time. The tourist center had undergone serious renovations in the past five years and was looking for a community recreation coordinator to oversee the planning and execution of a variety of events in the surrounding neighborhoods. I didn't feel particularly enthusiastic, but it was close enough to what I wanted.

The interview went like they always do. Tell us about yourself, what experience can you bring to the role?, what are your greatest weaknesses?, whatever corporate nonsense they needed to include.

"What does success look like for you?" one of the interviewers asked as we neared the end. I couldn't remember her role and she hadn't spoken much the whole time, so her voice was as jarring as the question.

"For me, success is excelling at a job that makes a positive impact on my community," I said, instantly hating that every candidate probably gave the same answer.

"And beyond work?" she pressed. "What is your full picture of success, Ms. Gold?"

Had this woman spoken to my mother before we got on this call? Was she wearing a wire?

"It's, uh . . ." I stalled. This should have been a layup. My whole life was constructed around my idea of success. Surely, I could verbalize what that was. "Balance," I said eventually, simply. "And the kind of confidence that comes with security," I added.

At the very moment she was thanking me, I realized I hadn't said a word about happiness. It was only her soft, sad smile that made me realize my answer was lacking. I'd answered in a way that would have made me proud five years ago. But right now, I felt embarrassed.

"As for Ireland," she said, dragging me from my introspection and back to the interview. "You're willing to relocate?"

"Oh, I don't live here," I said. "I mean, I do right now, but it's only for the summer. I'll be home to Boston in a month or so. And I'll be there for good."

"Oh! I'm sorry. I must have somehow overlooked that this was only temporary. My apologies. I'll make a note of your brief, uh, departure from your career in Boston and your intention to return."

Was she on the phone with my mother before the interview, asking for tips on passive aggression? I knew this was a risk, but surely I wasn't the first woman in her twenties to move away for a summer while she sorted her life out.

After a few awkward goodbyes we ended the call, agreeing they'd be in touch next week, and my thoughts continued to swirl. Was I finally defending my choice to come to the Wanderer? Collin's smiling face from the driver's seat, the Atlantic roaring behind him, flashed across my mind. The unfamiliar feeling that I *didn't want the summer to end* lingered in my chest.

No. I couldn't even entertain the thought. Boston was the right call, and one mildly awkward interview wasn't going to deter me from my plan.

I considered updating Ada right away, calling and telling her the interview was a bust, but I decided against it. We had another staff bonding activity tonight, and I promised Flo I would join as soon as the interview was over. Above all, I needed a drink.

I knew Collin was going to be at the function, and I was

grateful I didn't have time to dwell on what it would be like to see him after the kiss. Just thinking about it made my chest flutter, and any more time I spent on it would have me pulling out a diary like I was in middle school. The interview had been the only time I'd spent in the past twenty-four hours thinking about anything other than how much I wanted to kiss him again, and now that I no longer had that to distract me, I was hopelessly single-minded.

FORTUNATELY, I found Collin sitting on a makeshift stage tuning a banjo the second I walked into the multipurpose room. Was there anything this man couldn't do? He didn't see me right away, so I watched for a minute as he plucked strings and listened, turning knobs with nimble fingers.

He looked up at the exact second Flo called my name, and we made eye contact just long enough to ignite every nerve ending and send a raging blush to my cheeks.

"Thank god you made it," Flo said as I approached, kissing both of my cheeks. "I was getting nervous."

"Sorry, sorry," I said. "Just finished up the interview."

"How'd it go?"

I shook my hand side to side. "Eh," I said, searching for the words. "I felt like they were judging me for leaving Boston after I was let go."

"You were just giving yourself a hard time about the same thing, no?"

"Florence!"

"What? It's true, *tesoro*. Hard to convince them you didn't run away, if you can't even convince yourself. Here, help me with this." She handed me a case of beer, and I was grateful for her short attention span. Regardless, she was right. If I was berating myself for leaving Boston, why didn't I expect others to do the same?

"I didn't run away," I said, apparently willing to finish the conversation after all. "I'm going back. I'm just doing something else while I sort my life out." I busied myself with arranging the cans in a cooler as I spoke.

"You don't have to explain anything to me, Chels," she said. "I actually did run away. And it was the best decision I ever made. Who am I to judge? Also," she continued, "selfishly, I'm glad the interview was bad. I'm not ready for you to leave the Wanderer."

"I'm leaving either way," I reminded her.

"So you say," she said. "But do you have a backup plan? If you don't find a job, I mean. Then what?"

An image of my parents' office flashed behind my eyes, and I swallowed hard to stop a lump from forming in my throat.

"I'm going to find a job." We stood in silence for an uncomfortable beat, but I knew exactly what she was thinking. I was trying to convince *myself* that was true, not Flo. And I wasn't convincing at all.

"Remind me what all this is about?" I asked, gesturing to the stage and trying to change the subject for good.

"Variety show," she said. "Meaning: terrible stand-up comedy, some decent instrumentals, and whatever other talents are running wild in this place. And before you panic, it isn't mandatory. You can just sit in the back and get drunk with me."

Was I that predictable that she knew I was going to panic? And was I so boring that I clearly didn't have a talent for a variety show?

The rest of the staff rolled in after a few minutes, and Lars started a sound check.

"All right, all right, welcome," he said as everyone filed in. "Find yourselves a bevvy at the back and grab a seat for the Wanderer's annual Summer Staff Variety Show!"

Collin had since disappeared backstage, and I was grateful Flo hadn't seen me looking at him. I hadn't told her about the kiss, but I had a bad feeling it was only a matter of time before she—and the rest of our coworkers—found out.

Once everyone was settled, Lars welcomed the first act to the stage.

"Everyone please make a little noise for Marta, who will be opening our evening with some original slam poetry."

Marta, a petite blonde wearing a pair of corduroy overalls, took to the stage and began her set. She spoke in varying volumes about love, loss, and sex. We snapped after each poem, sipped room-temperature beer, and resisted the urge to whisper to each other as she continued.

Eventually, Flo gave in. "Collin seems engaged," she said, nodding in the direction of where he was sitting near the edge of the stage. As soon as I turned my head and caught his eye, I realized he was staring shamelessly in our direction. I tried to look away without seeming too obvious, but my cheeks flushed anyway.

"Oh my god," she said eventually, almost in disbelief.

"What?"

"Tell me everything right now."

I considered lying, or playing dumb, but I knew Flo wouldn't fall for either. I had no choice. "We kissed last night," I whispered.

"You what?"

Someone shushed us from the front row, and Flo waved them off as I tried to apologize.

"Don't make it a big thing," I said. "It was just one little kiss in the kitchen, then off to our separate beds like it never happened."

"You kissed in my kitchen?"

"Please," I said. "Keep your voice down."

"I cook in there, you know. For everyone. You included."

"Don't be gross," I said. "It was just a kiss."

"Now what?"

"Now nothing."

"Why nothing?"

"Because I'm only here for another month, so it doesn't make sense to start something."

"Isn't that how a fling works?"

"Have you been talking to Ada?"

"Who's Ada?"

Our whispered responses increased in speed and volume. I dropped my head into my hands, flustered and confused.

"It doesn't matter," she continued when I didn't respond. "What matters is it doesn't look like nothing." We both looked at Collin, who was successfully watching Marta. He was absentmindedly running his thumb over his bottom lip, forearm flexed beneath a rolled sleeve. "I bet he's thinking of the kiss right now."

"Florence."

"What? It was hot, wasn't it?"

I lowered my eyebrows as if to say *I won't dignify that with a response*, but the wicked gleam in her eye made me think maybe I should have responded after all.

On cue, Marta finished her set and the crowd applauded as Lars resumed his spot on the stage.

"And now, if you'll all lean in close for the storytelling styles of a Mr. Collin Finegan," he said, reigniting the applause.

"Oh, I'll pay attention, all right," Flo said, settling deeper into her chair. I glanced at her quickly before crossing my arms protectively over my chest.

Collin took to the stage with his banjo, fully attentive now in a way he wasn't a few minutes ago. He was focused and charming as ever, and I feared I might dissolve before his set was over.

"Thanks, Lars," he said, perching on a stool and lowering the microphone. "And thanks to everyone in the audience for being here and listening." There were a few snaps from the crowd, and I tried to keep my gaze on the stage without looking him directly in the eye.

He plucked a few strings on the banjo, and soft notes filled the room. "I'll admit I wasn't going to do this tonight," he began, "but you lot know how persuasive Lars can be, so here we are." The crowd chuckled, and I envied how easy it was for Collin to work a room. And how easy and carefree he seemed, when I'd been in a near twenty-four-hour whirlwind of suppressed feelings.

"I also know the power of a good fairy story here in Ireland," he continued, "and I know there are some people out there who might need to hear one." His eyes settled right where I was sitting, and I turned to liquid under his gaze. Unable to activate either fight or flight, I sat perfectly still, staring back at him.

Within the first few sentences he had the audience wrapped around his finger, and the gentle strumming of the banjo in the background all but lulled us into a trance.

"If we're to understand the fairy stories," he said, "first we must try to understand the fairies. There are different types, you see. And tonight, it'll be the Leannán Sídhe we try to understand." His eyes roamed the audience. "I see a few nods from the lot. Who'd like to do the introduction, then?"

"The fairy mistress?" came a voice from somewhere in the room I couldn't place.

"Aye, but could there be another translation, perhaps?" A smile played at Collin's lips as he plucked the banjo strings, and I followed his gaze around the crowd, silently begging for a distraction.

"The fairy sweetheart?" said a woman in the front row.

"The fairy lover," said a husky voice from back near the bar.

"Ah, lover, you say," Collin said, absentmindedly tuning a string. "I like the sound of that one. Ambiguous, isn't it? Proper range of things a lover could be."

He glanced back at me, and it took everything in me to stay upright when I was on the verge of melting.

"So, this fairy lover," he said, returning to the story with the full force of our attention. "Let's see what she's all about, shall we?"

A few chords later, he launched in. He told us of the life of Leannán Sídhe, a muse for her human lover, and the darkness often intertwined with infatuation.

He explained the exchange between Leannán Sídhe and the artist, life for inspiration. He described the romantics who don't believe that she sucks the life out of her lovers. He told us of the storytellers who do.

"Some say it's about whether she is honored," he continued. "If she is honored, the artist might just be spared. And if she is not, then artist be damned." There were a few more snaps from the crowd, undoubtedly from women who agreed with her behavior. This made Collin laugh, and the sound made me melt further into my seat.

"The worst fate for the artist, however, is her disappearance." I swallowed, and in a split second, his eyes found mine. "Once the artist is driven to madness, to a life full of longing, to the highest highs and the lowest lows, she might just disappear. And there is no recovery once Leannán Sídhe is gone."

If there was still a crowd around me, they ceased to exist. Everything beyond his spotlight turned to black, no matter how hard I tried to refocus. I felt his voice swimming beside the alcohol in my veins.

"It is a dangerous game with the fairy lovers," he said, shaking his head , his voice low. "Sure, she might draw the emotion out of the artist and into the art, but at what cost? The cost of his sanity? Of his life? How far is too far . . ." He played minor chords now, bringing the audience with him into the dark.

In typical Collin fashion, however, he didn't stay in the dark for long. In the short time he was on the stage, he told many iterations of stories of Leannán Sídhe. Dark ones. Lighter ones. Romantic ones. Fairy stories were usually open to interpretation, and Leannán Sídhe had more interpretations than most. He told each with a tone as wistful and nostalgic as the last, making it impossible to determine which iteration he most believed.

Though the look in his eyes threatened to give him away.

I wondered if the look in mine was the same. I was teetering on the brink of that rabbit hole again, dangerously close to overstepping. Memories of the last few weeks flashed in my mind as I felt myself tip over the edge; ticking clocks and flashing signs warned TOO FAST and TOO SOON and TOO GOOD and MORE MORE MORE.

"I'll give you one piece of advice here before I go," he said eventually, pulling me back to the present. I could have sworn the audience leaned in too. "If you are privileged enough to survive the Leannán Sídhe, honor and respect her while she is with you. Let her pull some emotion from the depths of its hiding place, and pray you'll never have to let her go."

With that, he dropped his head to the banjo and hummed a quiet tune that half the crowd seemed to know. A few other staff members sang the lyrics, and Collin's smile stretched across his face at the sound.

Lars thanked him as we applauded, and Collin shot me one last look before getting off the stage. One look that cut directly through me.

"Why don't we take a break, then?" Lars asked, looking around. "Feels like a good time for everyone to get another beer, or maybe cry in the toilet for a minute, doesn't it?" People laughed, leaving their seats to stretch their legs and grab fresh drinks.

"Well, that was—"

"Don't," I said, cutting off Flo before she could finish her thought.

"I won't," she said, "but only because I know we're both thinking the same thing, anyway."

"If you're thinking we could use another drink, then you're right," I said. I knew exactly where she was headed, and I didn't plan to give her an inch, no matter how much she rolled her eyes.

She eventually backed off, and the rest of the night crawled on like the beginning: an array of songs, obscure talents, gossip-whispering, and drink after drink, with Lars's Spotify playlist overtaking his hosting duties once the show ended.

"Another successful Variety Show, huh?" Lars asked, slinging his long arm around Flo's shoulders before either of us even noticed he was there.

"How do you even know all these people?" Flo asked. "Do they really all work here?"

"Of course they do." Lars laughed. "If you'd get out of the kitchen more often, maybe you'd get to know them."

"If someone hired another chef, maybe I'd have the chance."

"Touché," Lars said. "What about you, Chelsea? Did you enjoy the show?"

"I did," I said, fearful of how my voice would sound when I tried talking above a whisper. I still felt dizzy and unsteady from Collin's performance, and I was toeing the dangerous line between happily buzzed and too drunk.

"Did you have a favorite?" he asked.

"I think we all know the answer to that," Flo mumbled, not at all under her breath. I stepped on her foot, and Lars threw his head back, roaring.

"I should have known," he said.

"Marta *was* inspiring, wasn't she?" I said, finding my voice and trying to keep it from wobbling. "I thought her poetry was really powerful."

"Which parts?" Flo asked. "The parts about love or the parts about sex?"

"You're impossible," I said. "You know that?"

"You should talk."

"Keep it up and I'll leave Ireland right now," I said.

"D'you mean it?" Collin materialized beside Lars, and I had to remind myself how to breathe.

"Would it kill you if I did?" I could hear the gentle slur in my voice, but I hoped he couldn't do the same.

"Ah, you liked the Leannán Sídhe stories, did ya?"

"I *listened* to the Leannán Sídhe stories," I said, trying to keep us on solid ground, even if I couldn't quite feel it under my feet anymore. "I didn't say anything about liking them."

"You didn't have to. Your face gives everything away, remember?"

"What's it telling you now?"

"That we should talk," he said pointedly, glancing over my shoulder toward the door.

"On that note," Lars said to Flo, "feels like we should go get another drink, doesn't it?"

"We just got another drink," Flo said, obviously wanting to stay for whatever drama was unfolding.

"*You* just got another drink," Lars said, grabbing her arm. "I'm empty-handed. Let's go."

It only took a second after they were gone for Collin to close the space between us, resting his hands on my elbows and ducking his head slightly to meet my eyes. My head was a dangerous combination of beer, emotions, and loud Dutch club music.

"Are you okay?" he asked, tilting my chin up and clocking the way I held my hair off the back of my neck.

"Yeah," I said. "I just need some air, I think." His staring only amplified the spinning, and I had no choice but to let him lead me out of the party with a warm hand on my elbow.

When we finally made it outside, I took a breath so deep it made me lightheaded. I grabbed the back of a lawn chair to keep from wobbling and tried to focus on breathing normally, which was nearly impossible with Collin's hands on my waist holding me up.

"Here," he said, brushing some dirt off the chair and gesturing for me to sit.

"This is so dramatic," I moaned. "I'm fine now, really. Go back to the party."

He laughed, which only made me more embarrassed. "Like hell," he said. "At the very least not until you stop sounding like you have marbles in your mouth."

"You're the one with marbles in your mouth," I said, trying my hardest not to slur.

I wasn't looking at him, but I practically heard him roll his eyes.

"Sit on the ground," he said, grabbing my hands and pulling me up from the chair despite my weak protests. "I'm doing this for your benefit. Sit." He pointed to the ground right in front of us, and I obeyed.

What I didn't expect was for him to then sit in the chair right behind me. "Are you serious?" I asked. "You made me sit on the ground so you could sit in the chair? Even for you, Collin, this is—"

"Lean back," he said. I groaned like a child but ultimately did as I was told. I had no idea what he was getting at, but I was too drunk to care.

I nestled my shoulder blades between his knees, relieved I no longer had to look at his face in the moonlight. The distant thump of the bass was the only sound save for the animals in the garden, and I hoped the silence would make my ears stop ringing. I focused on the feeling of Collin at my back, his warm hands brushing my hair off my forehead, trailing down the sides of my neck.

"Is this another weird Irish old wives' tale?" I asked. "Are you casting a spell?"

He didn't answer; instead, he gathered my hair off my shoulders and split it through the center, working his fingers through the knots. It was impossible to ignore the gentle way he untangled them, especially compared to the way he pulled my hair in the kitchen the other night. How anyone could be both so soft and so rough was beyond me, and my stomach twisted at the thought. Eventually, he dropped one side of my hair back over my shoulder and began dividing the other into parts, and it was only then that I realized he was braiding.

"Coll, are you—"

"Just let me," he said. Of all the things I secretly wanted Collin Finegan to do to me, this hadn't even crossed my mind. For the first time in my life, a man French-braided my hair.

I watched the stars form in the clear sky as he turned lock over lock, winding my waves into two tight braids with expert fingers. He stopped periodically to run a hand through whatever hair was still loose, despite having already gotten the knots out, and I wasn't sure which of us was enjoying it more.

"How'd you learn to do this?" I whispered eventually, trying not to break the spell.

"Sisters," he said, and the silence returned for a while until he continued. "Our mam wasn't around much, and Da didn't have the foggiest how to do this stuff. They begged me to learn, and it's hard to say no to 'em."

I wasn't sure what answer I expected, but it wasn't that. I suspected Collin Finegan had a soft side, but not the braiding-your-sisters'-hair-because-mom-isn't-around kind.

"Is it working?" he asked.

"If I say yes, will it go straight to your ego?"

"You sound better already."

We both let out a gentle laugh that quickly disappeared into the night.

"Thank you," I said as he wound a rubber band around the

bottom of the second braid, letting his fingers linger against my back. "You didn't have to do this." I spun around to face him for the first time since we got outside. The heaviness of his gaze settled into my bones, and I wore it like a weighted blanket.

"Not doing it 'cause I have to, Chelsea," he said, pulling me to my feet. "Doing it 'cause I want to. 'Cause I want *you*, more specifically. And if you haven't already realized, there's very little I wouldn't do for ya."

His eyes were clear as day, even in the dark. Bright and honest and pleading, and I owed him the truth in return.

"Me too." I exhaled, and he raised his eyebrows. "I want you too." My voice was soft and small and hardly my own, but there was no mistaking my honesty. Especially because it was probably also written all over my face. Still, he looked surprised to hear me admit it. Hell, I was surprised to hear myself admit it.

He ran his fingers down my arms until they reached my hands, shaking them a little so I'd look up at him. "Is that why you looked so terrified when I was telling that story?" he asked, and I was both embarrassed he could see right through me and grateful I didn't have to confess anything on my own.

"It wasn't part of the plan." I laughed, and he did too. "And then you were telling such an emotional story, and I'd been trying to ignore my feelings for you all day, and it just felt like a lot all at once."

"I'm sorry," he said. "I didn't mean to scare you. It was just a story."

"You know better than I do that the fairy stories are never 'just stories,'" I whispered.

"And *you* know now they have a different meaning for everyone. It doesn't have to be so extreme as love and death. It can just be about inspiration, feeling, time." His tone slipped back into the hypnotic, lyrical voice he used onstage.

"What does it mean to you?" I asked.

"Right now, it's about cherishing the time I have with a beautiful woman before she's gone. It's about letting her in now, no matter what might happen later."

"Even if it's dangerous?"

"Especially if it's dangerous." He smiled, and I wanted to trace the lines of his lips with my fingers.

"And the kiss?" I knew I was asking too many questions, but his certainty was soothing.

"Doesn't have to mean anything if you don't want it to," he said, holding his palms up in surrender, "but I have a feeling you might, so I think we should make it mean something."

I swallowed. He watched. "What do you think it should mean?"

"A lot of questions tonight, huh?"

"You are the tour guide, aren't you?" He chuckled at that and I relaxed further, my shoulders dropping an inch.

"Fair play," he said. "I'm not proposing anything crazy here, Chels. I know you're planning to leave, but all summer flings end eventually, don't they? Doesn't make them any less worth it while they're happening."

The way he'd said *planning to leave* instead of *leaving* wasn't lost on me, but I didn't correct him.

"So you think we should just . . . have a fling?"

"Why are you saying it like I'm suggesting something insane?" He laughed. "Yes, Chels, I think we should have fun. I think we should stop fighting what's going on here and enjoy the next few weeks together. Feel however we feel, and let this run whatever course it's meant to run."

I mulled it over, trying to keep my face arranged in a way

that seemed totally cool and casual and not at all like I was freaking out.

"You make it sound so easy."

"It is so easy."

Silence stretched between us, long and charged, though Collin didn't look like he wanted to be anywhere else. No rush, no pressure, just patience.

"Where do we begin?" I asked eventually.

"Is that a yes?"

"Honestly, Collin, I couldn't say no even if I wanted to," I confessed. "But this is your territory, so you have to lead the way."

"Music to my ears," he said. "And we've already begun, don't you think?" He pulled me into him, resting a warm hand on the side of my neck.

"I'm serious," I said.

"You're always serious." Okay, rude. True, but rude. "So . . . We begin with a date. A real one."

"I can handle a date."

"But can you handle a ceilidh?"

Chapter 15

*T*ell me again what this is," I said as Flo played with my hair, trying to decide whether I should wear it up or down. She twirled individual curls around her fingers, holding them back from my face then dropping them again and pursing her lips.

"A ceilidh," she said. "Like, er, a dance. You're American. You've been to a dance?"

"In middle school." I laughed. "I doubt it's the same."

"Nothing compares to a ceilidh, anyway," she said, deciding to leave my hair down after all. "It's traditional Irish music, lots of dancing, even more drinking. It's a ton of fun. You'll love it."

I wasn't so sure about that last part, as I was notoriously a terrible dancer. Which meant there was absolutely no way I could have mentioned any of this to Ada. She'd remind me of the videos from our senior prom, where I looked like the inflatable men outside car dealerships. I'd back out of the ceilidh entirely.

"Trust me," Flo added, undoubtedly sensing my apprehension.

"I don't know any of the dances."

"You don't have to. There's a caller who's going to tell you what to do."

"I'm a lost cause."

"I'm sure someone will make sure you're just fine," she said, raising her brows and glancing down the hall from my room. "What kind of first date would it be if he didn't?"

"Remind me why I told you it was a date?"

"Because you were so excited you couldn't help yourself."

"Not quite how I remember it." I laughed, recalling how Flo had begged me to tell her every little thing that happened as soon as we left the variety show.

"I'm too happy you've both decided to give it a shot to care," she said. "You make a hot couple."

"I'm not sure we're a couple. Does a summer fling qualify as a relationship?"

"Stop overthinking it, *cara*. You'll enjoy it less. And the whole purpose is to enjoy, no?"

"You're right," I groaned. "I just happen to be great at overthinking. And terrible at casual flings. You guys are all much better at this than I am."

"What makes you so sure?"

"You're all so used to everyone coming and going, aren't you? You leave home, you meet new people, they leave, and everyone moves on. Everybody here seems to have a much more casual view of relationships in general."

"Look around," she said, gesturing vaguely at my room. "This looks a lot like coming and going and meeting and leaving and moving on to me. You might be more like us than you think, *tesoro*."

I did look around, struggling to come to grips with the fact she might be right. "Even if I am like you guys, I'm not nearly as good at it."

"Suddenly going back to Boston isn't so easy?"

"I didn't say that." *Out loud, anyway.*

"You didn't have to," she said. "I can see it in your eyes."

"So stop looking at me."

She rolled her eyes, and we both laughed despite ourselves.

"All I'm saying, Chels, is that it's okay if part of you changes while you're out here. Hell, it's okay if all of you changes while you're out here. Ireland has a way of doing that to people. And it's more than okay to indulge a little. Pleasure doesn't have to be logical, you know."

I opened my mouth, but she raised her hands in surrender, saving me from having to think of a response. "That's all I'm saying," she said again, and I nodded. Duly noted. I had a feeling I'd be pondering these words until my time at the Wanderer came to an end. And maybe even after that.

"Now," she said, grabbing my hands and looking from my head to my toes. "Are we ready?"

"You're the ceilidh expert," I said. "You tell me."

"Me? The Italian? Please. Let's get the real ceilidh expert in here."

"Flo, plea—"

"Collin!" she yelled down the hall. "Coll? Come in here!"

"Florence," I said.

"What? You were going to see him as soon as we went downstairs to leave, anyway."

"Yeah, but he wasn't going to approve of my appearance first."

"You rang?" Collin appeared in the doorway, and Flo and I were both stunned into silence. The edges of the tattoos lining his collarbones peeked out from an open white collar, and a deep-red plaid kilt hit the middle of his thighs, exposing knots of muscle in his legs. He leaned his forearm against the door-jamb, knowing full well we were staring.

"So this is why you invited Chelsea to a ceilidh," Flo said, gesturing to me. "You wanted to show off those legs, didn't you?"

"Flo, please," he said, lifting the kilt an inch higher. "If I wanted to show off my legs, I wouldn't need a ceilidh to do it."

"You're bad," she said.

"You started it."

"Good luck with this one, Chelsea," she said, patting his chest on her way out of my room. I wanted to kill her.

"Classic Flo," Collin said. "Calls me in here and leaves immediately. You two needed something?"

"Just to make sure Chelsea was ready!" Flo called from down the hall.

We jumped at the sound of her voice. Collin looked me up and down the way Flo had a minute earlier, undoubtedly assessing the black velvet shirtdress I borrowed from Flo and my platform Docs.

"Flo said to wear comfortable shoes," I said, hoping I didn't sound as self-conscious as I felt under his gaze.

"Flo could have said to wear a potato sack and you'd still look brilliant," he said, motioning for me to spin around. I obeyed. "That dress is class, Chelsea." He ran his thumb over his bottom lip as he looked at me.

"So, you'd say we're ready to go then?"

"Depends," he said. "Are you ready for everyone in the place to be having a look at ya?"

"Oh stop." I laughed. "It's going to be you they're looking at."

"We'll make one hell of a couple, then," he said. I stiffened at the word, thinking Flo might have been right. "Loosen up, Chels. A ceilidh is fun. And you can't dance if you're so stiff."

"I can't dance at all."

"Bollocks," he said. "Follow my lead. I'll take care of ya."

I did love the sound of that.

"Lead the way, then," I said, gesturing out of my room. If we stood in there staring at each other for another minute, I feared we'd never make it to the ceilidh at all.

ONCE WE RALLIED the rest of the staff who had the night off and a small handful of guests to whom Flo extended the invite, we caught a bus across town to the venue. From the outside, it looked like little more than an old barn, but the inside transformed into a scene from *Footloose*.

High-top tables lined the perimeter of a massive dance floor, giving way to a bar on either end. The string lights wrapped around the rafters had bulbs the size of golf balls, which bathed the barn in a warm, golden glow. Between the tartan tablecloths and burlap centerpieces, the whole thing felt a bit like stepping into another time.

"Grand, isn't it?" Collin said over my shoulder, watching me as I took in the scene.

"So grand, in fact, that I think I'm going to just observe the whole night. Really watch from the sidelines, take it all in. I don't want to miss anything, of course."

His laugh was so loud it got the bartender's attention. "Nice try," he said. "I appreciate the attempt, really. But no one comes to a ceilidh to sit on the sidelines. Especially not someone on a journey to embrace Irish culture."

"Perhaps we could start tonight's embracing with a drink?" I suggested, nodding toward the bar closest to us.

"Spoken like a true Irishman," he said. "That's a great start. Come on, then."

The rest of the group trickled in, meandering toward the bar and friends they recognized across the room. Their dispersal meant Collin and I were left alone, and the heat between us wasn't coming from the dance floor.

I approached the bar, looking around at the collection of bottles and taps, trying to decide what kind of buzz I needed. What drink would lower my inhibitions just enough to dance but not enough to make a fool of myself.

"What're you thinking?" he asked, leaning an elbow on the bar and bringing our faces close. I held back the urge to count his freckles.

I touched my fingertips to my lips while I considered my options, running them back and forth as I realized Collin's eyes were following their movements.

"Keep teasing me like that and we might not even make it to the dance floor," he mumbled with his lips pressed against my ear.

"How do you know that's not my plan?"

"Too soon." He pulled back from me, shaking his head. "Judging by our last kiss, you like a little delayed gratification."

"Collin!" I gasped, swatting his arm, which only made him chuckle.

"What?" he asked, feigning innocence. "Tell me I'm wrong and I'll believe you."

I opened and closed my mouth, searching for something to say that wasn't a lie and coming up empty.

"That's what I thought." He smiled, redirecting his attention to the bar. I had a feeling this would be a long night. "Fancy a Guinness?" he asked. "In honor of culture and all that."

"Can't say no to a Guinness, can I?"

"She's learning." He beamed at me, then signaled the bartender. When our drinks came and I reached for my wallet, Collin put a warm hand on my wrist. "I've got ya."

"At least let me get one round by the end of the night," I protested. "As an apology for the dancing."

"I'm sure you can find another way to repay me," he said, flicking his eyes almost imperceptibly to my mouth. "Besides, I feel like the dancing might be a proper gift in itself."

At that, I took a few solid gulps of my beer, prompting Collin to do the same. After which he licked his lips, and I was a goner.

I followed him through the crowd and back to some of our friends, who had found their own drinks and a high-top table on the side of the dance floor.

"Chels, there you are," Flo said as we approached. "Was beginning to think we'd already lost you two."

"Hardly," I said. "We were just at the bar."

"Good. I'm not ready for you to disappear quite yet. We've dancing to do."

Right on cue, the caller introduced herself and invited everyone to the dance floor. She was a tall woman clad in a pattern similar to Collin's kilt, her graying hair falling loose from its bun on the top of her head. She had the kind of voice that projected across town even without the microphone, so it didn't take long for everyone to make their way into the clearing and quiet down for her instructions.

All at once she named a dance and described a formation, and before I could decipher another word through her thick accent, Collin's arms slipped around my waist and whisked me into the commotion. I tried my best to listen to the steps, but Collin didn't give me much room to think. He pulled me around the dance floor like I weighed nothing at all. Catching my breath felt like a pipe dream.

"You two make a great couple," Flo said when I was flung into her arms as we changed partners. We swung around in a do-si-do, and I tried not to get dizzy, but I didn't think it was the dancing that was making my head spin.

"Then it's a shame we keep changing partners," I teased, trying to embrace the fun of having a friend on a date with me, without overthinking every minute. My new partner was a man, whom I might have noticed was vaguely handsome had I not been on a date. He twirled me with the same confidence Collin had, and for a moment I envied him.

All of them, really, who knew how to do this. Who had been doing this for generations. It was a past, present, and future cornerstone of their identities.

As I settled into a rhythm, I let my thoughts wander home to Boston. I tried to think of any traditions that had been passed down from generations of Bostonians before us, but I came up empty. Maybe it was because my parents had only moved to Boston after I was born. Or maybe we weren't as connected to the city as I thought we were.

Either way, we didn't have a melting pot of travelers coming together to dance in an old barn. We didn't grow up learning the same step. We didn't have a unified tradition just to celebrate being alive and together.

If someone visited Boston, would I bend over backward trying to make them fall in love with it? Was *I* even in love with it?

Before I could think of an answer, I was pulled back into Collin's arms to finish the dance the way we started.

"You have a good time with Declan, there?" he asked as we

made our way to the sidelines to reset for the next dance. God, they didn't waste any time.

"Declan?" I asked, trying not to pant.

"That tall bloke over there," he leaned and pointed to the man I'd been dancing with a minute ago. "Looked quite chuffed to be dancing with ya."

"Then maybe you should be asking Declan if he had a good time with me."

"I won't be asking him anything," he said.

"Collin Finegan, are you jealous?"

"Ach, me?" I raised my eyebrows. "Terribly," he whispered, brushing his lips against my ear. His voice was so soft I could hardly hear it above the noise in the bar, which only made me lean in closer. "I really don't fancy the thought of you with someone else."

"Makes you wish you hadn't delayed that gratification, huh?"

He faked a dagger to the heart. "Chelsea Gold, you are a cruel, cruel woman."

"Ready for another round?" I flashed my biggest smile, putting another few inches of distance between us. I was beginning to understand why he liked teasing me so much, and I was suddenly finding it hard to resist. Especially when it made him look at me the way he was looking at me: like he wanted to drag me off the dance floor and back to the privacy of one of our bedrooms.

The caller started up another dance to a new tune blaring from the band, full of lively fiddles, lilting tin whistles, rollicking accordions, and thumping drums, and once again we crowded the dance floor. The rest of the songs blurred into one another, and I was finding comfort in the pace. When I focused on the dances, I had little time or energy to focus on anything else. Like how impossibly good this was for a first date—or any date—and how I was beginning to fear this fling wasn't as casual as I thought.

So I channeled all my energy into the ceilidh. I studied the steps, how the words sounded with the Irish lilt, the way our bodies collided and pulled apart like magnets. I tried to memorize the faces of my various partners. I wondered if anyone, even briefly, thought I might belong here.

We'd traded partners with every song, so quite a few had passed without Collin and I finding each other on the dance floor. When we did, however, we crashed back into each other and found ourselves holding on just a bit too tight and for a second too long. His hands rested on my back inches lower than anyone else's had, and we managed to keep our eyes locked on each other despite the endless twisting and turning.

When we took a break for another round of drinks, I was thankful for the time to recover. My voice was getting hoarse from laughing and shouting over the music, and my initial buzz was wearing off.

"Looked like you were getting the hang of it pretty quick," Flo said, sidling up to me at the bar.

"She's a natural," Collin agreed before I could argue. "Looking more Irish by the day."

"Don't be fooled," I said, trying to conceal my blush at the compliment. "It's just the hair." I shook my crimson waves for effect, and Collin ruffled them with his hand.

"Of course," Collin said. "My mistake. It couldn't possibly have anything to do with all you're learning from your lovely tour guide."

"Didn't you just say I was a natural?"

"What I should have said was you're driving me crazy," he said, shaking his head and sinking his teeth into his lower lip.

"We're all still standing here, you know," Flo interrupted, gesturing around to the collection of guests and hostel staff crowding the bar.

"Make yourself useful and go get us a table, then," Collin said.

"Fine, but I'm taking this one with me." Flo grabbed my hand and I had no choice but to follow, though I did sneak a glance over my shoulder just in time to catch Collin doing the same.

"I'm not sure if I ever properly introduced everyone," Flo said as some of the others joined us at a high-top, "but I suppose you can do that yourselves." When we didn't move right away, she gestured to the lot of us as if to say *go on*. We obeyed, shaking hands and sharing names we wouldn't remember two minutes later. The mixture of accents made me instantly relieved I wasn't the only out-of-towner, and the flush on everyone's faces told me I wasn't the only one winded by the exertion of learning the steps either.

"You're the event planner, right?" a woman asked as I introduced myself. I wasn't quite sure how to answer, especially since I wasn't in the mood to think about work, but her shining brown eyes were too hopeful to ignore.

"I suppose I am," I said, waiting anxiously for her request and wondering how she knew. One look at Flo and her smug grin, however, answered my question.

"I'm Fayola, by the way," she said, and we exchanged polite smiles. "My friends and I are here to celebrate the end of our MBAs, and I was hoping you'd help us plan something special. We know those two do the outdoor and touristy stuff"—she tilted her head toward Collin and Lars—"but we've been told you're the person we want."

I glared at Flo, and she only winked in return.

"I'm sorry to ambush you at a ceilidh, and I know it's short notice," Fayola continued, "but we'd be so grateful if you could even point us in the right direction."

With her hands clasped together and her friends looking on with the same hopeful gaze, how could I have said no?

"It would be my pleasure," I said. "What sort of things do you like?"

"Getting dressed up."

"Cocktails."

"Being in bed early."

"Outdoors."

I looked at all four women, wondering desperately how I'd pull together anything that would please all four of them. "We're different, I know," Fayola said, something apologetic creeping into her tone. "If it's too much without enough time, I understand. I just figured we'd ask."

"No, no," I said before I could stop myself. I hated disappointing people, especially where a job was concerned, so I had to think of something. "Let's talk tomorrow. I'll put something together."

Fayola threw her lean arms around me in a hug. "Thank you, thank you, thank you," she said. We made plans to meet over coffee in the morning before she and her friends took to the dance floor for another round.

"What are you doing to me?" I asked Flo as soon as they were out of earshot.

"What?" she said, playing dumb. "I'm just trying to build your résumé, of course. I'm helping you get out of here."

"I think you're trying to do the exact opposite," I said, "and I won't fall for it."

"Would it be better if I told you I was just trying to get good reviews for the Wanderer?"

"Much."

"Then it's settled. Just in time too," she said, nodding behind me at Collin approaching with our drinks.

"What's settled?" he asked, setting the pints down on the table.

"That Chelsea is ready for another dance," Flo said.

"Can you ever just let me be?"

"Did you want to stand around here talking about work instead?"

"You started it," I argued.

"And I'm going to finish it." Collin said, pulling me back to the dance floor. "It's date night, Chels. Live a little."

One more glance at Collin in that kilt, his hungry, attentive gaze sweeping over my body, and I'd already forgotten about work altogether.

By the time we returned to the dance floor the caller had taken a break, so we were spared from the energy of the line dances. Instead, the band played a slower tune, a song both hopeful and melancholy. I dropped my head to Collin's shoulder as he swayed us back and forth in time to the music, letting myself get lost in his scent and the rhythm of his breathing.

"This is a really nice first date," I said against his chest, relishing the way his chuckle rumbled against my cheek. I'd spent so much of the summer lying to myself, it felt good to say something simple and honest.

"Reckon you might want to go on another?"

"If I can squeeze you into my schedule." I sighed. "I've been so busy seeing the country and appreciating the culture that I'm not sure when I can find time to date, and I just—"

He pinched my waist hard enough to make me squeal, then immediately softened his grip and ran his fingers over the spot that stung.

I risked another glance up at him, but the heat in his gaze was so intense I had to look away before I melted on the dance floor.

With my head against his chest and his strong hands tracing patterns over my back, everything outside that moment was forgotten. For a few blissful minutes there was no Boston, no job applications, no résumés or studio apartments I couldn't afford. There was only the ceilidh, the security of Collin's arms around me, and the rest of the summer stretching its languid arms out before us. And for the first time, it didn't feel so terrifying.

It felt *good*.

By the time the caller returned to her platform we'd been too deep in the bubble of our slow dance to recover that level of energy, and I was relieved to be ushered off the dance floor before the band restarted the upbeat trad music.

"What do you say we get out of here?" Collin whispered as we made our way back to the table where I'd left my bag.

"Are you propositioning me?" I teased.

"If the proposition is to get some fresh air and a moment alone, then yes. Very much so."

"Lead the way."

He pulled me by my hand through the crowd and out of the barn, looking around for spectators before dragging me around the side of the building and pushing me up against the wall.

"Collin," I said with a laugh as I took a second to look around myself. "There are tons of people out here."

"If by *tons* you mean those few smoking and that couple behind the tractor who may or may not be shagging, then yes, there are tons." He tightened his grip on my hips and dropped his forehead to mine, which instantly made me forget the people I'd been worried about a second ago.

"So you're the guy who kisses on the first date, huh?" I whispered.

"I'm whatever guy you want me to be." He touched our noses together, and my sharp inhale echoed in the silence. "Just say the word," he said. "Am I the guy who kisses on the first date?" His hands found their way up to my waist. "Yes"—he squeezed—"or no."

His breath tickled my lips, and I had to suppress a groan that almost escaped my throat. Our kiss the other night did nothing to dissolve my nerves, and the intimacy of the darkness outside the barn threatened to undo me before he could.

A month ago, I might have said there were a thousand versions of the man I wanted Collin to be. Someone who understood the city life I thought I wanted; someone who wasn't hell-bent on getting under my skin and keeping me up at night; someone who didn't draw me to him like a magnet no matter how hard I tried to resist.

But in that moment, pressed up against the barn with his lips an inch from mine, he was exactly who I wanted, exactly as he was.

"Yes," I breathed, and before the syllable was even out of my mouth, his lips were on mine, hot and desperate. The moan I'd tried to suppress rolled out of me the second he pressed the length of his body against mine. I laced my fingers through his hair, already wishing he was closer. Wishing there was nothing between us at all.

He ran his fingers down my body until they were under my thighs, lifting me so I was wrapped around him, holding me like I weighed nothing at all. His biceps flexed under my hands, and the noise he made when I trailed my fingernails up the back of his neck was enough to make me forget we were in public entirely.

"I've been wanting to do this all night," he mumbled with his lips against my jaw. "Watching you on that dance floor, the way you move your body—"

"Are you sure you were watching the right girl?" I teased. "Because the way I move my body on a dance floor is—"

"Intoxicating," he finished, kissing me again before I could argue. The firmness of his fingers on my thighs threatened to leave a bruise. While I was certain I'd never forget this kiss, I was secretly thrilled at the idea of having something tangible to remember it by in the morning.

As I wrapped my legs tighter around him, trying to feel every hard ridge of his body, we heard an unmistakable throat clearing entirely too close for comfort.

Flo stood nearby with her arms crossed, clucking her tongue and shaking her head slowly. "You two are lucky that was so hot." She looked amused as Collin set me back on the floor. "Otherwise, it's so cliché."

"Ah, Flo, hi, we were just—"

"You're right," Collin interrupted my fumbling. "We are lucky that was so hot."

I elbowed him in the ribs, but it did nothing to wipe the smirk off his face. Thankfully, it was impossible to scandalize Flo. I had a feeling she might have watched for a few minutes before making herself known.

"You two." More head shaking. "I came out to tell you that

we're leaving, just in case you wanted to head home together. But if you want to do your own thing, I can leave and pretend this never happened, yes?"

"Well, you've ruined the mood now, haven't ya?" Collin teased. "We'll meet you at the front in a minute."

"I'm holding you to a minute," Flo said. "Any longer and we're leaving without you."

Collin saluted her as she rolled her eyes and headed back to the entrance, then turned his gaze back to me.

"Some way to end a date," I said with a fake pout.

"Chelsea, this date could have ended in the apocalypse, and it still would have been the best date I've ever been on."

"Which is a good thing, I guess, since it would be your last."

"The thought of only getting one date with you is even more frightening than the apocalypse itself," he said, pushing a stray lock of hair behind my ear. "Especially if that one date ends with us being interrupted by Flo. Please say you want to do this again."

His candor was so disarming I would have been hopeless in resisting, even if I wanted to.

"I'd like that," I said without hesitation. After the whirlwind of the last few hours, agreeing to a second date was the easiest thing I'd done all night.

FORTUNATELY, our night ended alongside everyone else's when we returned to the Wanderer, which was for the best because anything more would have made me forget about Fayola altogether, and I needed to focus on my plans for her event.

Since reception was slow the morning after the ceilidh, I spent half my shift googling phrases like "can you drink alcohol at high tea," "champagne tea castle Ireland," and "custom vintage dress fitting." Eventually, Fayola's event began to materialize before me. There might be a way to please all four women after all.

Between checking in guests and answering the phone, I made a few of my own calls to set things in motion. My fingers hovered over Collin's name on my phone while I contemplated whether it was too soon to ask a favor. We hadn't spoken since we'd said good night in the hall, and I wasn't sure if it was tacky to ask for something before so much as saying good morning. Then I reminded myself it was a work-related favor, and we were, in fact, coworkers, so I called. While it was ringing, I chastised myself for nearly letting one good date interfere with my job.

Moments after I hung up the phone, Collin was leaning on the reception desk, wiping his hands on the bar rag hanging from his back pocket.

"You rang?" he asked, crossing his arms. His sleeves were rolled just above his elbows, exposing the ink that crept down his arms.

"You have that connection at the Kylemore Abbey, right?" I asked, trying to remind myself why I called in the first place.

"Ah, it's Eamon you're looking for, is it?" he said. "Just when you think a girl comes looking for you—"

"Oh, come off it." I laughed. "Can I ask a favor?"

"What's in it for me?"

"That's not how favors work."

"Suit yourself," he said, turning toward the door.

"Collin."

"I'm just taking the piss." He grinned, returning to the desk, shrinking the space between us. "What can I do for ya?"

I gave him the rundown of my plans for Fayola and her

friends, trying and failing to ignore the way he was smiling at me while I spoke.

"What?" I asked eventually. "Why are you looking at me like that?"

"You love it here," he said. "Deny it all you want, but the Wanderer is becoming just as much a part of you as the rest of us."

"It is not," I said, but I couldn't keep a straight face no matter how hard I tried. "I'm just doing my job."

"Like I said, deny it all you want. I know the truth, just know that." His smug grin made it even harder to suppress my smile.

"You don't know anything."

"Do you want the favor or not?" he said. "Last time I checked, only one of us had Eamon's number."

I groaned, having no choice but to admit he was right. About Eamon, anyway.

"That's what I thought." He beamed, pulling out his phone and making a show of calling Eamon. I tried not to roll my eyes, because I really was grateful he was phoning this in.

After a few minutes of enthusiastic conversation and a handful of Irish phrases I didn't recognize, Collin informed me we had a reservation for the brunch tent.

"You're all set then," he said, slipping his phone back into his pocket. Leading my eyes to the sliver of skin above his waistband.

"I can't thank you enough," I said. "Seriously. Fayola and her friends will be thrilled."

"I didn't do this for Fayola and her friends," he said, heat creeping into his gaze.

"Collin," I chastised, swatting at him, but failing when he caught my wrist in his hand.

"And I don't think you did either." I opened my mouth to respond, but he cut me off. "And don't even say you did it for your résumé, because we both know that isn't the truth. You did it because you love it here." He let go of my hand and pushed off the counter, heading back down the hallway before I could say another word. How it was possible for someone to be at once so charming and so infuriating, I had no idea.

But I did have work to do, and it didn't matter why I was doing it. There had to be some separation of church and state, or something like that. Except for the fact that I'd never been to church, the idea of Collin standing in for where I'd get on my knees and pray was doing the opposite of what I needed it to do.

I physically shook my head like the motion would somehow dislodge every indecent thought. I settled my hands over the keyboard like a pianist getting ready for a performance. In a way, this was my art, and I needed to treat it as such.

Fortunately, once things were settled at the abbey everything else fell into place. Since I'd grown accustomed to Boston attitudes over the years, it was a pleasant surprise to speak with vendors who seemed interested in pleasing their customers. Either that or I was just really getting the hang of my life here, which I wasn't prepared to acknowledge.

By the time Fayola and her friends returned from exploring the town, I was ready to present them with a plan.

"Oh, girl, you work fast," she said, complimenting me as they settled into the lobby. "You must have been made for this job."

I tried to laugh, but it got stuck in my throat. "I'd hold on to that endorsement until you see the plans," I said. "Let's make sure you're pleased first."

I was met with four pairs of expectant brown eyes, but I didn't feel nervous. I had a good feeling about this one.

"So," I continued, "I'm thinking champagne tea at the Kylemore Abbey. They do one on Thursdays, and I've secured a private tent for you in the garden."

"That's perfect," one of the women said, clapping her hands together.

"That's not all." I was suddenly giddy to give them the rest of the pitch. "I've also arranged for a vintage dress fitting. People often dress up for the champagne tea at the abbey, so I have some rental dresses arranged for the four of you. Period pieces, that kind of thing."

"Stop," Fayola gasped. "You're lying."

"Cross my heart." I smiled, and the women talked over one another sharing their excitement.

"And you just put this together this morning?" one asked, grabbing my forearm.

"Yeah, I mean, it was just a few calls, really, and—"

"Can I praise you now?" Fayola interrupted.

"Go to the event first," I said. "Then we can talk."

"And you're sure it was no problem to get us in on such short notice?"

"Positive," I said. "I have a connection."

Fayola jumped off the couch and threw her arms around me, pulling away only to thank me profusely on behalf of the four of them.

Maybe Collin was right. Maybe I wasn't giving myself enough credit, and I actually was better at making connections than I thought.

Chapter 16

All it took was one Instagram post from Fayola with a few hashtags about the Wanderer to gain immediate traction. A few other guests inquired about the dress rehearsals and tea at the abbey, and Eamon reached back out to arrange something more consistent.

"When will you just accept you're doing wonders for the hostel?" Flo said one morning over coffee in town. "You can be good at a job without being attached to it, you know."

I sipped my Americano and contemplated this idea. It seemed reasonable enough, except for the fact that this job happened to be three thousand miles from home, so if I was too good at it, I was bound to get attached eventually.

"That's what happens though, isn't it?" I said. "You get really good at a job, and then you get attached to the job, and then it just becomes your life?"

"You have it all wrong, *tesoro*," she said. "Too concerned that life is what you do for work. Or where you do it."

"And what is it if not those things?"

"It's everything in between!" The family of the crying baby looked over as Flo rattled her espresso mug in the saucer. "It's everything else you've done since you've been here. And more than that, it's everything you've *felt*. Your life isn't making reservations and booking events and answering phones, Chelsea. It's cliff jumping when you're scared and dancing when you don't know the steps and kissing men you think you shouldn't and screaming at the top of your lungs at a hurling match and speeding down the Wild Atlantic Way. Open your eyes."

Flo sank against the back of her chair like she was exhausted, muttering in Italian and signaling the barista for another espresso like we were at a cocktail bar. I was silent for a while, contemplating how I could possibly respond.

"I'm just saying you should consider letting go of these ideas about how you think life is supposed to go, that's all," she said after a minute, noticeably quieter than she'd been speaking before. "There's not even a 'supposed to' at all, really. There is only what is."

When I agreed to meet for a coffee, I didn't think I was agreeing to meet for *this*.

"You make it sound so easy," I moaned.

"It is," she said. "Once you surrender yourself to it, anyway. It's a mind-set. Americans always think you need to work to earn pleasure, when really pleasure is the only point of being alive."

"Have you always been so wise?"

"Ah, so you do see that it's wisdom," she said.

"Don't let it get to your head."

"It couldn't," she said. "No ego here. Another thing that's much bigger in America."

"All right, all right, I get it. You think America is the worst."

"I think American *ideals* are the worst," she clarified.

"Cheers," I said, clinking my coffee against hers and hoping vague agreement would put an end to this conversation.

"How are the applications going, anyway?" she asked, tanking my attempt at moving on.

I chewed my fingernail, trying to find a way to tell her I'd been deeply slacking on applying anywhere for lack of time and opportunity and fear of rejection.

"They're going," I said, though I knew it was lame. "I should carve out some time today to send a few more, actually."

"What does your friend think?"

"Ada?"

"*Sì.*"

"I should carve out some time today to call her too." Only then did I realize how caught up I'd been lately and how I'd been neglecting my usual priorities. I hadn't even looked at job sites or spoken to Ada before that interview, and that was nearly a week ago.

"The Wanderer sucks you in, doesn't it?" she said, reading my mind. "Tell you what. I'll leave you to it, and we can catch up later, yeah?"

I glanced across the coffee shop at the string of old-school computers, having no choice but to resign myself to a morning of trying to get my life back on track. Which I supposed was still the whole reason I was here, so perhaps I should have been taking it a bit more seriously.

Flo and I air-kissed goodbye, agreeing to find each other later for a few drinks. After she left, I ordered another iced Americano and dialed Ada.

"Chels?" Ada said after two rings. "Can you hear me?"

"Hardly. Why are you whispering?"

"I'm at Ben's sister's yoga thing."

I had no idea what that meant.

"Why don't you call me later, then?"

"No, no, I can chat. It's in the park, and I'm way in the back. And it's boring me to death. How's it going? I feel like I haven't heard from you in ages." For us, a week really was ages.

"I know, I know," I said. "I'm sorry. It's been weirdly busy here. I've learned to Irish dance. Sort of. And I sent some women to a castle for a champagne tea in old dresses and then people saw it on Instagram and it's been a whole thing."

"Sounds like you're making quite the impression over there," she said. "And Collin?"

"If I tell you something, can you promise not to freak out?"

"No," she said instantly, which made me laugh. I missed her. "But I can promise I'll freak out quietly, so I don't disrupt the rest of the class."

"I'll take it," I said, then launched in. The date, the kissing, the irresistible pull and tightening knot in my chest every time I remembered it was going to end. By the time I was done, I could practically hear her smug grin through the phone.

"It's even better than I hoped it would be," she said, and I was pretty sure I heard her clap her hands.

"Yeah, well, it still has an expiration date, so . . ." I tried to laugh, but it was hollow. "But it is nice for now. Really nice."

"Do you *want* it to end?"

"Of course not," I said before I could catch myself. "But I want to come home, which means it has to end, so in a way I guess I do? You know what I mean."

"Of course I do," she said. "I just wanted to hear you admit it."

"Why?"

"So I know Ireland is working."

"What is that supposed to mean?"

"Softening you up," she said. "Forcing you to let your guard down or whatever."

"Since when has that been the plan? Wasn't I just supposed to come here while I looked for a job back home?"

"Couldn't there be more than one reason you're there?"

"Not that we agreed upon."

"Things change, babe."

I could hear her smile through the phone, and for a minute or two neither of us said anything.

"I didn't think I would like him this much," I said eventually—quietly—like a confession.

"And we didn't think you'd move to Ireland, either, and yet . . ." She let her voice trail off into silence.

"What am I supposed to do?"

"Let yourself feel whatever you're feeling, Chels. These feelings are good. You don't have to fight them. And you definitely don't have to run from them. You can stay right where you are if you like."

"I thought you wanted me to come home," I said, "but lately it's feeling like you're trying to convince me to stay."

"I want you to be happy. Wherever that is."

"It's Boston."

"Great! Then I can't wait for you to come home."

I knew she meant it, but I also knew she wasn't satisfied. She knew me better than I knew myself, which meant she knew something had changed. Which meant I couldn't keep trying to pretend it hadn't. "I just don't want you to think you can't be happy in two places," she added when I said nothing.

"But I can't live in two places."

"Are you saying you're considering living there?"

"Isn't that what you just suggested?" I couldn't remember whose ideas were whose anymore.

"Is that what you want?"

"I don't know!" I didn't mean to shout, but I was pretty sure someone in Ben's sister's yoga thing shushed me through the line.

"That's okay, Chels," Ada said, returning to a whisper. "You don't have to know everything, all the time. But I'm always here to support you and we can always talk about it. That doesn't have to be right now. And it probably shouldn't be because you're messing up my flow."

I laughed at that. This was what best friends were for. They knew exactly how to rile you up and calm you back down.

"Like hell you know anything about flow," I said. "How's Ben's sister?"

"She's great! Really getting this yoga thing off the ground. I think their parents are still paying all her bills, but she's putting the work in."

"And how's Ben?"

Before she even answered I could *feel* her smiling, even from three thousand miles away. "We looked at rings this week."

"You what?!" People snapped their heads up to look at me, but I didn't care. "Why didn't you start with that?"

Ada laughed. "I don't know, we were on your thing!" I felt like such an idiot for rambling on about a job and a summer fling while she was on the brink of engagement.

"So, he's, like, about to propose then?"

"He's trying to be coy. Pretending he just wanted to gauge my taste, that's all. But I'm pretty sure he went right back to the jeweler with his credit card."

"Holy shit," I said.

"I know," she said.

"It's finally happening."

"Don't jinx it."

"Please," I said. "Ben's been madly in love with you since freshman year. I hardly think he's going to change his mind now."

"You're probably right," she said. "Who would have ever thought we'd both find love?"

"Ada! Oh my god. I have not found love."

"What was that? Sorry, you're breaking up. Service must be spotty."

"Don't make me scream so loud someone kicks you out of the class."

"You'd get kicked out wherever you are first," she said. "Besides, getting kicked out of the class would be a dream."

"Do it for your future sister-in-law."

"Fine," she grumbled, though I knew she was secretly thrilled by the phrase. "You do something for yourself then, yeah?"

"Fine."

We blew kisses through the phone and promised to call soon before hanging up. With a morning of job applications looming over me, I found myself envying her yoga class. And I hated yoga.

I booted up the old computer, staring at my reflection as I waited for the home screen to load. My freckles had multiplied tenfold since I'd gotten here, and I couldn't remember the last time I'd styled my hair beyond my air-dried waves. At first, it was because there weren't outlets in the bathroom here and the straightener cord didn't reach from the outlet in my room to the tiny mirror in the wardrobe. But now, dare I say it was because my natural hair might have suited me after all?

Fortunately, before I had time to answer that, the screen blinked to life. No more excuses. I was caffeinated, I had a boost from my best friend, and I desperately needed to get my life back on track before I was out of time.

I returned to the Google search bar and typed the phrase "event planning + hospitality + manager + director," then let my finger hover over the "B" for longer than necessary. I knew the next word in the search was Boston. It was a familiar search, bookmarked on my own computer, even, and there was no reason I should have hesitated before completing the phrase.

But I did.

I sat there for an extra second, weighing Ada's words, letting my gaze wander around the café. I scanned the families, first dates, tourists. But it was the solo woman in the corner behind a laptop who caught my eye.

Most of her dark hair was pulled off her face with a plastic clip, and beside her laptop sat an empty mug, a notebook, and two different colored pens. Large headphones covered her ears, and she rested her chin in her hand, visibly lost in whatever she was reading on the screen. She was undoubtedly working, or maybe studying, and the longer I stared at her, the more I realized what I was doing; I was imagining myself in her shoes. I was imagining myself in Galway, coming to the café in town to get some work done, maybe running some errands, meeting a friend for dinner, doing the kinds of things I did in Boston.

Then I thought again about Ada's words, and while she was right that maybe I could be happy in two places, I couldn't *be* in two places. I typed "Boston" at the end of the search bar and scrolled through the results.

A "guest services" position at a Four Seasons caught my eye, but only for long enough to force me back into a contemplative spiral. I didn't even want to go into corporate hospitality, did I? I'd loved O'Shea's because I was flexible in my work, and I knew

I wouldn't have the same at a big corporation. But I *would* have significantly more money, which would probably mean a nicer apartment and maybe even a chip at my student loans.

I wrote and rewrote my cover letters, customizing each for the job descriptions and poring over every word. Sure, event planning and hospitality might have been my "passion," and I was definitely keen on "improving communities," but did I really care about "exposing the magic of the greater Boston area"?

Beyond the first sentence, was my entire cover letter a lie? Was everything I'd been telling myself about what I wanted in a job a lie?

This morning had really gotten away from me.

In my last cover letter of the day, I tried to be more truthful. I tried to get to the root of what I was looking for in a job. How it felt to provide people with an experience that would change them in some way. Something that would bond them, challenge them, inspire them. How it felt to bring an idea to life, to know people are enjoying an experience I created for them.

And to tap into the root of those feelings, I was surprised to find myself thinking about my time at the Wanderer.

In the following days, I kept an eye on my email for responses to my applications. Two eventually rolled in: one informing me the position had been filled internally, the other requesting an interview. I replied, requesting a virtual interview and praying it would go better than the last one. When they accepted and I began my preparations, I vowed to spin my move to Ireland in a more positive direction.

It was a calculated career choice made to diversify my résumé and gain global hospitality experience. It was a way to broaden my skill set and apply to a wider range of positions and clientele. A privilege that allowed me an opportunity to be creative, innovative, and thoughtful in my work. That sounded good. Professional, reasonable.

True.

I was reviewing my notes the evening before our scheduled interview when Collin appeared in my doorway. We left our doors propped open sometimes, but this custom always seemed to come back to bite me. Especially when I was trying to be productive.

"Fancy a drink?"

I spun my tiny desk chair to face him, trying to keep my composure at the sight of his damp hair pushed behind his ears.

"I have to—"

"You can't say no," he said, stepping into my room. "It's part of your Irish education."

"I forgot that only happens on your schedule," I said.

"I'm going to ignore your sarcasm for once, but only for the sake of a lesson in spontaneity. And the Temple Bar."

My laugh was involuntary. "Sorry, you're saying this casual drink is in *Dublin*?"

"Would I lie?"

I narrowed my eyes, realizing I had no idea how to answer that question.

"Besides, I never said it was casual. And Flo already said yes," he added as leverage.

"Of course Flo said yes," I said. "Flo says yes to everything."

"Might not hurt you to do the same." His grin alone was almost enough to make me change my mind, which was exactly why I had to stand my ground.

"You haven't given me much of a choice thus far, have you?"

"Nope, and I don't intend on giving you one tonight, either."

"Well, unfortunately for you, you don't actually make all the rules. I'm sorry, but I can't go." I found myself genuinely disappointed. "I need to stay in and prepare for my interview."

"Interview?"

"Tomorrow at two with a high-end tourism organization in Boston. I'd actually like this one to go well, so I need to make sure I'm on my game."

"Still cracking on with that, are ya?" Collin walked over and sat on the edge of my desk, crossing his arms over his chest.

"With getting back to my life? Yeah, I am still cracking on with that." I chuckled, though as soon as the words left my lips I realized nothing about them was funny. Nothing about the interview was making me smile at all, if I was honest.

"Temple Bar will change your mind," he said, nudging my leg with his foot.

"Then it's a good thing I'm not going to Temple Bar."

"Chels," Collin said, getting off my desk and kneeling in front of me, taking my hands in his. It took everything in me not to pull away and hide from his gaze. I needed to stand my ground, and he was making it nearly impossible. "When else are you going to have the chance to drive across Ireland and drink in one of the most iconic bars in the world? With a proper Irishman to show you the way, no less." His lips curled into a smile on one side when he said this last part, and I was reminded how they felt against my own.

"I'm sure you'll find some other time for us to do exactly that," I said in a last-ditch effort to stand my ground, though my resolve was slipping through my fingers at warp speed.

"Nope," he said, getting back to his feet. "It's now or never.

One of our guests has an uncle who owns a hostel near the bar, and they're holding a few beds for us for the night. They're fully booked for the rest of the summer."

Shit.

"How am I supposed to interview after a night out?" I groaned, grasping at straws.

"I've seen you after a night out, Chelsea. You can interview in that state. Frankly, you could interview in any state, and they would be crazy not to offer you the job." He softened his voice, making a decent pitch at sincerity.

"You think flattery is going to convince me?"

"Is it working?" He reached out to push a piece of hair behind my ear, but I swatted his hand before he had the chance. "Ah, come on, Chels!" he pleaded. "You gotta come. It'll be minus craic without ya. We'll make sure you're all set for the interview."

"Oh, please," I said. "You'd be the first to sabotage the interview."

He made an X over his heart with his pointer finger: a wordless promise. "Listen, do I think it's ridiculous that anyone would leave this for American city life? Absolutely. But you really think I'd ruin something you care about?"

"You're really turning on the charm here, aren't you?" I crossed my arms if only to resist the urge to reach for him and bridge the gap between us.

"I'll turn it off if you agree."

"Bullshit."

"Guilty."

We exchanged smiles in the fading sunlight of my bedroom: his, suggestive; mine, reluctant. I weighed the circumstances. A good night's sleep was out of the question, but he was right about my ability to rally after a night out. I would have to finish my preparations from the car, which wasn't impossible, and I was now a pro at getting ready in a hostel bathroom. It was ridiculous, but he was also right about it being my only chance. Which was something that mattered to me now, apparently.

"One condition," I said.

"Anything."

"I'm riding with Flo."

By THE TIME we arrived in Dublin, I needed a drink. I'd spent the ride doing last-minute preparations, and I was feeling more unsure about the interview by the minute. And if I was still trying to convince myself it was a good idea, I had a feeling a night out in Dublin was going to do the opposite.

I contemplated asking Flo for advice, but I already knew what she would say. And I wasn't sure I was willing to put a point on the *Ireland* side of the board right before an interview. Maybe I should call my mom. She wouldn't entertain the idea of staying in Ireland for a second. It would be all Boston, and all business, and I could use that energy before the interview. I made a mental note to call her later, which would also hold me accountable not to drink too much.

Flo found parking in a dingy garage not far from the hostel with Collin and the rest of the gang pulling in behind us. Lars had to work tonight, and I didn't recognize the others who climbed from the back of Collin's truck, so I'd have to rely on Flo to keep me in check.

As we walked in the direction of the hostel, Collin dropped back so the two of us lagged behind the group.

"That's Reg, the one with the uncle," he said, indicating a guy with a buzz cut. His arm was linked with the woman next to him, and Flo seemed to have already met them both.

"There should be one more car following behind, and then that's everyone."

I made a noise to confirm I heard his voice, but I wasn't entirely focused. As Dublin unfurled beyond the parking garage, I began to realize what I was getting myself into. The city was more Boston than Galway, and I was at once at home and overwhelmed.

I hadn't been away from home for very long, but the size and scope of the city intimidated me in a way cities never had before. Was I already losing my edge? And if so, how badly did I want it back?

"This here is the Ha'Penny," Collin said as we approached a bridge, pulling me from my thoughts. "First iron bridge in the country. Used to cost a ha'penny to cross."

I was tempted to tease him as he turned on his Tour Guide Voice, but the echo of his accent over the water changed my mind. It was melodic, and I remembered that many come to Ireland to be inspired. People came to the Wanderer and to Collin to be inspired. As much as I tried not to admit it, he had a way of making people see Ireland the way he did. Myself included.

The hostel stood three stories tall and was unusually thin, sandwiched between an old pub and a cheap sushi restaurant. Curated graffiti splashed across the brick exterior, and a neon sign not unlike ours welcomed us above the door.

As we filed into the lobby, we were greeted by Reg's uncle. The man welcomed us to Dublin, told us we would be sharing a twelve-bed mixed dorm, then said a handful of other things that got lost in his accent.

"Did you get a word of that?" Flo whispered to me in the back of the group.

"Not one," I said. "You?"

"*Niente.*"

"Breakfast is from seven to nine, we should make use of all the amenities, and the Wi-Fi password is on the room key," Collin whispered. "Anything else I can do for you ladies?"

"Yeah, make yourself busy so we can get ready," Flo said, pretending to toss her hair over her shoulders.

"Easy enough. See you back down here in half an hour, then," he said, heading to the downstairs bar, but not without a glance over his shoulder.

"Oh, girl, you're never going to make that interview." Flo laughed, shaking her head and watching me watching Collin.

"I don't have a choice, remember?"

"There's always a choice, *cara.*"

For a second, Helen O'Shea flashed into my mind. *The choice is yours, Chelsea*, she'd said to me when she slid me the pamphlet for the Wanderer moments after she pulled the rug out from under me. At the time, choosing the Wanderer felt like upending my entire life. But that didn't mean choosing the Wanderer would *always* feel like upending my entire life. Maybe there could be a time when choosing the Wanderer would simply be choosing my life. But that time wasn't today, and I had to do what I told myself I would do.

"Well, either way, I need to choose myself," I said eventually, figuring that was the closest I could get to the truth. "And that means moving on with my life, which means doing this interview."

"Anything else you plan on doing?" She glanced in the direction we had just watched Collin depart, and I groaned so loud I was sure they could have heard me back in Galway.

"Yes, actually," I said. "I plan on getting ready and having a good time, so I don't regret this trip altogether."

"Let's do it, then," she said. "We can prep you for the interview while I do your hair."

"Your arms are finally rested from last time?" I teased.

"Don't remind me or I'll change my mind. And by the looks of you now, you can't afford for me to change my mind." I gasped and she grabbed my arm, dragging me up the stairs and toward the room.

Flo was reminding me more of Ada by the day. Riling me up, calming me down. She was stepping into dangerous close-friend territory, and I was suddenly aware Collin wasn't the only one it would be hard to leave.

FORTY MINUTES LATER, we were ready to go. I glanced at myself in the mirror, marveling at Flo's ability to create a salon-quality blowout in a hostel bathroom. She'd insisted her little black top would be perfect with the jeans I'd packed, and despite my protests, she was right. The asymmetrical neckline left one shoulder uncovered, which felt like just the right amount of exposure.

When we arrived back downstairs, Collin was sitting on a barstool with one ankle crossed over his knee, sipping a dark beer. I studied the faded ink on his ankles that I noticed the first night we met, wondering how it was possible he was ever a total stranger to me. Wondering what else about him would become this familiar by the time I left.

"It's about time," he said, swallowing the rest of the beer in one gulp as we approached.

"Seems like you kept yourself occupied just fine," I said.

"Lucky you two are worth the wait." He addressed us both but looked only at me. He wore a charcoal-gray shirt that changed the color of his eyes, turning them the same deep, stormy green as the Liffey.

The three of us made the short walk to the iconic bar together, winding down glistening side streets, under colorful awnings, and through groups of other twentysomethings looking for a good time. This corner of the city was so lively it was impossible not to get sucked in, and I could already feel the night taking hold.

As we turned the corner and the Temple Bar came into view, I was momentarily, unexpectedly stunned. I'd seen it in pictures, of course. It was one of the most famous bars in the world. But as I stood there on the cobblestones between Collin and Flo, staring up at its cherry-red exterior dripping in string lights, the reality of my circumstances set in.

I was in Ireland. *Living* in Ireland. I had made a temporary home in a place people dreamed of going. A place people came to be inspired, to spend time in nature, to be healed. A place people came for adventure. A place with culture and history and stories older than America itself.

And I'd been hell-bent on resisting that magic. Sure, I'd seen and experienced some of the country, but had I really taken it in? Had I really been present, or had I spent this much of the summer with one foot out the door?

A combination of shame and embarrassment washed over me, leaving me as open and exposed as the windows of the bar. I wanted nothing more than to lose myself in the people inside; I practically skipped over the cobbles as I followed Collin and Flo through the doors.

Inside, the bar was as loud and energetic as I'd hoped. A large band crowded a small stage, and everyone on the floor seemed lost in the music. Bartenders and servers performed a choreographed dance through the tight crowds, carrying trays of shots, Guinness, and gin and tonics high over their heads.

I let my eyes roam greedily, admiring the traditional dark wooden beams and the clutter over every inch of the walls: photos, bunting, flags, postcards, coins, advertisements. I roamed the faces of patrons, from all corners of the world, clinking glasses and dancing to the sound of an electric fiddle. Eventually, my gaze landed on a bronze statue of a well-dressed man in the middle of the room. With his arms raised in the air and his head low, he looked how I imagined we'd all look after a few drinks tonight.

"Who is that?" I asked Collin as we made our way toward the bar.

"Aye, that bloke there? They call him the unknown drinker."

"There's just a statue of a random drunk man in the middle of the bar?"

"Of course there is," he said. "You should know Ireland well enough by now not to be surprised."

I couldn't argue with that.

After Collin ordered us drinks (beer for him, gin and tonics for me and Flo), we took to the floor, milling around and finding a spot against the wall with a small ledge to rest our drinks.

"Should we find the others?" I shouted over the music. Unlike the night at the ceilidh, I had to avoid being alone with Collin if I wanted to stay focused on the interview, but I knew it was going to be harder than I'd hoped.

"I'm sure we'll see them eventually," Flo said, waving a nonchalant hand. I recognized the look in her eyes as she scanned the crowd, and I pulled her close to me by her elbow.

"Florence, you cannot hook up with someone tonight," I whispered.

"Why? Because we're in a dorm? People hook up in hostels all the time."

"No, because you can't leave me alone," I said, gesturing discreetly in Collin's direction. Fortunately, he was watching the band, ignoring our conversation.

"Did you not just hear me?" Flo said. "People hook up in hostels all the time."

When I glared at her she only smirked in response, sucking down half her drink through the tiny straw and returning her gaze to the crowd.

Once we had another round under our belts, we alternated comfortably between mindless chatter, people-watching, and dancing to the music. No overthinking. No thinking at all, really. Just friends, drinks, music, and the Temple Bar.

As the bands changed over, there was a brief lull during which we could actually hear one another. A man from a nearby table approached Flo, a shy smile on his face. I'd seen them looking at each other more than a handful of times, and I was thrilled that he'd finally come to introduce himself.

But I was afraid for myself, because it meant I'd be alone with Collin after all.

After a minute of small talk that I couldn't quite hear, Flo turned to me with pleading eyes. She'd been such a good friend to me from the moment I arrived at the Wanderer; it would be horribly selfish to ask her to stay. I nodded my consent and she kissed me on the cheek, then disappeared with the man onto the dance floor.

"Reckon that's the last we'll be seeing of her tonight?" Collin asked as we both watched her leave. We'd been alone less than a minute, and I could already feel him closing the space between us where Flo had stood.

"I reckon it isn't the last we'll be seeing of *him* tonight," I said. "Flo never stays out all night. I'm sure they'll both be back at the hostel some time before the morning."

"Hopefully not back in the dorm with the rest of us," he said, and I shook my head in agreement.

"Fancy another?" Collin asked, nodding to my empty glass. I was grateful for the change in topic but undecided about another drink. I tilted my head back and forth, debating. Another would make me comfortably drunk, but not too drunk that I'd be hungover. Yet, anyway.

"One more," I finally decided, holding up one finger in the air for effect. "Then I'm switching to club soda."

"It's a shame Flo isn't here to keep you honest," he said, snatching my empty glass from my hand and heading toward the bar before I could protest.

By the time he made his way back to where I stood a new band had started their set, and the energy in the bar shot back up to a ten. I turned my back to Collin and pretended to focus on the band, which turned out to be a mistake. His breath warmed the back of my neck, and I found myself leaning back into him the way I had the night he braided my hair.

After another song or two, we finally bridged the gap, and it was even more intoxicating than another drink. The night was slipping into dangerous territory, and I was an inch of contact away from losing my footing.

As the band played a slower song, Collin's fingertips trailed my hip, slipping in and out of my belt loops. With every inhale his back pressed against mine, and I could feel the pattern of his breathing. Like mine, it was fast and erratic.

I leaned my head back against his shoulder, closing my eyes to heighten my other senses. I basked in the sound of the band playing an Irish folk song and the crowd singing along, the lingering taste of gin on my tongue, the feeling of Collin's fingers now against my bare skin where my top met my jeans. My head spun, but in a way I wanted to savor.

"Chelsea," Collin said in the quiet between songs, with his lips right against my ear. I sucked in a breath, equal parts excited and terrified for what was coming next. "Can I ask you something?"

"Hmm?" I couldn't manage anything beyond that sound.

"Are you hungry? Because I would kill for a cheeky bite right now."

My breath rushed out of me like a gust of wind.

"Relieved, are ya?"

"Only because I'm starving," I said.

"Not because you thought I might say something else?"

"Like what?" I challenged, turning to face him.

He shrugged by way of response and slung his arm over my shoulders, pointing us in the direction of the door. "I guess we'll have to see," he said. "Come on. There's a chippy around the corner that should still be open. We can get a takeaway and eat it by the water."

"What about Flo? We can't just leave her."

He wiggled his phone in the air. "She texted us in a group chat twenty minutes ago. Said she'll meet us back at the hostel later but not to wait up."

"She did?" I said, fumbling in my bag for my phone. When I took it out, it flashed the dead battery icon instead of the home screen. *Shit.*

"I'll keep my phone volume on high in case she needs us," he said, sensing my apprehension about leaving a friend at the bar with no way to contact her. "I've got her too. Not to worry." He was becoming more attractive by the minute, and I needed to get out into the fresh air before I caught fire.

Collin stepped ahead of me, taking my hand in his and leading me out of the bar. His hand was warm but not clammy, and I held on tightly as we wove through the crowds.

The Temple Bar spit us outside into a much smaller throng of people crowded around barrels, smoking while they polished off the last of their pints. Collin extended his arm to me and I slipped my hand under his elbow, letting him guide us through the streets.

The chippy was just around the corner, and if he hadn't pointed it out I never would have noticed it. It was nothing more than a window with a red-and-white-striped awning, and the lights inside were so dim it looked closed. This did not stop Collin, however, from greeting the single employee like an old friend.

While he ordered, I studied the block on either side of us. Young people dragged their drunken feet over the cobblestone; fluorescent signs blinked over pubs and minimarts. Buses turned tight corners with tired passengers leaning their heads against the windows. If I didn't look in the direction of the river, I probably could have been convinced I was at home.

I used to be so certain I was only a city girl. Even a few days ago, I'd probably say I would always be more comfortable in the city. And eventually, in a suburb just a few minutes outside a city, where I would settle down for the rest of life. But surprisingly, I preferred Galway to Dublin. It was hard to hear myself think here, even after having left the bar, and I wondered if Boston would feel the same when I got home.

"Penny for your thoughts?" Collin asked, passing me a cardboard boat of fish and chips. The scent of malt vinegar wafted into my nose, making it impossible to resist popping a burning chip into my mouth.

While I chewed and contemplated what thoughts I was willing to share, I followed him to a spot on the ledge near the river Liffey.

The midnight water churned below our feet, carrying reflections of light on its journey through Dublin. For a second, I longed to be carried with them. To wind effortlessly on a dark path between the city and the country without having to decide which direction I should be going.

"It's not that different from Boston," I said eventually. "Dublin, I mean. This bit of the city kind of looks like home."

"I thought the same when I first arrived in Boston," he said. We both let out a laugh that was more of an exhale. "But does it feel like home?" he asked.

"Of course it doesn't," I said. "I still can't figure out how to cross the street because of the traffic patterns, I miss Whole Foods almost as much as I miss my bed, and my family isn't here."

"Well, your blood relatives aren't here," he said. "There's an important distinction."

"What are you saying?"

"Just that family doesn't only have to be people who share your DNA, that's all. There can be all kinds of families, really."

"And let me guess, the Wanderer is one?"

"You don't have to guess," he said. "You already know."

We both took a bite and stared back at the water, watching the ripples form and disappear beneath our feet.

"It's easy for you to say," I said. "Of course the Wanderer is your family. You've been there since, when? You were a teenager?"

"Time spent does not measure family, Chels."

For a reason unbeknownst to me, tears welled behind my eyes. I tried to place the feeling, but it was slipping through my fingers. It wasn't quite homesickness. Nor was it anxiety about the future. I wasn't sure they were sad tears at all.

"It's just a different way of thinking," Collin said in the silence, possibly in an attempt to assuage my emotional uprising. "It's not as serious as it is in the States. We're guided more by feeling here than by logic. So it doesn't matter if someone is *technically* your family. It just matters if someone *feels* like your family. We let the heart lead the way."

"Doesn't that make things harder?"

"Nah, not in the slightest," he said. I loved how his accent sounded any time he said a word with the letter *h* in it. "Much easier to trust your instincts. A bit of logic never did anyone any good, did it?"

"A *bit* of logic definitely does people some good." I gave him a pointed look, refusing to believe he was suggesting we throw it entirely to the wind.

"That's what got ya here then, is it?" He smiled. "Logic?"

I nudged him with my shoulder, and we lapsed back into silence. Conversations of passersby floated over our heads. A young couple kissed on the bridge nearby, and I averted my gaze for their privacy.

"Besides," Collin continued eventually, "we don't all have the luxury of having a home we want to go back to." I turned to face him and immediately wished it was lighter outside. His expression was unreadable in the dull glow of dying street-lights. "For some of us, the Wanderer is more stable than home ever was."

"Are you one of those people?" I asked, though I knew the answer. Since he offered the information in the first place, I hoped he wouldn't mind if I asked about it.

"Aye," he said. "I am. The Wanderer and its people have been there for me in ways my family hasn't always been. My family's grand, I don't mean to disparage them. Things just aren't always the easiest with the blood relatives, you know? There aren't so many expectations with chosen family. More support, less disappointment, that kind of thing."

"I can't imagine you not living up to anyone's expectations," I said before the thought fully cleared my brain. He smiled but kept his gaze out on the river.

"Because you've not met my family," he said. "But enough about them. It's just to say that the people you're related to aren't necessarily where your home has to be. If you have enough love for each other, it shouldn't matter where you are, so long as you're happy."

He sounded like Ada, and it made my heart clench. I'd been so attached to the idea that to be happy I had to have the job, apartment, and ten-year plan. I hadn't even realized it was possible for my happiness to come *first*, not as a result.

"Come on," Collin said before I could respond, wiping his hands on his pants and getting to his feet. "This night was supposed to be about having a proper good time in the city," he said, "and here we are carrying on about life and staring at the Liffey." He shook his head, extending a hand to help me up. "Let's end on a high."

We tossed our empty cardboard boats in a nearby bin, then linked our arms again to return to the city streets.

"Where to now?" I asked, resisting the urge to look at my watch. I hadn't forgotten about the interview, but I hadn't forgotten about my newfound resolve to actually embrace the night either. I also hadn't forgotten about Collin's fingertips on my skin, his breath on the back of my neck. The way his chest felt against my shoulder blades. His lips against my ear.

"Back to the hostel?" he said, and I tried to keep my sudden disappointment from creeping onto my face. "I heard they have a great little bar that's open nearly all night." This time, my face must have given me away, because he laughed and tightened his elbow around my hand. "And, since we'll already be back at the hostel, it'll be nice and easy to get up to bed and get a decent night's sleep for your interview."

I should have been relieved he remembered, but instead my disappointment reappeared. I thought we were supposed to be ending the night on a high, and thinking about an interview for a job I didn't even want was the opposite.

THE BAR IN THE HOSTEL LOBBY was little more than a counter with a handful of half-empty bottles on a shelf behind it. An older woman straightened when she saw us approaching, slinging a towel over her shoulder, and slapping her hands flat on the bar.

"What'll it be, then?" she asked. We eyed the small, lackluster collection of bottles before Collin ordered a local beer for himself and a club soda for me, both of which required no mixing from the bartender. All she had to do was pop the tops, and her relief was palpable.

"Long night?" Collin asked.

"Tending bar in a hostel is right brutal sometimes, you know that?"

We both laughed. "Actually, I do," Collin said. "Do the same thing myself over in Galway there."

The bartender turned back to face us, her gray eyes noticeably brighter than before. A hint of jealousy creeped in that Collin had that effect on everyone.

"Do ye really?" she said, looking him up and down. "A fine young thing like yerself probably has a better go of it though, I reckon."

"Ah, it's hell sometimes for all of us," he said, and she smiled, making her appear ten years younger.

"I'd drink to that," she said, raising the empty glass she'd been cleaning. "And what about you, dear? What do you do?"

"I'm the receptionist," I said. "And I do some event planning on the side." Or by now was I the event planner with some receptionist work on the side? Did it even matter?

"Aye, with this bloke, do ye? Hostel life for the lot of us then?"

"Oh, no. Not me. Just for the summer. Then I'm back to my life."

"Poor thing," she tsked. I tried not to be offended, but the pity in her eyes and the way Collin was holding in a laugh made it hard.

"Been tryin' to tell her just that," Collin said. "She doesn't listen."

"They never do, do they?"

"I'm right here," I reminded them, though neither seemed to care. "Though really I should be asleep, resting before tomorrow."

"What's that then?" the bartender asked.

"An interview," I said. "Part of the Back-to-Real-Life plan."

"Dear, I hate to be the one to tell ye"—she leaned in—"but wherever ye are is yer real life."

"If only it was that simple."

"It is."

I finished my club soda while I searched for something else to say. I settled on "thank you" as I rose from the stool, searching my bag for a few stray euros.

She dropped another beer and club soda on the counter. "On the house, it is," she said. I thanked her again and nudged Collin, suggesting it was time for both of us to leave.

"Right, then." He echoed my thanks and left a few euros on the bar anyway, then followed me from the lobby in the direction of our dorm.

"I didn't expect the bartender to also be a therapist," I said as soon as we were out of earshot.

"I don't know, Chels. Old Irish women are wise. I'd listen to her if I were you."

"Of course you would, because you've been saying the same thing for weeks."

"You think it would have sunk in by now."

"It's making a dent," I admitted, as much to his surprise as my own.

"Let's head up to the roof," he said. "You can tell me what's going on up here." He tapped my temple and sparks rained through my body. I nodded, wordlessly following him through a doorway up a stairwell.

The air was cooler on the roof than it had been on the ground, and I took a few steadying gulps before we sat. "So," he said after a moment, "talk to me."

"We've done a lot of talking tonight," I said. "You aren't sick of me?"

"Oh, no, I very much am, I'm just also very nosy."

I laughed, knocking my shoulder into his, making him smile. A knowing grin that saw right through me and was relentless in making me feel a rush of emotion I didn't even know I was capable of feeling. Like I was flying.

"It's making a dent," I said again, throwing my hands up. "Everything everyone has been saying since I got here, it's making a dent, that's all. I didn't even want to come to Ireland at the beginning of the summer, and now I'm not entirely sure I want to leave. I was so convinced I was happiest in Boston, but now that I'm here, I'm not so sure anymore." I rubbed my hands over my face, no longer caring what my makeup might look like. "It's just a lot. And it's not like I expected it to be a little, but I didn't expect it to be this hard."

"That means you're having a great trip, at least," he said, taking a long swig. "All good trips should subvert expectations, don't you think?"

"For you," I said, shaking my head. "But not for me. At least not where my future is concerned."

"What about where this is concerned?" he asked, noticeably quieter than a moment ago, gesturing back and forth between us. "You didn't expect this, did you?"

"No," I whispered. "I didn't."

"So the unexpected isn't all bad, then, is it?"

I opened my mouth to respond, but he pressed his lips to mine before words could come out. One single kiss, one hot sweep of his tongue, one deep exhale, and my body responded to him in a way that answered his question better than words could have.

"Come on," he said when he pulled away, far sooner than I wanted. "I promised we'd make sure you were well-rested for your interview, and we've kept you out late enough." He got to his feet and held out a hand to help me up, for which I was grateful. The kiss—and the mention of the interview—had turned my legs to jelly.

"Lead the way."

Collin slipped the key card from his back pocket as we approached the door, swiping it over the sensor and quietly letting us in. We made our way to the back of the room where we'd stored our bags when we'd first arrived, which felt like years ago by now.

The rest of the room was sleeping, so we were silent as we got ready for bed, stealing glances at each other while we changed our clothes. With Collin down to nothing but a pair of shorts, I couldn't help but sneak a peek, and he didn't seem to mind. His eyes sparkled even in the dark, and something about the silence heightened the rest of my senses. His gaze alone made me feel like I was on fire.

It wasn't long before I climbed up to the top bunk and he slid into the bottom, and we whispered good nights over the railing. With the rest of the room sound asleep in the darkness, we had no choice but to end our night.

Or so I thought.

I wasn't sure how long I'd been lying in bed before I heard Collin's voice. I wasn't sleeping, just lying there, staring at the ceiling, counting my breaths. Four seconds in, eight seconds out. Every time I heard him move on the mattress below, my heart rate skyrocketed, and I was more awake than I'd ever been.

"Chels," he whispered eventually.

"Coll," I whispered back.

"Are you awake?"

"Of course I'm awake."

His laughter was breathy, and it raised goose bumps along my arms. "I'm not ready for this night to be over," he said, his voice low and slow. "I don't want to be apart from you yet."

My breath hitched, and I was sure he heard it. "Me neither," I confessed, paralyzed by the thought of what might happen next. I didn't move a muscle, fearful of anything that would break the spell.

"C'mere to me," he whispered, and I unraveled.

I leaned over the side of the bed to get a glimpse of him, and a bar of neon light from the window split his face in two, illuminating one bottle-green eye and almost an entire summer of want.

Without another word, I lowered myself down the ladder and climbed into bed beside him. There was nothing left to say that couldn't be said with our bodies, even just with the simple act of sleeping side by side.

We folded ourselves into each other under the covers, and I savored the instant warmth of his arm around me as I settled my head on his chest. I was worried my mess of hair might be a nuisance, but the way he gently untangled the ends as he ran his fingers through it told me he didn't mind.

"Tell me another fairy story," I whispered after a while. My eyes were heavy, but I still wasn't ready to end the night. This was what I wanted to remember. "I'm starting to really like them, you know."

"Never thought I'd hear you say that." His soft laugh rumbled in my ear.

"Me neither," I said. "Though I also never would have thought we'd be here, so I guess we're full of surprises."

"Where, in Dublin you mean?" he asked, and I pinched his

ribs. He squirmed for a second, only to pull me closer when he recovered. "No, I know what you mean. Here in bed together, like."

"Exactly."

"You aren't wishing you were somewhere else, are ya?"

"No," I said, wondering if he could hear my smile. "I'm not. For what might be the first time since I've gotten to Ireland, I'm exactly where I want to be."

He pressed his lips to the top of my head, inhaling slowly in a way that told me I wasn't the only one savoring this.

"This is one I used to tell my sisters as a bedtime story when they were young," he said, slipping easily into the voice he saved for storytelling. "They were always asleep before the ending, and something tells me you might be the same. But I'll crack on."

I closed my eyes so the only sensations I noticed were the sound of his voice and the feel of his warm hand tracing idle patterns on my back as he spoke.

"This one'll be the story of Connla and the Fairy Maiden," he said. I tried hard to stay awake as I listened, imagining this man, this golden-haired son of a fighter, and his encounters with the Fairy Maiden.

I drifted in and out, catching something about the dreaded defiance of family but the undeniable allure of paradise. It would be the choice of a lifetime for Connla, between loyalty, logic, and the promise of pleasure. I couldn't decide what choice I hoped he would make. But, just like Collin's sisters, I was asleep before the end.

Chapter 17

I was awake an hour before my alarm. Rather than study my notes for the interview, I studied the way the sun cast a sliver of light across Collin's chest. For a few glorious minutes, it was like the interview didn't exist. Like the only things on Earth were that bar of sunlight and the freckles under Collin's eyes. There was a nearly unrecognizable feeling coursing through me, likely the result of the best night's sleep I'd gotten in months.

In those glorious minutes, I realized what I had to do.

Perhaps I'd even known it last night, only I wasn't ready to admit it then. Now, however, I didn't have the luxury of time. I had to make a decision, and it was as clear to me as the blue sky beyond the curtain.

I was canceling the interview.

Sending the email didn't take more than a minute or two, but I had a feeling it would take a little longer to unpack once I finally said it out loud. Collin must have felt me staring, because the room was otherwise still silent, but he stirred all the same, opening one clear eye and pinning me with his gaze.

"Why are you looking at me like that?" he asked, opening

the other eye and propping himself up on his elbows. "What's wrong?"

"I canceled the interview," I blurted.

He shot up, so close to me he nearly knocked our heads together. "You what?"

"It was a bullshit job, anyway." I shrugged, fighting a smile at the look on his face.

"The job you were so worried about yesterday? The one you've spent days preparing to interview for?" He rubbed his eyes, whether to rid them of sleep or to make sense of what I was saying I wasn't sure.

"I mean, the job isn't bullshit, but it was bullshit for *me*. It was in hospitality, sure, but it was on the corporate side, which I never even pictured myself doing. It's not like it's that event planning one I've been dying to interview for. It's just another random job in a series of random jobs."

"So why did you apply?"

"Haven't you been listening all summer?" I laughed. "To get my plan back on track."

"But I thought that plan was to get a job you *wanted*," he said. "Unless I'm wrong? Have I misunderstood something?"

"No, no. I think *I* misunderstood something," I said. "Or rather lost sight of something. I almost missed out on an incredible night because I've been so strung out over a job that I'm not even interested in just because it's in Boston."

"But you *didn't* miss out on the night," he said. "Chelsea of a month ago wouldn't have even considered it. You haven't lost sight of anything, you've just gained perspective."

"You don't think I've made the wrong decision?" I bit my lip. The decision came easily, but the aftermath had more waves than I'd anticipated. "Like I've changed too much and now I'm doing things that are out of character?"

"Of course you haven't failed, Chels. Traveling is *supposed* to change how we see things. That's why we do it. What good would seeing the world be if it didn't alter our perspectives? And besides, making a difficult decision in your best interest is the opposite of failing yourself."

"How do you always know the exact right thing to say?"

"Helps that you're letting me get to know you." His voice softened to match the morning light, and it took everything in me not to collapse back into his arms and spend the rest of the day in bed.

"They're going to think I'm such an idiot."

"Then it's a good thing you don't want the job, anyway." He smiled, pushing my hair out of my face. "Your perfect job is out there somewhere, Chelsea. And you're way too good to settle. It'll come."

Somewhere in the unseen depths of my brain, I wondered if it might already be here.

"Let's take your mind off it," he said suddenly, getting out of bed and running his hands through his hair. He was the embodiment of the energy coursing through me, and his suggestion made me eager to channel it into anything other than overthinking my decision.

"I like the sound of that. What do you have in mind?"

"How d'you feel about a roast?"

"A what?"

"God, Chels, could you even pretend you know anything about this country?" He shook his head. "A Sunday roast. Big bit of meat, roasted potatoes, some veg, that kind of thing.

Whole families get together, have some drinks. It's tradition. And I do think you could use something immersive today."

"And where do we do this roast?" I could feel the energy practically buzzing off his body. Whether it was from waking up next to each other or the adrenaline from canceling the interview, there was an undeniable energy to the morning neither of us could resist.

He sat back down next to me, leveling his eyes with mine. "I was thinking we could go to my family's house. Back out west, just past Limerick there, out in the countryside."

"Like . . . with your family?" Was this what I thought it was?

"I mean, yeah, it is their house and everything. And it's the best way to do a traditional roast. But it doesn't have to be a formal 'meet the family' kind of thing. It can just be a casual Irish education kind of thing. Though I do think it would be nice to introduce ya, while you're still here. Unless it's too much and you'd rather do it down the pub?"

"I'd love to," I said, surprising us both. "To do it at your family's house, I mean. Not the pub. If I'm going to have the experience, I want it to be authentic. And I think meeting them sounds nice."

"You don't think it'd be too much?"

"We've already shared a bed, haven't we? What's a little family time?" I shrugged to emphasize how not-a-big-deal this was, arguably more for my sake than Collin's.

"You know, Chels, you're being surprisingly casual about this."

"I'm a casual woman." He laughed a bit too hard for comfort. "Or at least I'm trying to be," I added.

"Since when? Five minutes ago?"

"People can change, can't they?"

"So it's a yes?"

"Will you stop looking at me like that if it is?"

"You don't like how I look at you?" He flicked his eyes down to my lips, almost imperceptibly, then back up to my eyes.

"It's a yes," I said, hoping to dodge his question.

"I should warn you though," he said. "They aren't perfect."

"No family is."

"They can just be a bit, I don't know, rough around the edges."

"All families are. Are you trying to change my mind?"

"No, no. I'm just trying to make sure you know what you're agreeing to."

"Are they ax murderers?"

"What? Of course not."

"Then I'm not worried about what I'm agreeing to," I said. I thought back to last night and our conversation about expectations and disappointments, and I tried not to hold it against them that they could possibly be disappointed by Collin.

Who cared if they were rough around the edges? The same could be said for my mother, especially when she met someone new. I didn't mind, because they were important to Collin, and what was important to Collin was quickly becoming important to me.

"Right, then." He exhaled, and a smile formed on his face. "I promised Lars my truck this afternoon though, so it'll be the train from Galway for us. But you'll love the ride."

If he'd been right about one thing, regardless of how hard I'd tried to fight it, it was that I'd been loving the ride.

On the drive back to Galway, I thought back to my own childhood home. One look at my small bedroom with its figure skating trophies, bat mitzvah photos, and the acoustic guitar I bought in high school but hardly ever played would tell you nearly everything you wanted to know about me. And that's without even talking to my parents. One conversation with them and you'd know more than I was ever willing to share. I wondered if Collin's home was the same way. I wondered if I was prepared to know him on a deeper level. And I wondered how much harder that would make leaving.

The train station was quiet on a Sunday morning, so we spoke in hushed tones as we grabbed two coffees for the ride and waited on the platform. When the train arrived, I watched the way the wind ruffled his hair, remembering how it felt in my hands the night of the ceilidh.

We wandered the length of a few cars, scanning either side to find two seats next to each other. The entire train was upholstered in a pattern likely chosen to hide any stains, but it was still cleaner and quieter than any form of public transportation I'd taken in the States.

"Aye, these are perfect," Collin said as we finally approached an empty pair. "Big nice window for ya. You'll get some brilliant views on this ride."

I slid into the window seat, shoving my tote under the seat in front of me and making myself comfortable. As the train dragged itself from the station, Collin nudged me with his shoulder. "All right, no going back now," he said.

"Should I want to?"

"I'd hope not." His eyes were so earnest it formed a knot in my chest.

"I'm sure it'll be grand," I said, trying to ease the tension in his shoulders.

"God, I love when you say that. *Grand.* Like you're a local."

His compliment, while it made my face warm, tightened the knot. I wasn't a local, and I could never be a local, and I feared he wished it was different. Wished I was different.

As the train reached a steady pace and the countryside began to stretch itself beyond the windows, he rested his hand on my knee, like it was something he'd been doing all his life. The weight of it steadied my nerves. I vowed to get carried away in the views, counting the shades of green to keep my brain from ruining the moment.

It only took a mile or so for Collin to be right about the landscape. The hills tumbled over one another, reaching higher as they moved farther away from the tracks. Farmland spread in all directions, and I allowed myself to slip into a daydream about what it might be like to live on the land. No corporate ladder, no coworkers, no ridiculously expensive Whole Foods groceries. Just land and sky and baking bread and drinking tea by the fireplace.

They might have been onto something after all.

"Brilliant, isn't it?" Collin whispered, like he was trying to wake me gently from my daydream.

"Seriously. The countryside in Massachusetts looks nothing like this. It's all grubby old farms and cemeteries and creepy abandoned houses."

"So you're finally seeing Ireland is better after all?"

"Just the countryside," I said. "Let's not get ahead of ourselves."

"Are you sure about that?" His voice was measured, and I knew what was coming.

"I used to be," I confessed.

"And now?"

"Now I do things like cancel interviews and have summer flings with men who ask too many questions."

"And how do you feel about that version of you?" He was obviously determined to live up to his reputation.

"It's unfamiliar," I said eventually. "This version of myself. If you told me a few months ago I'd be here with you, I would have said you were insane."

"And if I told you a few months ago that you'd be moving to Ireland? What would you have thought then?"

"Will I be meeting your sisters today?" I asked instead of answering his question. I didn't want to think about what my former self would think about Ireland.

"Yes, but you don't get to ask any other questions about them until you answer mine."

"That doesn't seem fair," I said.

"Nothing's fair," he said. "Something else I've learned from my sisters." I could see how much he loved them in his smile.

"I'd have thought you were insane then too," I answered. "So maybe the insane one is me."

"Surely there are worse things in the world than being a little insane. That's what got you here, isn't it?"

"Yes, but the effects of this whole experiment remain to be seen. This might have been a colossal mistake, and then my insanity would be working against me."

"Do you really believe that?" he asked. I knew his tone was hushed so as not to disturb other travelers, but it only added to the gravitas.

I sighed. "A mistake, no." I looked back out the window. "I'm beginning to think it's going to be a bit harder to go home than I originally planned," I said eventually. "I thought I would be running out of here and back to Boston, you know? That I'd be dying to get back to my real life. But the longer I'm here, and the more invested I get in the Wanderer, it's becoming harder to even determine which life is my 'real' one anymore."

"Why does it matter?" he asked. "What's the big concern with 'real'?"

"I can't live in a fantasy," I said.

"Is that what this is?" I opened my mouth, but he interrupted. "Don't try to convince me otherwise, Chels. Not if it's the truth. I don't know why you can't just admit you like it here."

"Because it wasn't the plan," I said, for the first time hating how it sounded. "And I know you think plans are stupid, but they're important to me. I had goals. I *have* goals. And the longer I spend here, the more they feel like they're slipping away."

"I don't think plans are stupid," he clarified, "but I do think plans can change. And I think it wouldn't kill ya to go easier on yourself. Be more flexible, you know? It's okay to have to adjust your plans."

I stared back out the window, watching heavy clouds darkening the sky. The weather moved twice as fast here as it did at home, but everything else moved twice as slow. This made the weather feel even more extreme, and I had a sinking feeling I'd miss it when I left. There was something cathartic about sudden heaving rain.

The more time I spent here, the less I understood why I was so desperate to get back to my stupid plans. They were nothing more than logical, calculated, tactical moves I'd attached myself to because I was convinced they would make me happy.

I wasn't ready to give them up entirely, but I might be ready to alter them. To loosen the reins a little. Consider other options. Maybe not Wanderer-related options, but options that include flexibility and grace and forgiveness.

"Why couldn't you stay?" he asked. "Would that really be so bad?"

I leaned my head against the back of the seat, closing my eyes for a few seconds to collect myself.

"It just wouldn't be realistic," I said, trying to tread lightly. "It would be a massive change. I can't just leave my friends and my family to work at a hostel halfway across the world just because I've had a fun summer."

"Why do you always say 'work at a hostel' like that?" His tone took a sharper edge.

"Like what?"

"Like it's beneath you."

"Collin, I didn't mean to," I said, wondering how many times he's had this thought before. My heart sped up at the thought. "There's nothing wrong with the work you do."

"I don't think I'm the one who needs convincing," he said, and we lapsed into silence while his words settled in my chest like bricks.

On cue, raindrops began pelting the windows of the train, and I tracked their movements as they raced to the bottom of the glass. Their paths were erratic. They changed direction halfway down the window, joined together and broke apart, sped up and slowed down with no real rhyme or reason.

"And if you think the reason we're all at the Wanderer is for work," Collin whispered after a moment, "then you haven't gotten to know us at all. And if you ever do decide to stay, it will be when *you* realize it isn't about the work either."

Nothing I could have said would have been adequate, so I didn't try. Instead, I settled lower in the seat and let my head drop to Collin's shoulder. His hand returned to my knee, and I was relieved he seemed to understand I had nothing left to say.

Most of the ride following our conversation passed in a comfortable silence, and he seemed to cheer up significantly as we approached his stop.

"All right," he said, sitting straight up in his seat and shaking the kinks from his neck. "Remember, Da can be a bit unpredictable, but it's nothing personal. He's harmless, really. Just a bit of an old bloke." I nodded. "And Aileen is going to act like my mam, as always, even though she's younger. And both she and Niamh are going to ask you a million questions that may or may not be appropriate, so feel free to ignore them. Especially Niamh."

I shifted uncomfortably, hating the idea of being asked inappropriate questions by strangers but hating the idea of ignoring any of Collin's family members even more. "Trust me," he said, sensing my discomfort. "I ignore them all the time. They're used to it by now. But they're excited to meet you. All of 'em. No need to be nervous. It'll be grand."

Something in his voice wasn't entirely convincing.

The train groaned to a stop beside a small redbrick structure that I'd hardly have described as a train station so much as a large toolshed. Inside was little more than a pair of turnstiles and an old woman dozing in a ticket booth.

"Welcome to the suburbs." Collin gestured with his arms in both directions. His wide, lopsided grin eased my increasing anxiety, and I accepted his proffered hand. "It's just a couple minutes down the road there," he said, handing me a newspaper from a stack near the exit. "And the rain isn't lashing yet or anything. All right for a walk?"

It was then that I realized the newspaper was to hold over my head to protect myself from the rain. He was right, it wasn't lashing, but it was definitely coming down hard enough to ruin my hair. "You can't be serious." I looked at him with disbelief. "I can't show up to meet your family for the first time like a wet shaggy dog."

"I've seen you after a rainstorm," he said, "and I can assure you, the rain works for ya."

The knot in my stomach turned to a flutter at the compliment then back to a knot when I realized he was serious. "We can't call an Uber or something?"

"Aye, sure, what with all the Ubers in the Irish suburbs. Shouldn't be a problem at all." He took out his phone and pretended to open an app I knew he didn't have. I nearly swatted it out of his hands.

"All right, all right," I said. "I get it. Walking it is, then. But give me another newspaper. My hair looks good today."

BEYOND THE STATION, the streets were a mix of paved roads and dirt-covered footpaths. We kicked mud into our shoes as we hustled in the direction of his house, sidestepping puddles and ducking under low-hanging tree branches. A collection of two-story homes lined the main road, smoke rising from their chimneys and mixing with the clouds. I wished it wasn't raining so hard so I could take a good look around. I imagined every iteration of Collin walking through these streets.

By the time we arrived on the doorstep, raindrops clung to our eyelashes, and our chests heaved with deep breaths from the run. I tried to get a good view of the house from the step, wanting to remember every detail. It was a humble whitewashed stone cottage off the main street, complete with window boxes and a thatched roof. The front garden was unruly; rusty tools littered the wet grass among giant weeds and overgrown shrubbery. There were only a few other cottages lining the street, and had I not done the walk myself I wouldn't have believed there was a train station only minutes away.

"It's not much," Collin said, watching me study the house. I hated how insecure he sounded.

"Collin," I said, "it's amazing. It's so charming. Every house in my neighborhood growing up looked exactly alike. Every house in America looks exactly alike, frankly. When you told me your family had a house outside the city, this is exactly what I hoped it would be."

"Let's see if you feel the same after we're done here." He smiled. "Ready?" I nodded, and he opened the front door.

We were greeted by the sound of Irish folk music and an intoxicating mixture of smells, both of which felt so homely I forgot I'd never been here before.

"Is that Collin there?" we heard a woman ask from the kitchen. "No, Da, at the door. You didn't hear the door? Niamh, did you hear the door? Coll, is that you there?"

"Aye, it is us!" Collin called back down the hallway, shaking water from his hair and leaving his shoes on a mat near the door. I did the same, stealing a glance at myself in the mirror on the wall and immediately regretting it. My hair was at once matted to my head and frizzing in all directions, and my mascara was halfway to my cheeks. With a quick swipe under both eyes and a claw clip in my hair, I was as presentable as I was going to get.

"He is here!" the woman, whom I assumed to be Aileen, shouted across the house. "I told you, Da. Niamh, they're here!"

"We hear ye, Aileen, we hear ye," Collin's dad answered from a room off the entryway. "What's the use for shoutin' in a house this small?"

"The use is that no one ever listens otherwise," Aileen said, rounding the corner of the kitchen and coming into view. Collin was right about her acting like a mother. She was about half Collin's height and wore messy, dark curls in a clip at the back of her head. "Look who made it down from the big city," she said, pulling him into a hug.

"I'd hardly call Galway 'the big city,'" he said with a chuckle. "Aileen, this is Chelsea."

"I bloody know who this is," she said, wiping her hands on her apron and pulling me into a hug the same way she did Collin. "Nice to meet ya, Chelsea."

"Nice to meet you too. Thank you so much for having me for the roast. The house smells incredible," I said.

"Aye, about time someone appreciates my cooking," she said, giving Collin a once-over. "I like her already."

"It's only because she hasn't eaten it yet," he said.

"Fuck off, then."

"You fuck off."

"Don't talk to yer sister like that," said Collin's dad, making his way into the foyer from what I glimpsed was a living room. "Welcome home, son." They clapped their hands together and leaned in for an awkward hug before Collin presented me the same way he had to Aileen. "Da, Chelsea. Chelsea, Da."

"Cormac," he said, extending his hand. "Pleasure to have ye. Where the hell is Niamh?" he asked before we finished shaking hands, turning his attention to the stairs. "Niamh, get down here. Yer brother and his girlfriend are here."

"Oh, I'm not—"

"Da, come on—"

Collin and I started at the same time, which made Aileen laugh. "Oh, boy," she said, turning back to the kitchen. "This is going to be fun."

I looked at Collin for reassurance, and he rolled his eyes behind his sister's back. "She's being dramatic," he whispered. "It's going to be fine."

"I heard that!" she called over her shoulder.

As I followed Collin down the hall and into the kitchen, I took stock of the photos on the walls and any evidence of his childhood. The frames were crooked and a layer of dust coated the glass, but I could make out a sandy-blond toddler with rolled pants and his hands in the mud, unmistakably the same Collin as the man standing in front of me. There were also a handful of photos of his sisters, clearly outside in their front yard, and even some of the four of them, but a noticeable lack of photos of his mother.

Her absence was not lost on me, and I remembered Collin telling me the night he braided my hair that she wasn't around much. I wondered if I might find out why today.

The kitchen was cozy and cluttered the way a kitchen is when it's been used for generations. Cookbooks sat atop the cabinets collecting the same dust as the frames in the hallway; pots and pans hung from the ceiling with rusted, chipped bottoms; sweaters draped over the backs of mismatched kitchen chairs; an ancient iron kettle boiled on the gas stove. It was like a painting.

"D'you cook, Chelsea?"

"Aye, we aren't starting—"

"I wasn't asking you," Aileen said, waving Collin off.

"Not well," I admitted. "But I'd be happy to help today wherever I can."

"But she won't, because she's the guest," Collin said to Aileen, throwing a glance over his shoulder at me. "Make yourself comfortable, Chels. I'll make you a tea."

"Tea sounds grand, thanks." Niamh appeared in the kitchen with soaking wet hair and an oversize hoodie, pinching Collin's cheek as she passed him. "Glad to see you haven't forgotten your family after all."

"I call you three all the time, do I not?"

"But ya never come around anymore, do ya? Maybe we have Chelsea to thank for this visit." She extended her hand to me and I shook it, feeling the weight of her rings against my fingers. "Niamh," she said.

"It's a pleasure."

"Tell us," she said. "How'd you convince our brother to get his arse back home for a roast? Unless, of course—as his family—we don't want to know." She wiggled her thick eyebrows, and Aileen elbowed her in the ribs.

"Niamh, be normal for once, would ya?" she said.

"No one in this house knows the meaning of normal," Niamh said. "Don't pretend."

They mumbled something to each other in Irish before Collin cleared his throat and changed the subject. I tried not to think about what they might have been saying.

"It really does smell great, Leen," Collin said, crossing to the stove. "What've you got on?"

"You know, the usual, there. Roast potatoes, turnips, and the like. It's beef this time. Hope you aren't a vegetarian, Chelsea."

"Nope." Even if I was, I'd have lied just to be agreeable.

"Grand," she said. "Coll, fix us some drinks, will you? I reckon we don't need to bother with a tea. Might as well get right to the good stuff."

Aileen was my kind of girl, after all. Nobody objected, so I figured we needed something to take the edge off. As Collin poured gin and tonics, we gathered around a small fireplace on sunken sofas and floor cushions while Aileen finished cooking.

Cormac hadn't said much since we arrived, but I could tell he was listening from the armchair in the corner. Niamh, on the other hand, was as intense as Collin had described.

"So, Chelsea, what is it that brought you to Galway?" She looked up from swirling her cocktail and locked eyes with me, taking a long, slow sip. I told her my story, trying to make it sound more like an adventure and less like a last resort.

"So you ran away," she said when I finished.

"Niamh," Collin said, his voice sterner than I'd heard it before.

"What? That's how it sounds, isn't it? Besides, there's nothing wrong with running away. Collin did the same thing years ago, didn't you, Coll?"

"I hardly ran away," Collin said, changing his position twice on the couch. "I took a job I was good at and made a life for myself. Shame on me if I didn't want to stay in this village forever."

"Reckon you're too good for this village, then, do ya?" she asked.

"That's enough, Niamh," Cormac said from his chair, looking up only to make eye contact with his daughter.

"Da's right," Collin said. "We've had this bloody conversation a million times, so we won't be doing it again." He looked at me and I tried to unclench my jaw so he wouldn't notice how tense I felt, but it wouldn't budge. And by the looks of him, neither would his. "Besides," he added, "it isn't running away if you plan on going back."

"I know you aren't talking about yourself, there," Niamh said, and Collin nodded, tight-lipped. "Where's home then, Chelsea?"

"Boston."

"And what's waiting for ya back there in Boston?"

That was the million-dollar question, wasn't it? I hesitated, unable to put together a semblance of an answer quick enough to appear engaged in this rapid-fire conversation.

"Her real life," Collin said, sarcastic emphasis on the word *real*. "The one with the job and the friends and family and that."

"And you didn't find that here?" Niamh asked. "I mean, you've been here, what? Since the start of summer? That's proper long enough, isn't it?"

I tried to laugh, but it came out forced and dry.

"It's been plenty long, actually. I've met some incredible people this summer." I nudged Collin with my knee, but he didn't move a muscle. My palms started to sweat, and I tried to regain my composure. "The plan was always just for this move to be a summer thing. It was never supposed to be full-time. And I like sticking to a plan. I'm not good with big life changes." I knew I was probably saying too much, but I was too nervous to stop myself.

"Moving to Ireland must have been a big life change though, was it not?"

"God, Niamh, must you ask so many questions?" Collin asked. "It's only a Sunday roast, like. It's not an interrogation."

"Forgive me, but it's the first time you've brought a girl home in—well—ever, so I'm sorry, but I'd like to get to know her."

He'd never brought anyone home before?

"Maybe there's a reason for that," he said. "And most people get to know people by asking about their hobbies or their interests or other normal things. Not their big life plans."

"I'm not most people."

Based on the way they were scowling at each other, if I didn't know Collin was years older, I'd have thought they were twins. I tried to focus on the similarities in their faces, their sharp jaws and faded freckles, so I wouldn't have to focus on how uncomfortable I was feeling.

"I could use a hand in here if anyone's got a minute," Aileen called from the kitchen.

"Coming!" I shouted, jumping up from the couch a bit too quickly.

"You don't have to," Collin said, doing the same.

"I want to."

An apology crossed his face, and I tried to communicate that I understood without either of us having to speak. He did warn me they were a bit tough, but I didn't expect unpacking my uncertain future with near strangers before we even sat down to eat.

"Chelsea, grand, come here," Aileen said as soon as I entered the kitchen. "Have you made custard before?"

"I'm not even sure I've even eaten custard before, if I'm honest."

"No bother," she said, laughing. "I'll teach you."

The kitchen already felt like much safer ground. While Aileen's maternal nature probably drove Collin insane, it felt like a warm blanket to me.

"We're going to cheat a bit here," she said, "because judging by the sound of the living room, we need to crack on." When I didn't answer right away, she rested a hand on my shoulder. "I'm sorry about Niamh. I'm sure Collin gave ya a warning, but she's been edgier than usual lately."

"Oh, it's fine," I said. "Really."

"Nah, it's a lot, I know. Our mam isn't around much, as I'm sure you know, and it's hit Niamh a bit harder than the rest of us, even as an adult." As she spoke, she produced a red canister from the cabinet and fished around the powder inside for a plastic scoop. "Here," she said, handing me the scoop and gesturing to the powder. "Drop two scoops of this into that bowl there."

I did as I was told, trying to figure out if there was a way to ask about their mother without seeming nosy. Fortunately, Aileen didn't need any prompting.

"She's got distant relatives all over the country," Aileen continued. "Our mam, I mean. Aunts, uncles, cousins. We've not met most of them. And she does some odd jobs on the road, like. Sales and stuff. Just one of those mams who isn't really keen on being a mam all the time, that's all. Been this way since we were weans. Collin and I got used to it, but I'm not sure Naimh ever will. Here, add this jug of milk."

"That must have been hard," I said as I stirred the milk into the powder. I watched it turn into a pudding-like texture, thankful to have a task to keep me occupied.

"I don't blame Collin for leaving," she said. "It was hard for him to stay here. He felt responsible for everyone, you know? That's a lot for a kid. So he left for Galway after he was done with school. And he comes home more often than we make it seem. We're just slagging him off. He's a good lad."

"He is," I agreed, handing her the bowl.

"D'you fancy each other?" she whispered. "I know we've all been a bit nosy, but I can't help myself." She ran a finger around the side of the bowl, tasting the custard.

"It's complicated," I whispered back, hoping he wouldn't hear. "Honestly, the fancying is the easy part. It's my impending return to America making it a bit more difficult."

"If you want my advice, which I doubt you do because you

didn't ask, it would be to focus on the easy part. Life is already so hard. If you have something easy, you should enjoy it."

She was right, wasn't she?

"Like this custard," she said, handing me a spoon. "Taste. Two ingredients and just a bit of mixing." I took a bite, letting the sweetness settle on my tongue. "Deadly, isn't it? And hardly any effort at all."

"I see what you're getting at." I smiled. "Very clever."

"Listen, Chelsea, you obviously know yourself. You seem terribly clever and I've only just met you this afternoon. But I've a good feeling about this, and I sense that you do too. I'd hate to see you two get in your own way."

I looked through the kitchen and into the living room, where Collin and Niamh had clearly made up. They were playing cards on the low coffee table while Cormac changed the record. While it might have looked like a snapshot of the perfect scene, it was just that: a snapshot. I understood what Collin meant when he said home wasn't stable for everyone. The love in the room was undeniable, but so was the tension, and I imagined returning to that would have been difficult for anybody.

Collin looked up just in time to catch my eye, and his wink warmed me to the core. If Aileen's warmth was a blanket, Collin's was a raging fire.

"Roast is on," Aileen called into the living room, saving me from having to respond. I had thought she'd called me into the kitchen to save me from the budding living room fiasco, but now I realized it might have been to share some insight on Collin. Smart woman. "Come on." She nudged me, nodding toward the table. "A little food should put everyone to rights. Let's eat."

WE CHATTED OVER ONE ANOTHER as we passed heaping serving dishes around the table, taking turns scooping roasted vegetables and pouring gravy onto each other's plates. "You gotta cover the whole thing," Collin said as he wielded the gravy boat over a plate that already had more food than I could eat in days. "That's the proper way to eat a roast."

"And that's why we're here, isn't it? For the authenticity?"

"Right you are," he said. "And spending time with this lot is about as authentic as it gets."

"I'm going to take that as a compliment." Aileen smiled. "Chelsea, spend a little more time with us and you'll be a proper Irishwoman in no time."

"Aye, they say it takes falling in love with an Irishman for that," Niamh said, shoving a piece of a potato into her mouth. Had I started eating yet, I would have choked.

"And they say ye have to see twelve wild horses first to fall in love with an Irishman, don't they, then?" Cormac said. "Have ye seen any horses, Chelsea?"

"She'll not be seeing any horses, and she'll not be worried about falling in love, either," Collin said, forcing a laugh and peeling a Yorkshire pudding apart with his long fingers. "I'm begging you lot to talk about something normal."

I could have kissed him right at the table for saving me. The last thing I needed was to be roped into a conversation about love with Collin's family when all this was supposed to be was a summer fling. As a notoriously terrible liar, there was no way to hide that I might be worried about falling in love after all.

Fortunately, Aileen was right about the meal. Once everyone started eating, the food did a better job taking the edge off than the booze. I savored the silence while we chewed, and

I listened while the Finegans told stories of past roasts and reminisced on cooking experiments gone wrong.

"Remember when Niamh didn't rinse any of the veg from the garden and there was a layer of dirt on the bottom of the roasting pan?" Collin chortled, leaning back in his chair.

"Oh, fuck off, would ya? It wasn't as bad as the time you were too cheap to go to the good butcher, so you bought that hunk of beef from the market by the train station."

Even Cormac laughed at this one, and I felt the tension from earlier easing with every bite shared and story told. It reminded me of my own family back in Boston. Meals were as essential to Jewish culture as they seemed to be for the Irish, and the moment of connection made me feel at once homesick and at home.

It was a complicated afternoon.

As we finished piling the last of the dishes on the counter, before Aileen shooed us from the kitchen so she could clean in peace, she grabbed my shoulders with damp hands and stared right at me. "It was grand having you here today, Chelsea," she said.

"It was great to be here. Thank you for having me. And for everything." We exchanged knowing smiles.

"You won't forget the recipe for the custard, will you?"

"Would it matter?" Collin added, joining us at the counter. "It's right on the side of the carton there."

"I won't," I said, ignoring his comment but leaning into his hand on my back.

"Right, then," Aileen smiled. "Off you go. Don't want to miss the train back to the big city."

"Do come back soon, will you?" Niamh asked. "Both of you."

"Aye," Cormac said from his chair.

We promised we would, but we both knew it wasn't the truth. I'd be back to Boston in a few short weeks, and all this would be behind me. Behind both of us.

THE JOURNEY BACK TO GALWAY was slow and quiet, and my heart was as heavy as my head on the train window.

That heaviness, I realized eventually, wasn't because of my uncertain future. It was because spending the day with Collin's family, piecing together the parts of his past that made him the way he is, only made me like him more.

Anyone who had a summer fling and came out unscathed couldn't have felt a fraction of how I was feeling. If I thought moving to Ireland alone was getting in over my head, it was only because I had no idea what falling for Collin Finegan would feel like.

By the time we returned to the Wanderer, my food hangover had subsided and newfound energy coursed through me. I'd spent too much of the day, too much of the summer, frankly, feeling pensive and confused and sorry for myself, and it was time I listened to Aileen and got out of my own way.

"Feel like another drink before we go up?" I asked Collin once we got into the lobby. If I'd learned anything so far, it was that if I was already in too deep, the least I could do was enjoy the ride. "I'd offer to buy you one as a thank-you, but you tend the bar, so."

"You know I'll never say no to that." He smiled. I'd hoped he hadn't wanted the night to end either. "And you don't have to thank me. If anything, I should thank you for putting up with them. I know they were a bit much today."

"I liked them," I said, turning toward the door that led to the bar. "Come on. We can thank each other."

"I like the sound of that." He pulled open the heavy door and ushered me inside.

Sunday nights were often quiet in the bar as most of our guests turned over Monday morning, and this Sunday was no different. A new hire was behind the bar, and a few tired guests occupied the stools.

"What d'you think about taking these drinks to go?" Collin asked, looking around. It wasn't crowded, but I didn't think that was why he asked.

"Sound," I said, precisely because I knew the effect the Irish slang would have on him.

"If you're talking like that, it's a right good thing we're getting out of here."

I swallowed the lump of anticipation in my throat, watching him order the drinks without making small talk with the bartender. He meant business.

We left with two bottles of something local, wordlessly making our way to the staff wing. I'd hoped we were heading to his room, because I left mine in a state of disarray trying to find something to wear to the roast.

When we got to the hallway, Collin took out his keys and I breathed a sigh of relief. He raised his eyebrows and nodded in the direction of his door, and I nodded in return.

I'd never seen the inside of his room, and it left me mildly surprised. It was immaculate, and the walls bore only a few faded postcards from faraway places and a framed print of the first page of a book I didn't recognize. The layout of our rooms was almost the same, except his had a window seat that overlooked the courtyard.

I made my way to the window and leaned out, using the fresh air to steady my nerves. "It's nice in here," I said. "You keep it so neat." I sat in the sill, bringing my knees up to my chest and leaning my head on the wall.

"After seeing my childhood home, I'm sure you can imagine why," he said. "Too much clutter growing up. Niamh had more stuff than the rest of us combined, so it was a proper treat to move away and have my own space."

"You didn't have a lot of that growing up?" I asked. "Space, I mean?"

"Unfortunately not," he said, shaking his head. "How about yourself?"

"I had too much space when I think about it. No siblings, just me and my parents. Well, Ada, who is basically like a sister, but no one else in the house. It was quiet."

"Ah, that explains why it was so difficult for you to adjust to hostel life," he said. I hadn't thought about it like that before, but he was right.

"And your upbringing explains why you like it so much, doesn't it?" I was working through the realization aloud, but he didn't seem to mind. "You grew up in a house that was noisy and dynamic, and even though you wanted to get away from them, you didn't want to escape that lifestyle entirely?"

"Bang on," he said. "Took me a while to admit that myself, if I'm honest."

"Things like that are always easier to see from the outside."

"By this point, Chels, I reckon you're on the inside."

I stared at him for a few seconds, trying to take in exactly how it felt to be let in by Collin Finegan. He seemed so open on the surface, but I was beginning to see layers beneath I knew weren't on display for everyone.

"I've been dreaming of this since the first night you got here," he said, pushing a curl behind my ear.

"You have not." I smiled, wanting him to tell me it was true.

"I swear," he said, crossing his heart. "I couldn't take my eyes off ya, Chels. Really. And it only got worse the more I got to know you."

"And where do you stand now?" I asked, holding my breath while I waited for a response. There was no going back. I'd gotten out of my own way, cleared a path, and now I had to see where it led.

"I think we both know the answer to that," he said. He put his drink on the desk and joined me at the window. I sat up straighter, and he closed the gap between us. "But in case you don't, I stand at a crossroads." He ran his thumb over my jaw, letting his hand linger on the back of my neck. "On one side of the road, I want to pull you into me and hold you close, and on the other, I want to keep you at arm's length because I know you're going to take a part of me with you when you leave." I wrapped my fingers around his wrist, trying to memorize the feel of it in my hand, the feel of his hand on my neck, the feel of my heart in my chest. "And on both sides," he continued, "you're the only thing I've thought about since the day you walked in here. I've been falling in love with you since that moment in the hallway, and I know whether I pull you close or push you away, nothing is going to change that."

Time stopped. All summer we'd either been moving at a glacial pace or hurtling toward the end. But in this moment, I felt the peace and chaos usually found in the eye of a storm. It was time I danced in the rain.

With words stuck in my throat, I answered in the next best way I knew how. I put my hand in the same spot on the back of his neck and pulled his lips to mine, standing up to reach him. In an instant he had me out of the windowsill and pinned against the wall, hungry kisses tracing a path from my jaw to my throat. When I raked my hands through his hair, scratching his scalp with my nails, he turned me around and laid me on the bed beneath him.

If there was anything that mattered beyond these four walls, I had zero interest in it. For the first time all summer, it was just me and Collin. And I was prepared to savor it.

I studied the weight of his body, the way he felt with our hips in line, the feel of his kisses as they dropped from my sternum to my stomach and lower still. I studied the sounds that came from deep in his chest, the needy grasp of his hands, and the map of ink across his skin. The more I studied, the more I knew he wouldn't be the only one losing a piece of himself when I left.

"I haven't been able to stop thinking about this," he mumbled against my skin, his voice hoarse in the silence. "You feel even better than I imagined."

"I thought you were supposed to be the resident storyteller," I teased, sucking in a sharp breath when he sat up and grabbed his shirt between his shoulder blades, pulling it over his head in one swift motion. "Isn't imagination your thing?" I let my fingertips wander over his firm stomach, tracing their path with my gaze.

"Even I couldn't dream of something that feels this good." He wrapped his fingers around my wrist, stopping my hand in its path. "Look at me," he whispered, and I snapped my eyes to his before he could say anything else that would undo me, even though looking at him did just that. Hair a mess, pupils blown, wet lips parted, inhaling ragged breaths. "You don't know how badly I want you, Chelsea."

"So, show me," I whispered, my voice hoarse.

After another second of smoldering eye contact, his lips were back on mine, and every inch of me sought his touch. I wanted to know his body better than I knew my own, starting with the rippling muscles in his back, down his toned arms and his ribs and the flexed muscles of his stomach, until I got to where he was pressed against me, both of us already breathless at the contact.

We moved together as if we had done this a thousand times before. There was no learning curve or awkward fumbling. We filled the dark silence of the room with whispers of each other's names, and we didn't stop our wandering hands from wherever they wanted to go. Every touch was more electric than the last, and the entire summer crumbled around us. And we crumbled with it.

When he sat up and pulled me onto his lap, my legs wrapped around his back and our foreheads pressed against each other, I was certain I'd never been so close to someone in my life. Any barriers between us, any walls I'd been focused on building, were long gone. Even I couldn't deny that I should have torn them down a long time ago. Despite our closeness, we pulled each other tighter still, desperate to erase any semblance of separation. I ground my hips into his, matching his rhythm, threading my fingers through the tangles of his hair. His moans were muffled against my collarbone, and I knew it would take my body a lifetime to forget how that felt.

He leaned back, pulling me on top of him without missing a beat. I pressed my lips to the sharp hinge of his jaw, relishing the way he pushed into me, harder from this angle. I felt each thrust all the way through to my chest, and when I sat up and let my head fall back, I saw stars. He raked his hands up my stomach, settling them firmly on my rib cage before pulling me back to him. The pressure inside me continued to build with each low groan, until I was on the edge of losing all control.

His breath quickened as my legs started to shake, his fingers pressed hard enough into my hips to leave a bruise, and I wanted us to finish just as badly as I didn't. The night was passing in slow motion, and it still didn't feel long enough.

"God, Chelsea," he groaned at the exact moment a cry escaped my lips. I tried to keep my eyes open if only to watch the way his rolled back, but it wasn't long before I followed him into the dark.

I wasn't sure how long it was before our breathing slowed and we returned to Earth.

Eventually I pulled his shirt on and settled against him. With my head on his chest, I traced the eucalyptus leaves I'd been staring at all summer. I finally had answers. I knew how Collin's skin felt under my fingers, how he looked without clothes, what he sounded like in bed. And I knew I couldn't forget any of it if I wanted to. But at that moment, I couldn't imagine ever wanting to.

"What's this one?" I asked, running my fingers over a harp just below his ribs.

"That the harp there, is it?" His eyes were closed, and I was grateful I could stare undisturbed. I nodded against his chest, and he continued. "Another fairy story," he said, and I could hear his smile. "About the Harp of Dagda."

"Go on," I said.

"Dagda was one of the gods," he began. "Protected his tribe, like. And he had a harp that played only for him. The music made people feel things, you know? Transformed them. Until there was a proper battle with another tribe, and they got a hold of the harp. But eventually Dadga did what he had to do, got it back, and played them to sleep, returning to his tribe having won the battle and guaranteed their freedom."

"And the meaning of the tattoo?" I asked.

"Aye, telling the story is the easy part," he said. "The tattoo is just, ah, like a reminder to be more like Dadga. To protect people. To transform them, if I can."

I sat up on my elbows to look at him. "You don't sound as confident when you talk about yourself as you do when you tell the stories."

"Of course not," he said, finally opening his eyes. "The stories are easy. Nothing personal, just a bit of Irish folklore. Everyone can interpret them however they wish. Telling my own stories isn't quite the same."

"Do all the tattoos have a meaning like that?"

"Most," he said. "The Irish are symbolic people."

"So I'm learning."

"And I'm chuffed, Chels. I really am. I'd have hated if you'd spent this entire summer here and not embraced the country at all. It really is a beautiful place."

"It is," I agreed, dropping my head back to his chest and nestling back in the crook of his arm, "but I think I love the people more."

I could feel his smile against the top of my head. "Maybe you Americans aren't so bad either."

We drifted to sleep around sunrise, unable to hold off any longer. No matter how hard we tried to fight it, the morning was bound to come eventually.

Chapter 18

I was at the reception desk a few days after my night with Collin when my phone rang. I'd been floating in a heady cloud since then, vaguely disconnected from reality, so the professional tone on the other end of the line came as a shock.

"Good morning. This is Bridgette Gantz, hiring manager at Hotel Blue, calling for Ms. Chelsea Gold, please."

"This is she," I said, sitting bolt upright in the chair and trying to make sense of what I was hearing.

"Ms. Gold, hi." Her deep voice sounded like honey through the phone. "I'm glad I caught you. Do you have a minute?"

"I, uh, yes," I said, turning on the answering machine and stepping outside. "I do. Thanks so much for calling." I steeled myself for a rejection. It had been ages since I'd applied for the senior events planner job, and, surely, she was calling to inform me they'd given it to someone else.

"The pleasure is all mine. I want to apologize for the delay in our reaching back out to you regarding the senior events planner position. We had to put our hiring process on hold for some unforeseen renovations, but I hope you're still interested."

"I am, very much so," I assured her automatically, before I could consider the weight of my words. The new plan was only pursuing jobs I really wanted, wasn't it? And hadn't this been *the* job?

"Excellent," she said, her relief audible. "When will you be back in the country? Given the innately personal nature of our business, we generally do not conduct virtual interviews. We'd love to have you in for an interview on Friday, if at all possible."

Friday. Three days from today. Three days earlier than I'd planned to leave.

For the one job I'd been dreaming of since I'd seen the posting at the start of the summer.

"Friday sounds great," I assured her. "I'll be back by then, and I'm very much looking forward to it."

"As am I," she said. "I'll reach out via email this afternoon to confirm the timing. Between now and then, if you have any questions, please don't hesitate to reach out."

"Thank you."

"Thank *you* for your understanding and flexibility. I'll see you Friday. Safe travels home."

Home.

I wasn't sure how exactly we ended the call, because I nearly blacked out as reality set in. If I was going to fly home in time for the interview, that meant today was my last day working at the Wanderer.

I walked back inside on autopilot, returning to my body only when I registered Flo calling my name.

"Chelsea, hey." She put her hand to my elbow like she was approaching a wild animal. "What's going on?"

"I can't tell you," I whispered, looking around the lobby to see if anyone was listening.

"What do you mean you can't tell me? We keep secrets now?"

"I just can't," I said.

"Can you tell me why you can't?"

"Because I will cry at this desk and I'm so not prepared to cry at this desk today," I said, voice already wobbly. Her expression softened, which didn't help my case.

"Put the answering machine on," she said, abruptly grabbing my hand and pulling me around from the back of the desk. "We need pastries for this."

I did as I was told, letting her drag me down the hallway and into the kitchen.

In the kitchen, she shooed a prep cook out the side door, handed me a pain au chocolat, and hopped up on the steel workbench. "Okay," she said. "Talk to me, *cara*. What's going on?"

"I got an interview for that job," I whispered. "The one I thought I was underqualified for."

"The dream job?"

"That's the one," I said. She blew air through her full lips, trying as hard as I was to process what this meant. I figured the least I could do was help her along. "And I have to fly home on Thursday to interview on Friday."

"*Merda*."

"*Merda* is right." I dropped my head onto my folded arms. "If this was what I wanted the whole time, Flo, why does it hurt so bad to leave?"

"Oh, Chelsea. Look around. Whether you can admit it or not, you've built quite a life here in the past few months. Goodbyes are never easy."

"I can't believe I thought it would be," I said. "I feel so stupid." I thought back to that day in Boston when Helen and Jack told me they were closing O'Shea's. When I'd woken up thinking it was going to be such a good day. I should have learned then there was no use in trying to predict the future.

"No sense in any of that," Flo said, waving her hand. "When you first got here from Boston, you were only thinking about getting yourself back to America. How could you have known all you'd do for this place? How could you have known you'd fall in love?"

"Flo!" I sat up straight.

She laughed. "You've fallen in love with *Ireland*, at least. But it's obvious you've fallen for Collin too, Chelsea. I've seen you two together. And I've heard you talk about each other. *And* I saw you sneaking out of his room the other morning, which I will forgive you for not telling me. But it doesn't look like just a summer fling."

"He talks about me?" I asked.

"If you could see your face right now." She smiled, shaking her head.

"What does he say?"

"Same thing we're all thinking, really. He wishes you wouldn't leave. He can't imagine the Wanderer without you."

It was a good thing we had left the lobby, because I couldn't keep the tears back for much longer. The end of my time here had come even sooner than I'd expected, and it was a lot to bear.

"Was this whole thing so selfish?" I asked. "Getting involved with him, knowing I was going to leave?"

"You wouldn't be hurting this much if it was selfish," she said. "And besides, he's an adult. He knew what he was getting himself into and made the choice anyway. Though I don't know how much of a choice it was for either of you, judging by how hard you tried to resist but ending up falling anyway."

I was so embarrassed by how I'd acted when I'd first gotten here, I almost had to laugh. I had no intention of getting involved, or making connections, or doing anything beyond the job I was required to do. But everyone who came to work at the Wanderer left as part of the family, and I was the only one who couldn't see it. I was the only one who had been determined to resist what everyone else knew was inevitable. And had I known then what I know now, about how special this family really is, how special Collin is, I never would have resisted it in the first place.

"How do you always know the right thing to say?"

"I'm Italian, *tesoro*." Flo laughed. "We know about love. And I've seen enough people come through this place thinking they're one thing and leaving another."

I took a deep breath, but it didn't make me feel any steadier. "I'd have been so lost without you this summer."

"Oh, trust me, I know. You're still lost even with me."

I dropped my head again onto my folded arms. "You've been such a good friend since I've gotten here, and I've been such a basket case."

She reached out and squeezed my arm. "Basket case or not, you've been equally good as a friend," she said. "But I'm not sure why we're talking in the past tense, like we aren't going to be friends after you leave."

"That would be a nightmare," I said. "I'm not sure I could manage."

"Which is why we'll keep in touch," she said. "You're stuck with me now, *cara*."

The idea of being stuck with anyone other than Ada was so foreign it made my heart ache. Flo and I had only known each other for two months, during most of which I was certifiably insane, and she didn't want to get rid of me.

"It's an honor," I said.

"So, you're really leaving, huh?"

"I was looking for the dream job, and I finally have a shot at it," I said, trying hard to picture Hotel Blue and not the very place I was sitting. "And my time here is up, so, yeah, I suppose I am."

She jumped off the table and threw her arms around me.

"I'm proud of you," she said into my hair. "As long as you don't forget about us and come back to visit, yes? Maybe for a long time, like, say, another summer?" She pulled away and wiggled her perfect brows, and I was grateful to be laughing instead of crying.

"Let's not get ahead of ourselves," I said. "And don't tell the others yet, will you?"

"My lips are sealed. Now get out of here. I also don't want to cry this early in the morning, so I need to get back to work."

I pushed through the swinging kitchen doors before either of us succumbed to the wave of emotion, returning to my desk only in body. My mind couldn't have been farther away.

I'd been in such a daze, so different from the one I'd been in when I started the day, that it had taken me almost an hour to realize I'd gotten a text from Collin.

> Last day off tomorrow. Reckon you're finally ready for the Cliffs?

I nearly dropped my phone on the floor fumbling to answer. I thought that was up to you, I replied.

> You're right.

> And I've made up my mind. You're ready. Be ready tomorrow morning by 10.

With braids, he added in another message. It's windy. And you know I quite like you in them.

I'D SPENT MOST of the morning trying to decide how I was going to tell Collin the news, only to decide I wouldn't tell him right away. I didn't want to ruin the Cliffs, or our last day together. If I was going to make it through the day without unraveling entirely, I would have to avoid all thoughts of my departure until then.

"There she is," Collin said when I walked into the lobby at a quarter to ten. "Big day ahead of us, haven't we?"

His smile was becoming so familiar to me I couldn't imagine a time in the past when I hadn't known him. Which only made me hate imagining a future without him even more.

"How do you always beat me down here?" I said.

"I get impatient waiting."

"Are you ready, then?"

"The question is, are you?"

Our eyes locked together like magnets. I was both woefully unprepared and as ready as I could ever be, and the sensation made me feel like I was already on the edge of a cliff.

I nodded instead of speaking and followed him out the door, breathing in the warm air of a late summer morning. I was close enough to my flight home that I could check what the weather would be in Boston when I got back, but I had to force the thought from my mind before I threw up.

The Cliffs were a shockingly short drive away, and we were in the parking lot before I knew it. It seemed odd that such an iconic landscape had a parking lot, but I supposed that was a necessary evil.

Before we got out of the truck, Collin turned in his seat

to face me. This move pulled his T-shirt halfway around his body, making the eucalyptus leaves visible just under his collar. I was instantly reminded of how his tattoos felt under my fingers, some of them raised just enough to feel in the dark. I wondered if I'd ever forget.

"This is a big moment," he said, completely genuine and completely unaware of my inner turmoil. "You only get one first go at the Cliffs, so you have to be in the right frame of mind to really embrace their effect."

"Is this the speech you give before you let the guests off the van?" I said.

"Of course it is," he replied with a smile. "Only difference is I don't quite give a shit whether they listen. You, on the other hand . . ." He trailed off. "Well, it's important."

"So, guide me," I said. "It is your job, after all. How do I get in the right frame of mind?"

"If you're asking a question like that, I reckon you're already there. The Chelsea of two months ago didn't want my advice, remember?"

I thought back to that first night in the bar, and I wondered if seeing the Cliffs for the first time would be like seeing Collin for the first time. Only then, I had no idea he would become so significant, and now, I had a feeling I would never be the same after this afternoon.

"I couldn't forget even if I wanted to," I said. "After that night I thought you were going to be the biggest pain in my ass all summer."

"And now?"

"I know I was right," I teased.

"I walked right into that one, there, didn't I? Come on," he said, opening the door. "You're open to the magic of the Cliffs, which means you're ready for the magic of the Cliffs."

I followed him from the truck up a small hill, with my heart in my throat. This was our last adventure before I left, and the thought was almost too much to bear. So instead of dwelling on it, I tried to memorize the sound of his breathing, the rippling muscles in his legs as he climbed the hill, the space between his shoulders, and the smattering of ink over his forearms. I already missed the security that came with having Collin Finnegan at the wheel, and how it had nothing to do with jobs, money, or material things.

When we got to the top, however, even those feelings melted away. The stress and the hope surrounding the interview, the heartbreak of leaving Flo and Collin, the sense of self that had been dissolving and rebuilding itself since I first got to the Wanderer. The feelings I'd been wrestling with for months were whisked away by the wind, replaced only by a sense of wonder I hadn't felt since I was a child.

The jagged coastline sat seven hundred feet under the cliffs, which stood proudly against the wide-open sky. A narrow dirt path lined itself along the edge, so onlookers could wander at what felt like the edge of the world. From where we stood, they looked like specks of color splattered against a painting. The cliffs themselves towered over the ocean, rock formations like stacks of earth built up or worn down since as far back as anyone could remember, and further back than that.

"Proper sight, aren't they?"

"Do people usually answer that when you ask?" I said, hoping he could hear my voice above the wind. "And if so, what do they say? And how do they manage to string words together at all?"

He laughed, swinging an arm around my shoulders and leading me in the direction of another small hill, which I figured would provide an even better view. "Nothing insightful," he said. "Most everyone is stunned into silence. Or they try to say something meaningful, but it comes out like something they read on a brochure before they got here."

"Holy shit," I said as we reached the top of the second hill, hardly listening to a word.

"Or that," he said. "Take it all in, Chels. The Cliffs will always be here, but never with quite the same magic as this time. Let the moment happen to you."

His words washed over me with the sound of the waves, but for once I wasn't tempted to look at him. I couldn't take my eyes off the landscape before me, even if I felt like crying.

The cerulean ocean stretched to the horizon on one end and crashed against the cliffs on the other, settling into gentle rolling waves in between. The only interruption in the endless blue was that shade of green I realized I might never see again outside of Galway, blanketing the expanse of cliffside just before it dropped fearlessly into the sea.

Standing on the steep edge of the cliffs served as both a literal and metaphorical precipice, and I was thankful I could blame my teary eyes on the wind. I understood why Collin waited to take me here. Had we done this at the start of the summer, I would have been standing here as the version of myself I'd been on arrival. Cynical, cranky, full to the brim with self-pity.

Instead, I stood here as, well, whoever this version of myself was. Open? Vulnerable, even? Mildly terrified? She was not the same Chelsea from the start of the summer.

That version might have been unrecognizable to me, but one look at Collin told me this change was as familiar to him as the back of his hand. He'd seen the Cliffs change people before, or even seen Ireland change people before, and he knew I was no different.

"Ready for a walk?" he asked, offering me his hand. "There's a great spot to sit a bit down the way. Dodge the tourists for a minute, really give us some time to sit and enjoy if you'd like."

"Lead the way," I said, grabbing his hand and letting the weight of it ground me. We wandered along the edge of the cliffs without speaking, instead alternating between watching the path and staring out over the edge. With every step the landscape seemed to change, new cliffs forming and overlapping one another, the tides receding and crashing back against the shore, the entire coastline warped and ambiguous.

"Here we are, then," Collin said, gesturing to a patch of grass just beyond the path. He stepped over the rope, which was supposed to serve as a barrier, and motioned for me to do the same. When I hesitated, he only laughed. "Relax, Chels. No one is here to yell at ya. And the cliff isn't going to, like, crumble into the sea there. Trust me."

Maybe this was another reason he waited. Had he told me to trust him two months ago, I would have laughed in his face.

I followed him over the rope and settled beside him on the damp grass, letting my head drop to his shoulder as I returned my gaze to the sea.

"Is this the part where we talk about you leaving?" he asked eventually, barely loud enough to be heard over the wind. We both knew this conversation was coming, but that wasn't going to make it any easier .

"We can't put it off a little longer?" I knew this was the time to tell him about the job, but the words were already lodged in my throat.

"We're out of time, Chels." We both knew he wasn't just talking about having this conversation. Except only I knew we had even less time than we'd thought.

"This summer was more than I ever could have imagined," I said eventually. "I mean, I thought I was going to hate it here. All I wanted to do was get home to Boston. And now I'm sitting here at the Cliffs with you, trying not to cry at the thought of doing exactly what I'd planned all along." I tried to laugh, but it got lost in the wind.

"And you don't think that means anything?" he asked.

"Of course it does," I said, wary of his tone. "Are you saying I think it doesn't?" I angled my body to face him. "Collin, this summer, especially the past few weeks, has meant more to me than you know."

"Not enough to change your plans, though, is it?"

"Coll," I started, hating that we were going there. "I can't stay here. You know that."

"You keep saying that, but I'm still not quite sure why. You could easily get a visa. Lori would sponsor you."

"It isn't about the visa."

"What's it about, then? I need it to make sense to me. Is it just about familiarity? Family and friends? You have both right here, do you not?"

"It's more than that," I said, trying to keep my footing. "It's stability. It's making a living." I knew I was dancing around the truth, but I wasn't ready to stick the landing.

"And what's wrong with the living we make here?" He angled his body this time, away from me and back to the edge of the cliff and the Atlantic beyond. "If it's not good enough for you, Chelsea, I wish you'd just say that. It's what you've been thinking since you got here, isn't it? That you're above hostel life."

"I'm not above it, Collin, and you know that."

"Of course *I* know it," he said, "but do you?"

"I thought we'd gotten past this?" Frustration crept in where sadness used to be, and I didn't like the direction this conversation was headed. This wasn't what this afternoon was supposed to be about, and I hated the dark turn it was taking. "It just isn't for me. That's it. I'm not cut out for this kind of life."

"But you've done it the whole summer," he said, relaxing his tone. "That's where I'm lost. You keep saying how much you aren't like us, how much you can't just do something new every day, how you can't manage hostel life. But you've been doing exactly that every day since you got here. And you've been doing a brilliant job." Hearing the kindness return to his voice made my chest hurt. "You've changed so much since the start of this summer, Chelsea, and I know you can see that too."

"I have, I know I have. And in some ways, it's been for the best. But in other ways, I've just . . . I've gotten away from myself. And I have to bridge the gap. The ways I've changed since I've been here are what have given me the confidence to actively pursue the life I really want in the first place, but now I need to see it through."

"And you're sure going back is the life you really want, then?"

"I'm sure," I whispered, letting my words get carried away on the wind, wishing I could follow them. He ran both hands roughly through his hair, dropping his head briefly between his knees.

"Then I'm happy for you, Chels. Really, I am."

"Then why don't you sound happy for me?"

"Because it turned out I was the one who was a bit thick, after all. Letting myself get my hopes up that you might stay."

"Collin—"

"I just want to make sure you're really happy there, you know?"

"Do you think I won't be?"

"I think you haven't once sounded happy when you've talked about Boston," he said, and I froze, keeping my eyes locked on the horizon even though I could feel his on me. "You don't talk about Boston with any joy, not like the joy I've seen you feel here. At Blackrock, cheering on the hurlers, dancing at the ceilidh. I've seen you come alive, and you don't so much as smile when you talk about going home.

"So, I want to think you'll be happy because I've fallen in love with you, Chelsea. I want nothing but the very best for you, but I'm not convinced the very best thing for you is to go back." He paused, taking a deep breath. "But that doesn't mean I won't support you. If you really think this is best for you, then I will always support that."

Any hope of blaming my tears on the wind was long gone. With every word he spoke my heart turned further in on itself.

"I'm sorry," I said after what felt like an eternity.

"You've nothing to apologize for," he said before I could continue. "You made it clear this was your plan from the start. You were always going to leave. It's my fault I let myself get carried away."

"You aren't the only one," I said.

"I just wish we could have been carried away a little while longer." A few more tears slid down my cheeks, and I tried to wipe them away before he could see. "We have a few days left, right?"

Pain radiated from my chest. "Just one," I said, still afraid to meet his gaze, even though I could feel the confusion in the way he was looking at me. "I got the interview for that job, my dream job, really, that I thought I was underqualified for. They want me in on Friday, so I'm leaving tomorrow."

Eventually, he cleared his throat. "That's grand, Chelsea. I'm chuffed for ya. You're going to smash it. And I guess that means we better get you back to get packed, huh," he said, brushing off his hands as he stood, like suddenly he was like the picture of nonchalance. Like we hadn't both been ripping our own hearts to pieces on a sweeping, dramatic cliffside. Like we hadn't backed ourselves into a corner. I didn't know what I'd expected him to say, but I couldn't believe this was it.

What I *did* know was that I couldn't falter now. Despite the pain, I had to follow through. My dream was still my dream, wasn't it?

I followed Collin back down the hill and to the parking lot, equally speechless as when I arrived, only for entirely different reasons. The sinking feeling in my stomach dropped lower and lower until it threatened to drag me straight into the ground. I knew sometimes doing the right thing meant doing the hard thing, but in that moment, I wasn't sure I was doing the right thing at all.

"So, those are the Cliffs, then," Collin said as we neared the truck, dragging me back into reality.

"They're magical, Collin. They really are."

"I'm not sure if they've changed you or brought you back to yourself, but I'm glad you got to see how special they are before you left. They're the proper final piece to your Irish education."

I managed a hoarse, humorless laugh. Leave it to Collin to still have made this a lesson. And just like every other adventure we'd been on, everything I learned only tied the string between me and Ireland tighter, rendering it nearly impossible now to undo the knot.

"This isn't goodbye, is it?" I asked when he finally turned to face me. "I'll see you again before I leave, won't I?"

"It's possible," he said, "but I'm quite busy with a tour to-morrow. Supposed to be decent weather, so trying to make the most of it. But I'm sure we'll bump into each other."

Perfect. A whole summer reduced to a chance goodbye in a corridor.

"Grand," I said, getting into the truck. With nothing else left to say, I felt the chasm left behind by Collin and the rest of the Wanderer open inside me before I was even packed.

Chapter 19

Still reeling from the pain of my final afternoon with Collin, I wondered if it would be easier to leave everyone else without saying goodbye. Slip out unnoticed in the morning and send a text from home, dodging sad hugs and thinly veiled judgments and pleas not to go.

My daydream was cut short by the crushing reality that the only thing worse than saying goodbye would be leaving without doing so. Flo would kill me, and I needed to thank Lori, and Lars, so I flopped on my bed beside a pile of clothes, sent two texts, then immediately returned to packing to distract myself from the impending responses.

Before I'd even finished emptying the wardrobe, Flo appeared in my doorway. She was out of breath and wiping greasy hands on her apron, surely having run from the kitchen the second she saw my text. For someone who loved cooking, she jumped at any chance to put off doing it.

"So this is it, then?" she asked. "Lori said you're leaving first thing in the morning."

"Afraid so." I shrugged, and she was hugging me before I could even drop my shoulders.

"Good luck, Chelsea. They'd be crazy not to hire you," she said. "Anyone would."

"Thanks, Flo. For everything, I mean. I'm really going to miss you."

"Are you trying to make me cry?" She made a dramatic show of wiping away tears, which made us both laugh. Then cry a little more. "People come and go here all the time, Chels. But you made yourself an institution."

"Oh, stop."

"I'm serious. It isn't going to be the same here without you."

"You'll all be just fine," I said.

"And will you?"

"Of course I will."

"I'm going to pretend I believe you," she said, "but you need to work on your acting."

I swatted her arm, and she pulled me into another hug. "If you ever aren't, you know where to find us," she whispered.

"Thank you."

"Good luck, *amore mio*."

With one more squeeze she was out the door, and I was left standing tearfully in front of the empty wardrobe. It took everything in me not to crumple to the floor, but I had to keep moving. This was what I wanted.

When I arrived at the Wanderer a few months ago, I was already counting the minutes until I left. I would have jumped at the chance to bump my flight home a day earlier, but now that I only had a few hours between me and that flight, I'd have killed for an extra day. It was beginning to feel like I was convincing myself this was the right idea just as much as I was convincing everyone else, and an extra day to get my head on straight would have been a gift.

I took out my phone and pulled up the website for Hotel Blue, swiping through the gallery and reminding myself why it was my dream to work in a place like this. I thought of the events I could plan in their outdoor spaces and the kind of people I would meet. I thought of how inspired I'd be with the myriad of colors, tumbling plants, and the trendy stretches of patterned wallpaper. How much I'd enjoy working with the young, creative-looking people I saw in the photos. How I could find an apartment within cycling distance and maybe even ride to work.

My new life unfurled before me with a few swipes of my thumb, and I released a dramatic exhale. If I was going to prove this was the right decision, I needed to make it work.

By the time I was fully packed with alarms set for an ungodly hour of the morning, Lori appeared in my doorway the same way Flo had hours earlier: out of breath and a little teary-eyed.

"Chelsea, dear," she said, holding me at arm's length like an old relative she hadn't seen in ages. "You've been such an asset to the Wanderer this summer. My sister wasn't lying when she said you'd be irreplaceable."

"Oh, please," I said, fighting the blush creeping onto my face. "You'll have someone new in no time."

"Someone new, maybe, but no one near as good. Hard to find people who really embrace the spirit of this place, you know?" She shook her head, waving off her own words. "Though I'm sure that's not helping you leave, is it? You'll be grand in whatever you go on to do, Chelsea. I wish you all the best."

"Thank you, Lori," I said. "For giving me this opportunity. And for saying yes to all my last-minute plans."

"I'll miss those plans," she said. "And I hope you know there is always a place for you here if you change your mind. The Wanderer never forgets the good ones."

Lori and I hadn't spent much time together this summer, but she had never hesitated to send an encouraging email or drop a kind word when we passed each other in the lobby. She had a way about her that really made you believe every word she said, and that only made this conversation hurt more. Being trusted so thoroughly by someone who hardly knew me struck a chord deep in my chest.

Lars came by only a few minutes later, and I was more grateful than ever for his levity. We hugged, we laughed, we briefly reminisced, I thanked him for my training, and he was out of my doorway and off to a volleyball tournament before either of us could get too emotional. If only it could have been so easy with the others.

My only goodbye left was Collin. We hadn't run into each other, and I had a feeling it was by design. We'd already said goodbye. Maybe I'd tied up my time at the Wanderer with a sloppy bow, and the only thing left to do was leave.

I shook the thought from my mind, remembering the words of the people I've met here and the constant urge to embrace how I felt. I couldn't bring myself to just disappear.

I dug through my carry-on for the almost-empty journal, tearing out a page and sitting at my desk for the last time. After nearly twenty minutes of staring out the window and trying to determine what was left to say and exactly how to say it, I scribbled a note to Collin that I'd slide under his door on my way out.

My LAST NIGHT in the Wanderer passed much like my first: restless, anxious, unsure of what was ahead. I was awake when my alarm went off, staring mindlessly at the ceiling, but that didn't make it any easier to get out of bed and take the necessary steps to the door. I reread the texts from Ada and my parents expressing their excitement to have me home, trying to psych myself up for the journey.

The sound of my door closing behind me was so final, I heard it rattling around in my brain for the long walk down the hallway. I stopped outside of Collin's room to listen for the silence inside. He was still asleep, which I'd hoped for, so I slipped the note under the crack, dragged my feet down the stairs, and walked out the door and into the car waiting for me.

It wasn't until we were halfway to the airport that I allowed myself to feel the weight of leaving Collin behind with nothing more than an awkward afternoon and a last-minute note, and before I knew it: I was the Girl Who Cries in an Uber.

And then: the Girl Who Cries in Airport Security, and the Girl Who Cries on the Plane. Every time I went through the mental montage of the summer—the picnic at Glendalough, the rain at the hurling match, spinning freely in Collin's arms at the ceilidh, falling asleep to the sound of his voice—I broke my own heart all over again.

Sleep evaded me on the flight much as it had the night before, so I arrived home in a daze. Tired, uncertain, in need of both caffeine and a two-day nap. I only had to scan the passenger pickup area for a minute or so before I spotted my parents, waving frantically while people honked and shouted at them to get out of the way.

"Chelsea, girl!" My dad called across traffic, holding his arms open and waiting for me to step into them. I was overcome by a wave of emotion and instantly felt like a kid again, wanting them to protect me from the troubles of the world. "Welcome home," he said as I approached, pulling me into his embrace.

"Hi," I said, but it came out muffled from my face being pressed into his shoulder. When I pulled away to hug my mother, she held me the same way Lori had the night before.

"Look at you," she said. "My baby is home. Have you been crying? Your face is puffy, but you look thin. What's that about?"

"Nice to see you too," I said, letting her pull me into a hug. "I'm just tired, that's all. Been a long day."

"We've got a whole spread at home," she said, leading me toward the car. "Bagels, lox, the whole nine. Even that babka you like from Falk and Rosen's. Maybe that'll put a little meat back on your bones."

"Don't listen to her," my dad whispered as he loaded my luggage into the trunk. "You look lovely."

We shared a knowing smile before getting into the car, and it made me feel good to be home. I stared out the window on the ride, basking in the familiarity of the roads. In no time at all our neighborhood came into view, brick colonial after brick colonial, welcoming me home like soldiers at attention.

"Did you miss it?" my dad asked as he pulled into the driveway.

"Of course I missed it," I said. "But I got used to missing it, so I didn't think much about it after a while."

"Good," he said. "That's how it should be."

"How long do you think you'll be living at home now that you're back?"

"Wendy," my dad scolded, "she's hardly through the door. Let her get her bearings for a minute, will you? Chelsea girl, you can be home as long as you need."

"I wasn't saying you couldn't," my mother added. "I was just asking. Of course you're always welcome here. You know we love having you at home, don't you?"

I smiled, already making a mental note to start looking for apartments no later than the minute I walked through the door.

Unsurprisingly, nothing had changed since I'd been gone. Their house had the same smell, the same spotless entryway leading to the same full kitchen, with the same pile of clean linens on the bottom of the stairs for the next person to take up with them. It was the same old life I'd always known.

Only it didn't feel quite the way I thought it would. It must have been reverse culture shock or whatever happened when people were gone for long periods of time. Or maybe it was just dehydration and exhaustion from the flight. Either way, I was sure a Falk and Rosen's babka would sort me out.

We stood around the kitchen island piling lox onto bagels and peeling flaking, chocolaty pieces of babka from the loaf. I'd been decent at keeping in touch with my parents via email while I was away, so they were mostly up to speed with the past two months of my life, barring specifics that would send a Jewish mother over the edge.

"You must be exhausted," my dad said as we cleaned, noting my head slipping lower into my hands on the counter. "Why don't you go up and get some rest for tomorrow's interview?"

I was so excited at the prospect of getting into bed and being done with this day I could have cried all over again.

"Do you know what you're wearing?" my mother asked. "It's obviously too late to have it dry-cleaned but I'll steam it for you if you bring it down to me."

"Thank you," I said, equally grateful for her affection and annoyed at her prying. "This was a really nice afternoon. I'm glad to be home."

"We're glad to have you back," my dad said, flashing the

same knowing smile he did at the airport. Only this time, it felt less like a comfort and more like a challenge: Was I really glad to be home?

I had just enough energy to change my clothes and brush my teeth before collapsing into bed, promising myself I'd get up extra early to wash my hair before the interview. After a few minutes of scrolling my phone, I texted Ada to confirm that we'd meet for drinks after the interview tomorrow, like I'd never left.

THE LOBBY OF HOTEL BLUE was even more gorgeous in person than it was in photos. Eclectic wallpaper stretched behind the reception desk, which had gold flecks in the marble countertops that reflected rainbows of light from the massive windows making up the opposite wall. A few guests mingled in a lounge off the lobby, turning in my direction at the sound of my heels clicking across the floor. I tried to appear powerful and confident before I stepped into what might have been the most important interview of my life so far.

With every step, I reminded myself how much I wanted this. I repeated it like a mantra. *This is exactly what I want. This is the dream job. This is exactly what I want.* The voice in my head was so loud I wondered if onlookers could hear.

"Welcome to Hotel Blue," said the receptionist when I approached the desk. "I hope you've had an easy journey here. How can we help you today?" Her name tag told me her name was Iris, and for a second I was so distracted by her cropped curly hair and deep golden skin that I didn't respond. She could have been Flo in another lifetime. I almost laughed.

I almost laughed again when I thought about anyone describing my journey as "easy." If she only knew what it had taken me to get here.

"Hi, sorry," I said when I realized I'd been silent for a moment too long. "I'm Chelsea Gold. I'm here for an interview with Bridgette Gantz."

"Ah, yes, from Ireland, right?" She picked up the phone and dialed a few numbers, wedging the phone between her ear and her shoulder.

"I mean, directly, yes, but really from Boston."

She offered a polite smile, and I wondered if she also heard the strange note of disappointment in my tone.

"Bridgette, hi. Ms. Gold is here for your meeting," she said into the receiver, still smiling at me. She hung up a second later, clapping her manicured hands together. "She's ready for you. Right this way."

Iris came around the front of the desk and motioned for me to follow, and together we walked the length of a hallway off the lobby. I tried to sneak peeks at everything we passed along the way: a cozy bar with wingback chairs, an indoor pool with a smattering of fake palm trees, and the entrance to a sort of garden. The wallpaper from the lobby changed twice on our walk, splashing deep green leaves and faded lilac petals across the hallway.

"Just in here," Iris said, opening a door and gesturing inside. "Good luck."

I thanked her and followed the direction of her arm, letting the door close behind me. The conference room was neutral in comparison to the rest of the hotel, but there was still an eclectic gallery wall coloring one side and mismatched, colorful chairs surrounding the table. Bridgette sat at the far end but stood to greet me as soon as I was inside.

"Ms. Gold, welcome. Thank you for making this work on such short notice. I'm glad you were able to come in." We shook hands, and I hoped my smile looked genuine and approachable and not at all insane.

Bridgette wore a linen tent dress with buttons down the front of varying colors and sizes. Her hair was wrapped in a patterned scarf not unlike the wallpaper. She looked nothing like anyone on any other hiring committee I'd seen all summer, which I took as a good sign.

"It's so nice to meet you," I said. "Thank you for making the time to meet with me."

"Oh, please," she said, pulling out a chair, "the pleasure is mine. Have a seat."

She had a casual air about her that made me relax instantly, and I tried to channel her confidence for my benefit. As she shuffled a few papers, my résumé included, I watched a few employees pass by the window. They wore blazers of assorted colors with shimmering gold ID badges pinned to the lapels and laughed over clipboards and tumblers of iced coffee.

I tried to imagine myself as one of them. What color would I wear? Would I be the one making people laugh or the one laughing in the background? Who would I be here? Who would I *become* here?

"So, Ms. Gold," Bridgette said, pulling me from my reverie. "Tell me a bit about yourself. Who are you? Beyond what's on the résumé." She laced her fingers in her lap and leaned back in her chair, giving me the floor.

When I had prepared for this interview, I practiced talking about my time at O'Shea's. I planned to spin my move to Ireland as adventurous and impressive. I even was primed to talk about some of the work I did at the Wanderer. But after all that, I didn't know exactly who I was. Or, at least, who was the version of myself she wanted to meet.

That question hung between us like a rain cloud, and I had to take a few deep breaths before I responded.

"Well," I said, "I'm a Boston native, so after a summer away I'm looking forward to getting back to my roots. I'm also from a tight-knit Jewish family, so it's a priority of mine to bring that close family feel to my clients and their events." That much was easy. Those were facts. And they made me seem like a good candidate for the job. I was on solid ground, and I was determined to resist sliding into *I have no idea who I am* territory, no matter how open her face was.

"Yes, yes." Bridgette nodded. "And what brings you to Hotel Blue? After a bed-and-breakfast and a hostel, I imagine this is a bit of a change."

"That's exactly what brings me here," I said. "I'm ready for the next step of my career. I'm looking to bring what I've learned during my time at those places to a higher-end location. I think there's value in synthesizing the culture of different styles of accommodation. It'll allow me to plan events for different types of guests looking for different kinds of experiences."

The longer I spoke, the more I wanted to throw up. I sounded like a robot. If I wanted this so badly, couldn't I talk about it organically? Could she tell how much I had to rehearse for this?

"Tell me about the Wanderer," she said, once again interrupting an inward spiral. I spun the claddagh around on my finger, a gesture I'd been doing absentmindedly all summer, only now it transported me back to Galway so fiercely I had to remind myself I was actually in Boston. I had to convince myself this was still what I wanted, despite my composure slipping away at an alarming rate. Thankfully, if Bridgette knew I was struggling, she wasn't showing it. "Your portfolio is quite impressive," she continued.

"The Wanderer was— I'm sorry, my portfolio?" Surely there had been a mistake. I didn't submit a portfolio. Had she confused me with someone else?

She shuffled through her stack once more, presenting me with a stack of papers bound together with a gold clip. "This one," she said. "I received it late last night. The email address didn't match that on your résumé, but I assumed you knew it was sent over on your behalf. Has there been a mistake?"

I flipped through the papers, only half listening. Sure enough, it was a packet of events I'd planned at the Wanderer. Photos, descriptions, testimonies. The movie night, the cooking classes, the high tea in period dress. A group of guests headed to a ceilidh.

"No, no mistake," I said, still flipping the pages and trying to make sense of what I was seeing. "This is definitely my work. I just . . . I'm sorry, who did you say sent this over?"

"I have the email correspondence right here," she said, thumbing through her stack and producing a sheet of paper. "Have a look."

I took the paper, scanning frantically for the email address. When I found it, I had to stop an audible gasp from escaping my lips: collintours@thewanderer.ie. I willed the room to stop spinning so I could read the rest of the email.

To whom it may concern,

We hope this finds you well, and we hope you'll excuse the late submission. Attached please find the portfolio of applicant Chelsea Gold. She has made an invaluable impact on not only The Wanderer as an institution, but also on the staff and guests she worked with during her short time here. Our events calendar is fuller and more vibrant than it's been in years, and we have only Chelsea to thank. Since she has done so much for us, it is our hope we can do the same for her in her future endeavors. Please consider this our heartfelt recommendation.

Sláinte,
Lori O'Shea (Owner), Collin Finegan (Tours),
and Florence Rossi (House Chef)

"You had no idea they sent this, did you?" Bridgette asked as she watched me read and reread the email.

"No, it's, uh, no," I said. "I didn't." I was too stunned to pretend I wasn't. After all the fuss about me leaving, they went through the trouble of putting together this portfolio and recommending me for the job?

"Seems like you made quite the impression," she said. "Which makes me wonder, Chelsea, why did you leave?"

"The summer ended," I said automatically. Another fact. "It was the end of my contract."

"Doesn't sound like it had to be," she said. "Let me ask you one more question. Not as a potential employer, but woman to woman." She leaned her forearms on the table, bringing her face closer to mine. "Is this really what you want?"

In the silence that followed, we both had our answer. There was only one thing I wanted, and once again, everyone had seen it before me. But I was done being the last to know.

"Ms. Gantz, I'm so sorry."

"I understand," she said, a smile creasing her eyes. "I think you would have been great here based on this portfolio. I really do. And maybe our paths will cross again someday. But it doesn't seem like you would be happy here. At least not as happy as you'd be there. And that really is what's important, isn't it?"

"I'm so embarrassed," I said, pinching the bridge of my nose. "I shouldn't have wasted your time. And I should have had this conversation with myself a long time ago." I tried to laugh, and the warmth in her eyes glowed brightly. "Please know how sorry I am."

"No apologies necessary," she said with a smile. "Only to yourself, perhaps." Her kindness made me feel even guiltier for wasting her time.

"It's a beautiful hotel," I said as I gathered my things, slightly nostalgic already for a life that could have been.

"Ah, this old thing?" She waved her hand around. "It isn't much. You won't be missing anything."

I could have hugged her for how easy she was making this experience, which for her was a minor inconvenience and me a monumental life change.

"Thank you," I said, praying she knew how much I meant it. "Not only for your time, but for your forgiveness. And for the push in the right direction."

"That's what hospitality is about, isn't it? Taking care of each other?"

I was too overwhelmed to respond properly, so instead I followed her to the door and tried to contemplate what would happen when I left. "Take care, Chelsea," she said, shaking my hand once more.

"You too, Ms. Gantz."

The conference room door clicked behind me, and my legs carried my back through the lobby and out to my car independent of my brain. I sat behind the wheel for a few minutes resisting the urge to scream at the top of my lungs or burst into tears.

Where do you go when you realize your dream isn't your dream at all? When you realize your new dream is the exact thing you thought you never wanted?

When you thought your ideal future was the metropolitan city you'd grown up in, a senior position and a husband and a picket fence by thirty-five, and instead it was an unruly hostel on the Irish coast with a patchwork family and no real plan beyond each day?

If I knew one thing, it was that the answer wasn't *back to your parents' house.* Ada would know what to do. I picked up the phone, and she answered on the second ring.

"Welcome home!" she shouted as soon as she picked up. "How was the interview? Don't answer that, actually. Are we still on for drinks? I want to hear all about it in person. Was that a sigh? What's wrong? Was it horrible?"

I laughed, and I could almost hear her relax on the other end of the phone. "It was . . . something," I said. "Are you busy? Or can you meet me at the bar right now?"

"I'm on my way," she said, and I almost laughed. There was no better friend than Ada. "You're freaking me out, Chels."

"I'm fine," I said, surprised that I actually meant it. "I'll see you at Jefferson's in a few. I'll tell you everything, promise."

I WAS ALREADY on a barstool when Ada came crashing through the door, hair a mess and tote bag falling off her shoulder. She ordered a vodka Diet Coke from the bartender with a wide smile before snapping her attention to me, brows furrowed and smile turned into a line.

"I think I have to go back to Ireland," I blurted before she could say anything. And for what might have been the first time in her entire life, Ada was speechless.

"Please say something," I said after an agonizing minute of silence.

"You need to go back, like, for good?" she asked, drink halfway to her mouth.

"I do," I said, trying to maintain some resolve. "I mean, not forever. But at least for right now."

"What happened at the interview?"

"I just realized it wasn't the dream I thought it was," I said. "I was so concerned with getting back here to the life I thought I was *supposed* to have that I didn't even realize it was becoming less and less the life I *wanted*. I know it sounds crazy. I really do. But sitting in that conference room, it just didn't feel like my life anymore. It felt like someone else's."

"Wow," she said, accompanied by a slow exhale. "You're serious about this?"

"I know how it sounds," I said. "But I am."

"What does this mean for you and Collin, then?"

Goose bumps covered my body at the sound of his name, and I was relieved to finally see her smile. "Okay, first of all, you know this isn't about him, right? I don't want you to think I'm moving halfway across the world for a boy."

"Of course not," she said. "That's more something I would do." We both laughed. "But it is a perk, isn't it? That there will be a gorgeous Irishman who loves you there when you get back?"

"I don't know that he'll be there. Or that he still loves me."

"Because I'm a good friend, I'll pretend to believe you."

"Seriously, Ada. I mean, physically he will be, obviously.

He'll probably be at the Wanderer until end of days. But we didn't end on a great note, so I'm not sure he'll be thrilled to see me."

"Okay, I can't pretend anymore."

"That was short-lived."

"The man loves you, Chels. He spent all his days off this summer trotting you around a country you thought you hated, trying to convince you to love it. You didn't end on a great note because he couldn't bear to see you leave. He'll be thrilled to see you. He'd be crazy not to be."

My skin was crawling with anticipation. If I could have snapped my fingers and been back at the Wanderer in an instant, I'd have already been gone.

"Am I really doing this?"

"Leaving me, you mean?" she said. "Leaving your dear best friend behind?"

"Ada! Don't do that, please."

"I'm kidding, I'm kidding. Yes, Chelsea. You are doing this. And you *can* do this. And I'll remind you of that every step of the way if that's what you need."

"How am I going to live across an ocean from you?" I said, fighting the prickly onslaught of tears.

"We made it through the summer, didn't we? What's another, you know, indefinite amount of time?" We tried to laugh, but I could tell she was fighting the same tears. "Chels, you are my sister. No stretch of ocean is going to make that any less true. We have technology, and I'll come out to visit! If any friendship can withstand this, it's ours."

We were both freely crying now, but they weren't just sad tears. We'd seen each other through every stage of life so far, and this was just another piece of our story.

"I never could have done any of this without you," I said.

"Oh, stop. Give yourself some credit. You've done huge things here! You've taken risks, you've put yourself out there, you've trusted your intuition. I'm really, really proud of you, babe."

"Thank you," I sniffled.

"It's an honor," she said. "I canceled the rest of the meetings I had today. What do you say we go back to your parents' house, order Thai from that place down the street, and get you ready to go?"

The relief of having Ada's support, having someone beside me while I figured out my next step, was almost too much to bear. All I could do was nod.

"I love you," I said eventually, reaching out to squeeze her hand.

"I love you more."

I sniffled once more at the familiar refrain and pulled her into my arms. We laughed at ourselves, at the scene we were making in public, before paying the bill and heading in the direction of my parents' house.

ADA AND I spent the night much like we had two months ago, before I left for Ireland the first time. Only this one had none of the uncertainty, none of the anxiety, none of the fear. Galway was no longer the unknown.

Together, we ticked off everything on my checklist: call Lori and take her up on her offer to return, talk to my parents, book a five a.m. flight, gather my still-packed luggage, and spend one more night in Boston before I left on a new adventure.

She was right. I could do this.

Chapter 20

As we taxied around the terminal at the Shannon Airport, I cataloged the differences between this arrival and my last: anxious versus eager, foreign versus familiar. Still buzzing with nervous energy. Still unsure of the future that awaits me. Dreading it versus desperately looking forward to it.

If all went to plan, that is.

When I called Flo on the way to the airport she screamed for about a minute at the news of my return, then informed me Lars convinced Collin to do another open-mic performance tonight, this time at the pub, so I could find him there. I wasn't sure surprising him was the best idea, but a Grand Gesture felt like my best bet.

The ride from the airport to Galway would have felt excruciatingly long if not for the scenery. I'd only been in the States for thirty-six hours but it felt like a lifetime without this view. Was anything in Boston this green?

I let my memories wind back to the first ride from the airport to the Wanderer, when I'd been too jaded to care about the grass and the hills, too overwhelmed to look beyond the gray sky, and too tired to register the beauty that had been right in front of me.

Now I watched the shades of green turn from emerald to sage and back again as the clouds took turns eclipsing the setting sun.

The reality settled in as the bus slowed to a stop a few minutes' walk from the Wanderer, spitting me out onto the pavement with only my luggage. I stood in a cloud of exhaust and watched the bus rattle along down the road before turning myself in the direction of the hostel. The only way to go now was forward.

All my doubts were expelled the minute the Wanderer came into view. I felt what I was looking for when I returned to Boston: feeling like I was coming home.

Before I even crossed the street, Lori and Flo came crashing through the door and running across the road, shouting my name.

"I can't believe you came back!" Flo threw her arms around my neck, and I dropped my luggage to return the hug. "I mean, I totally can, because you obviously love it here, but it's amazing that you actually did it."

She released me, and Lori stepped in for a hug that was a bit more awkward, but the sentiment was all the same. "Welcome back, Chelsea. I'm thrilled you're here."

Lori had been beside herself when I called. She'd said there would always be a room for me at the Wanderer, even if it wasn't totally up to my standards. I hated myself for how snobby I'd been when I arrived, and I'd told her the room was perfect, and I'd meant it.

"Well, you know the way," she said, handing me the key. "I'm sure you have quite a bit of settling to do, but we'll see you down the pub for open mic in an hour?"

"Wouldn't miss it," I told her, leaving out the real reason I was going, although I was sure it was no secret. Flo mentioned on the phone that Collin had been sulking in my absence, and given how fast word traveled in this place, I was sure everyone knew every detail of our summer by now.

I followed the familiar path to my room, nearly collapsing on the bed when I arrived. Even though I'd orchestrated my return, I still couldn't quite believe any of this was real. It felt at once like I'd been gone for years and like I never left.

Unpacking didn't take long as my parents planned to ship the rest of my clothes when the seasons changed. Within an hour, my room looked exactly as it had a few days earlier: full wardrobe, faded quilt from a local market splayed across the bed, empty journals taunting me from the desk, the same string lights dripping from the window frame that I forgot to take down before I left. It felt more like mine than my room at my parents', and it wasn't just because they put the elliptical in there over the summer.

This was home now.

As I got ready for the open mic, the nerves I'd successfully distracted myself from resurfaced. I hoped Flo and Lori kept their promise not to tell Collin I was coming back. I wanted him to hear it from me.

I texted Flo that I'd meet her at the pub, wanting a few more minutes alone to collect myself.

The pub was packed when I arrived, so I slipped into a dark corner near the bar undetected. I wasn't exactly sure of my plan of action now that I was here, but whatever it was definitely required a drink first.

I leaned on the bar and sipped a light beer and combed the crowd for familiar faces while a trio of women performed a slam poem. Eventually, I made out the back of Flo's head squished between Lars and someone I didn't recognize, nodding toward the wings of the stage. I followed their gaze . . . and saw him.

I was grateful for the cover of darkness at the back of the bar because I wasn't ready for him to see me yet. But from where I stood, I could see the veins in his hand gripping the banjo, the crinkles in the corners of his eyes while he smiled at someone else backstage, and the faded ink just below his shirtsleeves. Unlike the Cliffs, Collin Finegan could be seen for the first time over and over again.

The crowd applauded the women, and Collin shook their hands as they traded places on the stage. I held my breath, trying to prepare for the sound of his voice.

"Right, then," he began. "Tough act to follow, that, isn't it?" The crowd chuckled, and I tightened my grip on my glass. It'd only been a few days, but I missed the sound of his accent. His storytelling. His quiet jokes. The fact that I ever thought I would just carry on with life three thousand miles away from him felt unfathomable to me now.

"I do suppose I have to try, however, so let's crack on." He strummed a few chords, and the crowd settled in. "This one is a bit interactive," he said, "so I'll need your participation. You think you can do that for me?" Murmurs of affirmation floated from the audience, and he smiled at the sound. "Good. I was hoping you'd be keen. Here's how we'll go. This one's about a knight, as they often are, but our ancestors didn't do a great job of passing down this story, so there are quite a few blanks. When we reach them, I'll need your help filling them in." More plucking. Minor chords.

"So, our story begins close to home. This one starts in our dear Oranmore, right there on the bay. On a quiet summer evening by the water, we see a tortured knight, staring up at the moon. He has lost something. Mates, tell me, what do you reckon he's lost?"

"A battle!"

"His mind."

"A fair maiden!"

"Aye, a fair maiden," Collin said, his voice amplified by the microphone, twice as loud as those from the crowd. "What would a bit of Irish folklore be without a fair maiden?" More murmurs of affirmation. "He stands by the water there, asking for a sign. Something to show him how to carry on. Or perhaps how to find his maiden. What kind of sign do we think he receives?"

Every time he scanned the crowd for a response, everything inside me tightened into a knot. Would his eyes catch on mine? What would we do if they did?

Once again, a few voices stood out from the general murmur of the crowd.

"The shape of the moon."

"A voice from the trees."

"A red fox!"

"You said a fox, there, did you?" He lifted the minor chords just enough for us to notice. "The color of her hair, I reckon." I instinctively reached for my own, twirling a single crimson lock around my finger.

"He follows the fox, he does. For days and nights, he follows this fox through the forest and along the edge of water, toward what he cannot be sure. He only hopes the fox is leading him to an absolution. The maiden, if he's lucky. Or at the very least toward freedom from his own pain."

The audience was rapt, leaning closer with every word,

and their unwavering interest in him only reaffirmed mine. Strengthened it. Reminded me that it was not every day you got the privilege of being told a story by Collin Finegan, so when you did, you needed to savor it.

"After what feels like an eternity," he continued, "the fox leads the knight . . ."

"Down the pub," someone shouted, and others laughed.

"Aye, of course." Collin laughed too. "Where else is there to be when trying to cure a broken heart?" Collin picked up a pint off the floor and raised it to the crowd, and everyone with a drink mirrored his gesture. We took a collective sip, and I wondered how many of us could see ourselves in his story.

"When they reach the pub and the man looks down to the fox, he finds it has disappeared. The man is alone in the doorway, so he does the only thing he can think to do. He goes inside, sits on a stool, and orders a pint of the black stuff."

"Slàinte!" someone shouted from the crowd, and Collin winked in their direction.

In my dark corner of the pub, I was reaching a boiling point. The more he spun this story, the more glimpses of us I found between the lines. I needed confirmation that I wasn't the only one still reeling from our fallout. I needed to know in some recess of his mind he was still thinking about me. Still feeling the same things we'd been feeling only days ago. Still secretly holding out hope for my return, even if he'd tried to make it easier for me to leave.

"He drinks pint after pint, wondering after the fox. Why had it led him to this very pub? What was he supposed to do next? He fears he isn't strong enough to make the decision on his own, so he looks around for what might be the next guide on his journey. Or what might be the answer.

"When he finishes his pint he swivels his stool in the direction of the door, willing something to happen. He isn't sure for how long he sits and stares at the dark wood, counting the bolts in the iron hinges, sending his prayers to the gods, but eventually it swings open, and, mates, what does it reveal?"

"The fox."

"A witch!"

"The maiden," I called. Perhaps it was my voice that drew the attention of the crowd, or maybe the flash of recognition on Collin's face, but in a split second, the entire audience had turned to face me instead of the stage.

"The maiden," he repeated, slowing his strumming until it ceased altogether. I took a few steps in his direction, hoping his expression would become readable if I moved a little closer. Whispers rippled through the crowd, and I could have sworn I heard a gentle gasp from where Flo sat with Lars near the stage. "But the knight is wary," he continued, keeping his tone consistent with that of the story. "He's had quite a few pints, and he worries his eyes might deceive him. Was she really there?"

"She was!" This time the voice was unmistakably Flo's.

"She was," I repeated. The audience darted their eyes back and forth between us like they were at a tennis match. The strumming returned, tentative.

"But what for?" he asked. "The knight had been nearly certain he'd never see her again. How could he be sure of the intentions for her return?"

"Maybe he could buy her a pint and ask," I said, fully aware by now the audience knew we were no longer making up a story.

A few whistles sounded from the crowd, and Collin shook

his head, fighting a smile. I willed that smile to form. *Let me back in*, I wanted to say. *Come on*.

"Well, mates," he said, returning to his storytelling volume. "What do we think? Does the knight invite the maiden in, buy her a pint? Or does he assume she's a mirage, something too good to be true, and try to find a way to move on?"

Conflicting suggestions overlapped across the crowd, people shouting over one another and raising pints in the air. Much to my advantage, the raised pints edged out the sad, broken-hearted voices. Collin kept his eyes locked on mine, and I shrugged, palms in the air. "Sounds like he buys her a pint," I said. Another shake of his head. Another half smile.

"And so he does," Collin said, playing a few final chords. "He invites her in, and he buys her a pint. And since our dear ancestors left too many holes in this story, we are left without an ending. That part, mates, I'm afraid you'll have to make up on your own. You decide their fate." Silence from the banjo. "And whatever you decide, do make it a good one? The knight could use a win."

Applause filled the room, and Collin thanked his audience with a raise of his hand, handing his banjo to someone backstage and disappearing behind the curtain. I swallowed the rest of my beer in one gulp, trying to prepare for his reappearance on this side of the stage.

As I turned to put my empty glass on the bar, I heard his voice behind me. Normal volume, no microphone, inches from me instead of miles. "I guess he has to follow through on that promise to buy the maiden a pint, then, doesn't he?"

"Collin," I said, turning to face him. We were both breathless, like we'd run a marathon to get here.

"Hi, Chels." He signaled to the bartender for two more beers then slid onto the stool beside me. I wanted to wrap my arms around him, inhale his familiar scent, feel his heartbeat against me, and see if it was pounding the same way mine was. Instead, I kept to my barstool, following his lead.

"You've become a knight in my absence, have you?" I thanked the bartender and took a sip, hoping the light banter would soften him.

"Hardly," he said. "I didn't quite think I was going to become the subject of that one." I nodded, taking another sip. He did the same. "Why are you here, Chels?"

If he was going to get right to the point, I might as well do the same. "Why'd you send the portfolio?"

"Because you wanted the gig."

"But you wanted me to stay."

"But you wanted to leave," he said. "All we wanted was to see you happy. And if that meant going back to Boston and getting that job, we wanted to help you get there."

I was overwhelmed with both gratitude and that same selfish feeling I had that day in the kitchen with Flo, momentarily speechless. "I don't know how to thank you," I said eventually.

"It doesn't seem like it did you much good, did it? Not if you're back here, anyway."

"It's actually exactly what got me back here," I said. "It was in the interview when I realized that job wasn't at all what I wanted. The concrete city, the trendy new hotel job, the endless extension of the only life I'd ever known. And then as soon as I saw your name on the bottom of that email, it was over."

"But you didn't want to be here," he said, staring into the darkness of his pint. "You said a million times that this life wasn't for you."

"It wasn't for an old version of me," I said. "It wasn't for the version of me I was when I arrived. But now, I'm not even sure who she is anymore. That version of myself is unrecognizable, and I have no intention of bringing her back."

He lifted his eyes to mine, and the tangle in my chest loosened just slightly.

"What version of you is here now, then?"

"The one you fell for," I said. "Hell, the one I owe to you, in fact. The one who jumps off cliffs and dances without knowing the steps and speeds down coastal highways. The one who's learned to love Galway more than Boston, and who's learned stability does not equal success. And that happiness doesn't have to look anything like a corporate job and a white picket fence."

"I quite like that one." He swirled the beer in his glass, and I willed him to look at me. "So, what?" he asked, still apprehensive. "You're here just for another season, then?"

"Coll, I'm here for good," I said, letting the words settle between us. "I don't have a return ticket. There's no date of termination on my contract. No replacement lined up for when I leave. I'm staying this time. I mean it."

For the first time since we locked eyes during his story, his expression softened completely. No ridge between his eyebrows, no suppressing a smile. He was letting me back in. "You've decided to live in the fantasy after all." He raised his glass to me and took a swig. "God, Chelsea. It better be true. You remember the story of Leannán Sídhe, don't you?"

The fairy lover who served as a muse then turned her human lover to dust when she left. "How could I forget?"

"Aye, you love the fairy stories, don't you?"

"Among other things." I smiled. It was something I should

have confessed the night after the roast. I'd been as sure about it then as I was now.

"So tell me." He angled his body toward mine, filling the space between us. "What does happiness look like now?"

I hummed, pretending to think. "Well, it looks like endless stretches of green," I started, "picnics near lakes, drives along the water."

"Go on."

"It also looks like neon signs in hostel lobbies, plates of roast potatoes"—I leaned in—"Irishmen with that sparkle in their eyes."

"Anything else?" he probed, parting his lips just slightly.

"Look around," I said. Together we scanned the bar, clocking our friends, the warmth of the atmosphere, the clink of glasses in celebration, and the misty Irish rain outside the windows. The scene that had become so familiar I couldn't imagine a life without it.

He took my hand in his, spinning the claddagh around a few times the same way I had in the interview. "You remember how this works, don't you?" he asked, sliding it off my finger. I nodded, sensing exactly where he was going. He turned the heart so it was facing me and slipped it back on, and the rest of the crowd melted away.

"I haven't seen twelve wild horses yet," I said, still staring at my hand, "but if Niamh is right and all it takes is falling in love with an Irishman, I believe I might just be a proper Irishwoman after all."

"In that case," he said, pulling me into him so close I could feel his smile against my lips, "welcome home."

Acknowledgments

*W*riting the acknowledgments for my debut novel was a daunting task. I didn't know where to begin, I couldn't even believe the book actually existed, and I was afraid somehow I'd do it wrong, even though this bit has no rules.

This time, it's something I've been looking forward to since I started writing the first draft. How lucky am I to have space to express my gratitude for the people who have made this possible? (Even if no one ever reads it.)

To my agent, Hannah Todd. Can you hear me shouting my thanks from across the Atlantic, or should I get on a plane and come back to London? Maybe I should come back . . . just in case. Thank you for entertaining me every time I say, "Wait . . . I have an idea," for championing my work, for reminding me there's nothing to be nervous about (even when there is), and for being the reason my books are out in the world. There's no one else I'd rather have in my corner.

To my editor, Ariana Sinclair. I'm sure you can hear my yelling from New York, but that's not going to stop me. Thank you for the time, attention, and care you give to every draft—without you, my drafts would remain drafts forever (and my characters would be laughing nine hundred times on every page). Thank you for never judging my spelling errors (or at the very least not telling me you're judging my spelling errors), for your expert guidance, your talent, and your dedication. I'd be lost without you.

To every other crucial member of the team who brought this book to life, I'll never be able to thank you enough for your hard work. I am the luckiest writer in the world to be backed by such a talented group of people—because of you, I get to hold my books in my hands, and I can't think of anything more special than that.

To the tour guides on my first ever trip to Ireland who told me my first fairy stories as we drove the Wild Atlantic Way, to the kind people of the country who welcomed me into pubs and shared their culture and inspired these characters, to everyone in my life who's been listening to me bang on about how much I love Ireland ever since, and to the fairies themselves for letting me borrow their lore for the sake of love and storytelling. I hope they don't mind.

And to my friends who feel like family (you know who you are), for the support, the encouragement, the preorders, the inspiration, and for letting me yap incessantly about my writing without complaining (at least to my face). This is all so much fun because I get to share it, and there's no one I'd rather share it with.

And to my family: my favorite people, my closest friends, and my loudest cheerleaders.

To my mom, Hillary, for believing in everything I do and reading every draft and keeping me calm and asking hard questions even when I don't want to answer them. My books will always be better because of it.

To my siblings, Jake Rosone, Steph Rosone, and Daniel "Big

Bobby Chuckie Diesel" Rosone, for the constant celebrations and the social media promo, and for suffering through reading romance (which is especially gross because your sister wrote it). I love and appreciate you more than you know! (And Jake, the offer still stands: anytime you want to make the trip to Ireland, just say the word.)

To my dad, Mike, and my stepmom, Kristen, for the manifestations, the energy, the affirmations, and the unwavering confidence. Because of you two, I know the universe is on my side.

And to Adam, for being one of the most unexpected, inevitable, life-changing things to happen to me. The Collin to my Chelsea. Steadfast, joyful, kind. Here's to our own great adventure.

About the Author

Alexandra Paige is a novelist and a marketing copywriter. Her debut novel was *Weekends with You*. She currently writes in the apartment she shares with her boyfriend in a cozy New Jersey suburb or in the coffee shop down the street, though her stories are always taking her elsewhere. She has a BA from Moravian University and an MFA from Lindenwood University.